TOUCH OF THE BONE

BAXTER CLARE TRAUTMAN

2023

Bywater Books

Copyright 2023 Baxter Clare Trautman

Print ISBN: 978-1-61294-271-1

Bywater Books First Edition: August 2023

Printed in the United States of America on acid-free paper.

Cover design by TreeHouse Studio

Bywater Books
PO Box 3671
Ann Arbor MI 48106-3671

www.bywaterbooks.com

*To the unending line of women who have always healed,
who still heal, and will continue to heal.
And yet they persist.*

CHAPTER 1

Rain enfolded the winter. It fell constantly, softly, soaking far beneath the ground to replenish each mountain root, spring and seep. The grass grew higher than any of the old ranchers could recall and the cobbled streams ran fat with trout.

Every day of that long, wet season Frank saddled Buttons and rode into the mountains. She started in the green meadows surrounding the ranch, exploring each side canyon as far as it would go. She carried a map; some of the canyons had names, most didn't. If there was soft ground with good fodder and the rain was not too hard, she would hobble Buttons and camp the night. More often she rode home in a dusk indistinguishable from day to give the old horse a long rub and hot mash.

After the dogs were fed and chickens locked up, she would stoke a fire and spend the long nights reading. Every wall in the cabin that wasn't window, door or mantel was shelved and every shelf groaned with books. Frank had often wondered: if she were to spend the rest of her life here would she ever get through them all? It was an idle question that seemed to match her days, but those winter days on the ranch were anything but idle for each one was spent steeped in the atoms, grains, and fibers of the mountains. Ridge and peak, portrero and canyon, creek and field, each feature of the land was absorbed into Frank's bones as was the rain into the ground.

With the spring came the sun, and with the sun a blaze of birdsong and bud. Frank had spent hours hunched over flowers, finding their names in tattered field guides—Johnny-jump-ups and popcorn flower, loco weed and coral bells, poppies, fiddleneck, and houndstooth. She spent just as many hours squinting through binoculars, learning birds and their songs: bluebirds and jays, sparrows and towhees, finches and warblers. She was alone but never lonely. The dogs and horses, the chickens and wild animals, all the flowers, bushes, and trees were the only company she wanted. She had never known solitude, nor what a hunger she had for it until a body found in the crowded, clamoring heart of Los Angeles had led her to "Sal" Saladino and this mountain redoubt.

She thought often of that miserable day when she'd thought she was leaving the ranch for good, how heartsick she'd felt until Pete Mazetti grabbed her hand and slapped a set of keys into it.

"This is for Sal," he'd hissed. "Not you."

She'd immediately recognized the keys to all the gates on the twisty ranch road that led to the Mazetti cabin. It was the cabin Sal had spent her whole life in before leaping from an overlook facing the vastness of the Pacific Ocean. Before she jumped Sal had left three letters—one each for her daughter, Pete, and Frank.

In Frank's she wrote that she'd asked Pete to let her stay on but didn't know if he would. Frank hadn't known either and guessed the answer was no—until the investigation into Sal's death was finally wrapped up and he had given her the keys. She'd been stunned, driving back to LA laughing all the way. She had a moving truck deliver everything in her Pasadena house to a local thrift store and let a property manager rent the house out. After that, the only thing standing between her and the mountains was the cursory Internal Affairs inquisition.

She replayed that in her head a lot, too, never tiring of the relief of that last day.

"Lieutenant Franco."

"Retired," she'd corrected, with hidden joy.

"Lieutenant Franco, *retired*," the IA detective said. "Have you ever spent the night at a suspect's home before?"

"I've never had a suspect as remote as Diana Saladino."

"So in your mind that made it okay?"

"I needed to interview her and I thought it was the best way."

"Why not just question her at the local station? Why did you have to follow her out to such a remote location?"

Frank reined in her impatience and resisted shifting in the hard chair. She explained again, "Ms. Saladino was reluctant to talk. I thought I'd get better results if she was on her own turf."

"And did you?"

"Yes."

"And what exactly were those results?"

Frank reiterated the highlights of the case, how the body found in South Central had led straight to Saladino's cabin deep in the mountains of Big Sur. How she had sussed out Sal's confession there.

"Tell us again why you didn't immediately take Ms. Saladino into custody."

Frank ticked off on her fingers, "She wasn't a flight risk. She'd been living in that cabin her entire life. There was nowhere for her to go. She wasn't a violent suspect. Had no history of premeditation." She shrugged. "It was a calculated risk."

"The records indicate you spent considerable time with Ms. Saladino at her cabin. Would it be safe to say that by now you had a personal relationship with the prime suspect in your homicide investigation?"

"I developed a personal relationship with a lot of my suspects. It's how I got 'em to talk."

"Would it be safe to say you willfully disregarded the rules because of this particular relationship?"

There was no way these guys could know about the brief, dire coupling on that last night of Sal's subtle—and to Frank, unknown—passing of the mantle.

"The woman had lived there for sixty-two years. I didn't

think letting her have one more night would be a problem. I know it was wrong. I knew spending that much time there was wrong. It's why I hung up my badge. Look, how many times are we gonna do this? Crucify me if you have to. My story's not gonna change."

The detective shook his head with a disgusted noise and looked at his partner. "Why are we wasting time on this?"

The partner had shrugged. Banging his notes into a neat square he said, "We're done here. You'd just better hope no one comes after us for your fuck-up."

Walking out of LAPD headquarters for the last time, she fingered the fob in her pocket like a talisman. Down in the parking basement she pressed it and a brand new Tacoma sang out. Lights flashing, doors unlocking, it welcomed her into the cocoon that would take her from the City of Angels back to the mountains. She hadn't been able to drive fast enough, getting a speeding ticket in Santa Barbara, then slowing only after she crested the grade dividing north San Luis Obispo County from south. There, at the trailing end of the Santa Lucia Range, with her mountains finally in sight, she reset the cruise control from ninety to seventy and relaxed. Steering with her knee, she rolled a cigarette. The sky was muddled, only a few stars showing through the clouds, but they were her stars. Frank had never felt more at home.

"And the rest, Kook," she said to the curly white dog in her lap, "is history."

She was sitting by the fire pit, coffee in one hand, the other stroking Kook. At her feet, a sleek black dog lifted his head. Bone heard it before Frank did, a truck grinding up the jeep trail that led to the cabin. It sounded like Pete's old V-8. As she wondered what had prompted her landlord's rare visit Frank braced for the worst-case scenario—Pete was done humoring a dead woman and was finally going to kick her off the ranch. She wondered if he'd let her keep Kook and Bone.

When he rumbled over the creek bridge Kook leapt from her lap and raced with Bone to greet the ranch dogs barking in the bed of his truck.

"Quiet!" he yelled, stopping in the dirt yard. All the dogs settled to whining, tails frenzied as they stretched to sniff each other. A fireplug of a man and twice as hard, he told her, "Get in. I gotta show you something."

She put her cup on the chair arm and asked, "Bring the dogs or pen 'em?"

His door squealed open and he said, "They can come. But Little Bo Peep's gotta ride in back with the real dogs."

He dropped the tailgate, growling for his dogs to stay. Bone put his feet up and looked expectantly at Pete.

"What's this?" he asked her.

"He's been having trouble jumping up. He's waiting for a lift."

"Jesus." Pete shook his head but obliged the older dog and Frank dropped Kook over the side.

They bounced past Pete's peeling Victorian ranch house and down the mountain. The seatbelts were long shot and Frank clung to the roof grip to keep from concussing herself. The dogs scrabbled on the metal bed. A couple times she caught Pete glancing at them. Frank couldn't imagine where he was taking her, but refused to give him the satisfaction of asking. She studied the view out the window, the rippling fields of yellow grass studded with dark oaks. When Pete pulled up to the first gate she dutifully got out and unlocked it.

"You can leave it open," he called out the window. Frank lifted a brow; he'd told her never to do that. Right after the last gate, he turned into the dirt lot of the Celadores Store and cut the engine. They sat under a massive oak, studying the old store and listening to the engine cool. The dogs paced.

"What?" she finally bit.

He jutted his chin toward two women sitting on a bench against the store. They were watching the truck intently. The women were middle-aged, each with a purse on her lap and a plastic bag beside her.

Frank frowned. "What about 'em?"

"They're waiting."

"I see that. What for?"

"Not what. Who."

"All right," Frank played along. "Who?"

Pete spat tobacco out the window then turned his squinty gaze all over her. "You, Chief. They're waitin' for you."

"Me?" She looked hard at the women. "Why?"

He flapped a hand. "They're waiting for you to do whatever it was Sal did."

"Oh, no, no." She shook her head. "I don't do that."

"Then go tell 'em. They come every Saturday. Just sit here waitin' for you."

The women stared at her. Frank shook her head again and looked away. "Uh-uh."

"Well, Lolly said to show you and I did."

He got out and limped into the store. Frank waited in the truck, turning her eyes everywhere but to the waiting women.

The locals had called Sal a *curandera*, a healing woman. Every Saturday she had held office hours in a lean-to behind the store. Every Saturday there had been a stream of clients, mostly women, mostly Hispanic, who came to see her. One by one they walked around to the back of the store then left through the front. Needing to question Sal about a case, Frank had patiently taken her turn in line one Saturday. Even now it gave her a shiver to remember how Sal had told her things about herself that would have been impossible for anyone to know, at least without some serious research, and some things not even then.

As Pete came out of the store Frank made the mistake of glancing at the women. Their stare burned like a branding iron.

Tucking yesterday's paper and mail onto the dashboard he chuckled. "You okay there, Chief? You look a little pale."

He walked around the back of the truck, still grinning.

"Here." He opened her door and dumped Kook onto her lap. "Little Bo Peep's gettin' trampled back there."

Glad to have somewhere to look, she smoothed the dog's curls, feeling the women's eyes even after Pete turned and started back up the mountain. They made the drive up in the same silence they had coming down. Pete dropped her at the cabin but before he left, he leaned out the window.

"That's how it started for Sal. They just started showin' up like that." He grinned. "She didn't want to do it either."

CHAPTER 2

Frank made herself a second cup of coffee. She paced outside the cabin, drifting from barn to corral, over to the bridge, around the fire pit, back again. It didn't make sense, Pete showing her the women, them waiting for her. She wasn't a witch doctor. She wasn't anything anymore. Just a retired homicide detective soaking up life after too many years steeped in death.

Figuring if she was going to pace this much, she ought to do it while washing her laundry. She rinsed her cup in the sink, then ran water into the tub and added a good shake of detergent. With nowhere to go and no one to impress, Frank's accumulation of laundry was minimal. She dropped it all in the tub and took her jeans off. Stepping in, she waded among the clothes, swishing and swirling them in the soapy water.

She was curious how long the women would wait. Surely they'd have realized she wasn't coming back and had left by now. She thought about making a trip into Soledad and driving by. Her library books were all past due. They were mostly special-order poetry books and likely unmissed. She'd always wanted to read poetry but until now hadn't had the time or patience for it. Now she had both and spent long hours marveling over the exquisitely crafted words of Doty, Dove, and Sarton; Marilyn Nelson and Mary Oliver; Rich and Brooks and Bishop. Just as the depth and variety of the natural world continued to amaze her so was she amazed by the scope and complexity of poetry.

Frank drained the dirty water, filled the tub with clean, and started her rinse cycle. The dogs watched from the doorway, hoping domestic chores would give way to something more fun.

"Go to town or go for a ride?" she asked.

Bone cocked his head 45 degrees and Kook's tail swept the floor.

In addition to taking the books back, she needed to sit down at the library computers to check her email and bank statements, make sure the property manager was getting paid and that rent was coming in from the LA house. Not that Frank needed the money. Her pension was generous and largely unspent as Pete was letting her stay for free.

She had an easy relationship with the ranch foreman, Pork Chop, and had asked him if he knew why Pete let her stay on if he didn't even like her.

"He likes having someone here. Keeps the rats and squirrels out. Keeps the place livable."

"Why doesn't he just rent it to someone?"

Pork Chop shook his head. "Pete don't like strangers on his land."

"I'm a stranger."

"Yeah. But you're different. If Sal wanted you here I guess that was good enough for Pete."

Whatever his reasons, Frank was happy with them. She wrung the clothes and while she pinned them onto the line behind the cabin she decided it was too pretty a day to waste driving into town. Besides, if the women were still there she didn't want to see them.

"Let's go get Buttons," she said to the dogs. They raced ahead of her to the barn and pranced around while she saddled Sal's steady old mare. After she'd double-checked the girth and the stirrups Frank cautiously mounted. It was still the scariest part of riding for her even though Buttons was calmer than a pond on a windless day.

Relieved to be securely in the saddle, she turned to the

foothills. It was an easy ride to one of Frank's favorite watering holes. There she skinny-dipped with the dogs, splashing and playing chase with them. By the time they rode back to the cabin she'd dismissed the sharp-eyed women at the store.

Folding a slice of bread around a couple apple slices and a slab of cheese, she ate the makeshift sandwich on the bridge, legs swinging above the water. The dogs sat to either side, waiting for something to drop, until Bone stood. He looked expectantly toward the ranch end of the bridge. Frank saw nothing but a minute later Pork Chop appeared on his horse.

"Hi." He lifted a hand. "Am I bothering you?"

"Not at all." She crammed the last bite into her mouth and waved him over. "I'm just trying to figure what that is."

She pointed to a black and orange bird singing lustily from a willow.

"That's a *picogrueso*," he said without even looking. "They come back every spring and have their babies here."

"Come back from where?"

He shrugged. "I dunno. Down south somewhere. Mexico?"

"Huh. Amazing. All that without a map or GPS. We couldn't do that."

He grinned, one dark eye on her, the other pointing at sky. "They do lots we can't do." Pork Chop tied his horse on the ranch side of the bridge and pulled something out of his saddlebag.

"I just finished a sandwich. You hungry? I could make you one."

"Nah, I'm good. Thank you." He sat beside her holding a long flat box, like a safe-deposit box. After he petted the dogs and they laid back down he told her, "I found this. Up at the overlook. I think…I started to read it, but I think it's for you."

He handed her the box but she didn't open it. Frank hadn't been to the overlook since the investigation ended but she thought about it plenty—racing up the mountain in the dark, letting Buttons lead the way, running into Sal's horse on the impossibly skinny cliff, the sun coming up as she tried to persuade Sal not to jump, the whisper in the air after she had.

"There were sheriffs and Search and Rescue all over that place. Where was it?"

More than a hand, Pork Chop was Pete's right arm, because as Pete had explained, "He's got one eye on the cattle and the other on everything else." Frank scrutinized the wiry, walleyed man. Found him guileless.

"One of my dogs dug it out from under the old manzanita up there. You know that big one with all the dead branches? Must be at least a hundred years old."

Frank thought she knew which one. The dogs had sought shade under it when she'd gone up there with Sal.

"It was wrapped in one of her shirts," he said shyly. From the way he talked about Sal it was clear he'd had a crush on her and Frank was glad he had something to remember her by, even if it was just an old shirt. She had the cabin, Sal's books, everything she'd left, and it still wasn't enough. There was still so much more she wanted to know that only Sal could have told her.

Frank ran her fingers along the cool edge of the box. Sal had taken so many secrets with her, so many mysteries. They had had that one night but it had been nothing to do with love and everything to do with sorrow and goodbyes.

"I miss her."

Pork Chop nodded at the water. It rolled beneath them, not at all concerned with their woes. The bird sang above its babble.

"*Picogrueso.*"

"Yup." Pork Chop bobbed his head.

"And they come back every summer?"

"Yup."

"Nothing ever really leaves, does it?"

They shared a smile and Frank opened the box. Inside was a scrap of sheepskin, still smelling of lanolin. A sheet of paper lay on the skin. Frank recognized Sal's handwriting. She looked at Pork Chop. He nodded and she picked up the paper. Quiet as a whisper, the wind ruffled Frank's hair.

There are only three people I can think of who

*will find this. Only one of you may understand
what to do with it. I hope you're the one that finds
it. I couldn't leave it for you because I wasn't sure
what you'd do with it but if you're here, if you've
found this, then I think you will know what to do.
I hope you will.*

*I have been a coward in so many things and
what's written in here is one more instance of
that. A rough justice was served, which I couldn't
condemn, having served such justice myself. I also
know the server of such justice makes a prison of
her secrets and that others become locked inside that
prison with her. But I didn't have the courage to
deliver any of them, just as I never had the courage
to deliver myself. But you do. It's your gift. You can
set them free, just as you did me.*

—Forever, Sal

The day was warm but a chill traveled Frank's spine. She
pulled the bundle of sheepskin from the box. A dime store
composition notebook was wrapped inside, like the ones Frank
had used throughout school. Every fall she had lobbied her
mother to buy spiral-bound notebooks, the sort you could rip
pages from, and every year her mother insisted on the cheap
comp books.

She flipped to the first page. It was dated five years ago.

*All the promise of a new journal! Fresh, clean,
white pages, so many possibilities! What will take
place in here between this first page and the last?
Seven people today –*
KF – just a head cold – cold herbs
*HG – lost her boyfriend; grief, but not for him
I don't think. It was deeper. Still think she lost?*

aborted? a child and has never told anyone. Will
sit with W.

>*D - limpia (oh she makes me laugh!)*
>*ID - heart*
>*DD - broken arm/trauma - I know boyfriend*
>*did it. Insists she fell. Spent a lot of time with her*
>*AS - susto, slight accident with kids in car*
>*FrRa - neuropathy - nerve herbs*

>*Promised W elderberries for her cold syrups.*
>*Thought there would be some fruiting by Viejo*
>*Rock and was there ever! Collected two gallons. I*
>*think she will be pleased. Note: there will be a good*
>*crop of rose hips there in 5 or 6 weeks.*

>*A long delayed trip to town to deliver Ws*
>*berries. Sat with her about HG. She gave me a*
>*tincture of linden, hawthorn and roses. What W*
>*doesn't have in her garage hasn't been grown yet!*
>*What a marvel she is.*

"Who's W?"

"I dunno."

Frank read a couple more short, dated entries. "Seems like a combination of patient records and a journal."

"That's like a diary, right? I only read a little. It felt like I was spying on people."

Frank closed the notebook. She reread the letter and Pork Chop asked, "You think she meant her father? That part about being a coward? 'Cause she was one of the bravest ladies I ever met."

"I guess."

"The part about justice, and you being a cop and all, that's why I figured you should have it."

Frank nodded.

"The only other person I can think that mighta found it

would be Pete. You think she meant him?"

"I guess," she repeated.

They hunched over the water, each with their own thoughts. Finally Pork Chop said, "Pete told me he showed you those ladies down to the store."

"Yeah. How long they been coming?"

He made a whistle through pursed lips. "About a month or so? Maybe six weeks?"

"Always the same ones?"

"I think so. Maybe. I don't know."

After a minute, he asked, "Are you gonna do it?"

She gave a snort. "Pretend to be Sal? I don't think so."

"Not to be her," he protested. "To be you."

"Okay, so what I don't get is why they're waiting for a white woman with absolutely no street cred to come and do what Sal did. I mean, Sal had a track record. Me, I'm no one. Those women don't know me from Adam, and I can't do what they think I can. They're mistaken."

"How do you know?" Pork Chop trained a curious eye on her. "Have you ever tried?"

When she didn't answer, he pressed, "Sal told me once that you belonged here."

She followed the flight of a phoebe snapping the bugs that flitted over the water.

"She happen to mention why?"

"Actually, yeah, she did. I was really sad when she told me, I thought maybe she had cancer or somethin', but she said she wouldn't always be here. And if you listened to your heart you could take her place. But she was afraid you wouldn't. She said she was afraid your brain would be stronger than your heart."

Frank's lips twitched. That sounded like something Sal would say.

"What do you think?"

"Oh, I don't know. There's a lotta things I don't know. But Sal said it and she never lied to me so I believe her."

Their gazes stayed on the rushing creek until Pork Chop

brushed his palms on his pants and stood. "How you set for meat?"

Pork Chop earned his name by hunting the feral pigs that roamed the ranch. Since she'd moved in he'd kept her tiny freezer jammed with ribs and chops.

"I'm good. Thanks."

"Okay then. Just holler if you need more. I shot a big boar a couple weeks ago so I got plenty."

"Hey," she called after him. "What's your real name?"

He grinned, his bad eye on the treetops. "I'm Frank, just like you. Francisco. Pete and the guys call me Pork Chop. My family calls me Pancho."

"What do you like to be called?"

His face dropped. "I don't know. No one's ever asked me." Then he brightened just as suddenly. "But here on the ranch I'm just Pork Chop."

He waved and rode off. She watched him go. The dogs rose when she did. She considered the notebook lying at her feet. Nothing in her life had ever been as easy, as peaceful as these last nine months. She didn't want to jeopardize that by opening Sal's journal and taking on a problem that wasn't hers. It would be easy to just boot the notebook into the creek. Let it get tumbled away down to the Salinas River and out to the ocean. Food for the fishes.

Instead Frank stooped to pick it up.

CHAPTER 3

The dogs had been fed their kibble and the horses their hay. The chickens were done scratching in the yard and waddled into their coop to roost. Frank kindled a small fire in the mortared stone fire pit. She fried a couple chops over the low flame and chewed them right off the grill with handfuls of dried apple. Occasionally she spit a piece of gristle out to Kook and Bone.

The sun was easing down over the ridge of mountains, ready to sink into the ocean on the other side. Sal had insisted each sunrise and sunset were different and that she never wanted to miss a single one. So Frank watched them for her though she had a feeling Sal still watched them too. Somehow, from somewhere. She'd even hinted as much in her closing salutation. *Forever, Sal.*

After licking her fingers clean, Frank pulled a pouch from her shirt pocket and rolled a smoke. The box Pork Chop had given her sat on the edge of the fire pit. Frank considered it as she smoked.

She'd never been one for religion or belief in an afterlife yet she felt certain Sal was still around. The search teams had never recovered her body. From the overlook it was about a quarter-mile fall. Below, ridges and steep redwood canyons serrated the base. A determined effort had been made to find Sal but as the search captain noted, probably no human had ever set foot in any of that terrain. Sal had probably jumped from the overlook for that very reason, knowing no one would ever be able to take her from the land she loved.

There was no way she could have survived the fall. Even in the extreme case she had, she would have been far too hurt to live long. Frank had no illusions Sal was still alive in body, but in spirit? That was entirely another matter.

Kook interrupted her thoughts. He delicately placed his forepaws on the edge of her chair and wagged his tail hopefully.

"You want up?"

He wagged harder.

"What about Bone? Where's he gonna sit?"

The tail went faster.

She eyed the little dog until his whole back end wiggled and pleaded. When she patted her thigh Kook jumped into her lap and licked her chin before curling into a tight ball.

"Pete's right. You're spoiled."

Frank felt his tail wag between her leg and his body. She petted him and watched the sky fade over the ridge. From mauve to purple to almost black. It was never pure black, never as black as the mountains in their cloak of night, always standing guard, always on duty. She and Sal had spent their few evenings together doing exactly this, saying goodbye to the day and hello to the night.

As the stars and constellations came out she noted them by name—Cassiopeia, Ursas Major and Minor, Regulus, Arcturus. She had learned the biggest and brightest, and when it had been too cold to sleep outside Frank had pushed Sal's bed under the window so she could follow their mute transit through the night. Like the dogs, they had become trusted and loyal companions.

She listened to the creek rolling by. The treefrogs were in full throat, calling for females. Behind her there was a small rustle from the row of sheds. A mouse or woodrat? Maybe the skunk that lived under the woodshed waking up? She smiled, astonished that all this—the stars, the wild beasts, the mountains—had existed all her life and she'd never known it was here. It had all been background, mere scenery to be ignored. Even more mind-boggling was that somehow she had at last stumbled onto it, and that maybe because she'd made such a clean break from her old life it hadn't taken her more than a minute to get used to her new one.

She remembered how much she'd slept after getting to the ranch. She hadn't realized until then how exhausted she'd been. The first couple of weeks she'd slept twelve-, fourteen-hour nights. There were still the nightmares, the same theme nightmares she'd always had. They'd probably never go away, but they didn't come quite as often. It had taken her a good month to shake off her lassitude. After that she had slipped into an easy rhythm of rising with the sun and settling down with it at night.

On mornings she didn't ride, Frank and the dogs would amble the trails around the cabin scaring up jackrabbits and quail. Riding had been the best way to learn the ranch but boots on the ground with Sal's ancient field guides taught her about the plants and animals that shared their home with her. She learned to split wood and build fires, how to groom a horse and ride one. She discovered the hard way what stinging nettle looked like, and the bare stems of poison oak in winter. She could tell a valley oak from a blue oak, a raven from a crow, a jay from a bluebird.

She hadn't for a minute doubted Sal's pronouncement that she was supposed to be on the ranch but the *why* had started to nag her. Why was she here other than for her own sensual delight in the land, her own healing after almost thirty years of dealing with the worst that humans did to each other? In the early slow-motion days that had been enough. The land had taken her like a gentle lover and she had blossomed under its touch. In the process she had become someone else. But Frank wasn't sure who that someone else was.

She reached toward the box, pulled it closer. An owl called, "Who-who?"

"Who-who, indeed," she replied softly.

She was sure the answer was out there, somewhere on the

land. Or maybe, she thought, eyes on the flat shiny box, maybe the answer was in there.

CHAPTER 4

The nights were warm enough again to sleep outside and Frank woke in a pile of blankets a little after the first sunrise. She watched as trees and landmarks became distinguishable. At second sunrise, when it was light enough to see details, she rolled up her sheepskin pallet and made coffee. She sat with it on the cabin steps waiting for third sunrise, when the sun at last cleared the horizon.

Content to let each day unfold on its own she didn't usually wake with plans, but this morning after her cup was empty she walked to the enclosed pasture and rattled a tin of oats. Buttons and the lame gelding looked up from across the field and trotted over.

They nibbled from her palm as she scratched their chins. As bad as Pete was with people he sure had a soft spot for animals; Buttons was a herd animal and knowing she'd be lonely without another horse around he'd left the gelding for her. Frank slid a halter on the old mare and led her to the barn. The dogs wrestled while she saddled up. Frank would have liked to canter across the pasture and start climbing into the mountains right away but Buttons needed a slow start. Bone couldn't stand a fast pace, either. As it was, he'd be limping by the end of the day.

A cow path rose steadily through the foothill chaparral into a thick canopy of buckeye, oak, and maple. Buttons' steps were muted in the fat carpet of duff and leaf. She barely needed guidance but when they came to a narrow canyon of fern and redwood Frank tugged her to a stop. Water plunged from a fall that Frank had only seen once. It had been dry then, at the end of summer, and Sal had told her she'd have to come back in the spring when it was running fresh.

"I'm back," she said, her words swallowed in the churchy gloom.

Except for a creepy southeast corner of the ranch that Pete had warned her away from ("too many crazies with too many guns on the other side"), Frank had traveled most of the Mazetti acreage. Yet she had shied from the ridge tops with their ever-brooding, ever-watching peaks. Even now she felt a flutter of trepidation but pressed on.

They came to the pond where she and Sal had stripped and swam one hot afternoon. She let Buttons drink while Bone and Kook waded in to their chests, then they rode on until they reached a cliffside trail. One side was sheer face and the other nothing but space. The bones of a good horse at the bottom of the cliff told of its danger. It was impossible not to remember how she'd raced after Sal, finding her way here in the dark by giving Buttons her lead, only to run into Sal's horse halfway across. The trail was too narrow to turn around on so the only options had been to advance or back up one agonizing step at a time. Frank hadn't been about to retreat and had inched Buttons forward. Sal's horse backed slowly, one hoof at a time, until it lost its footing. She shook away the memory of its screams, the desperate scrabbling of its hooves, and focused on the thin trail. It wasn't too late to turn around. She didn't have to keep going. But her need to continue had nothing to do with reason.

Leaning forward she scratched Buttons's ears. "Whaddaya say, old girl?"

Buttons offered no advice but Kook whined and danced on his hind legs.

"Ready to ride?"

It would be safer to have him in the saddle than underfoot

so Frank dismounted and put on his harness. She clipped the lead to it and remounted, hoisting him easily into the saddle. He melted into her and stared up with liquid brown eyes, tail in a frenzy of joy.

She petted him, studying the chamise and buckbrush hanging from the cliff wall. Bone stood and looked up curiously. "You want a ride, too?"

His little nub of a tail shook and Frank smiled. "You're a good boy. Ready to go?"

At the word "go" he moved off onto the trail. Frank took a deep breath and gave Buttons a slight squeeze. Sal had assured her the mare could navigate the narrow track half asleep. Frank had counted on it the night she'd chased after Sal, and now again. She wondered what would happen if they ran into a rattlesnake sunning itself, or worse, what if the winter rains had eroded the trail away, or left an impassable mudslide, a deadfall?

She swore, wishing she'd asked Pork Chop how long ago he'd been up here. She studied the ground. There wasn't a trace of hoofprints. The trail wasn't that long and she should have walked it before setting out on an irrevocable course but now she was committed. The only way off was to back up or power through. Despite the full sun in her face Frank broke into a cold sweat.

"Goddamnit, Sal. You better not let anything happen to us." And Sal didn't.

The trail soon widened into a small portrero where Frank shakily dismounted. She bent over, not sure if she was going to puke or not. After a couple minutes her stomach settled and she stopped trembling. She took in the dogs, sprawled and panting. Buttons munched the winter-lush browse. Frank was the only one of the foursome at all concerned. She took a pull from Sal's battered canteen, grateful for the tinny, warm water. Working the adrenaline out of her system she led Buttons the rest of the way.

Just before the overlook she tied the mare to a stunted pine and walked around an ancient manzanita. She could see where

Pork Chop had broken some branches and disturbed the ground beneath. She wondered if Sal had planted the journal the night she'd died or before. Because of the care and deliberation she'd taken in hiding it, Frank decided before.

The bush towered over her head, its limbs as thick as her legs. The older branches were rough and gray but the new ones a satiny red. Frank rubbed her hand against the smooth bark. The plant had to be at least a century old and Frank marveled at all it had seen over the years, the last of the grizzlies, maybe. Certainly the disappearance then return of the condor, what Sal had called the *zopilote*. Had an Esselen, one of the land's first human occupants, brushed by it when it was barely knee high? Surely it had seen generations of Mazettis. It had attended Frank and Sal's first visit here and borne silent witness to their last.

"You didn't have to go," she whispered, knowing even as she said it that it wasn't true. Sal couldn't have lived anywhere else. Just as she'd written, it was best for her to die here and remain forever.

Frank stepped away from the manzanita into the shallow bowl of the overlook. Beyond was a blue-gray horizon of sea and air. She stood close to the edge and looked down. A lone condor sailed over the redwoods below.

"*Zopilote*," she called softly.

Sal had told her that the big vultures sailed over the Santa Lucias looking for lost souls, and that the *abuelas*, the old grandmothers, swore that if a person was ever in trouble all they had to do was appeal to the *zopilote* and they would come to her aid.

Frank watched the bird disappear, then she sat on a sun-warmed boulder. Sprinkling tobacco into a creased paper, she recalled the visions she'd had between finding Sal's father and settling on the ranch, visions of circling high above a twilit land of mountain, sea and canyon. Frank stopped making her cigarette. She closed her eyes, remembering the sensation of wheeling in a blood-red sky, a tableau of darkening earth below. While the fact that she had been suffering from hallucinations was unsettling, the visions themselves had been profoundly peaceful. They'd had a timeless quality, as if whatever, or whoever, was, circling and wheeling above the earth, she had been immortal.

"*Zopilote,*" she said to the endless blue. "Why am I here?"

Her only answer was a groaning stretch from Bone. A buzzing fly. The mild ocean breeze.

She finished the cigarette and stuck it in her pocket. Scooting to the edge of the overlook, she dangled her legs into the void.

There were only two types of evidence—the evidence you had and the evidence you wanted. The evidence Frank had was that by completely unforeseeable circumstances she was living at the ranch. Sal had insisted she belonged here and here she was. Sal had even told Pete and Pork Chop as much.

There was the fact of the visions, the fact of Sal reading her as easily as a college grad read a picture book. There was all that weird hoodoo business years ago with Darcy and Mother Love, and that no matter how hard Frank had tried she just couldn't squeeze all those inexplicable events into tidy boxes labeled "Logic" and "Reason."

There was her history of fighting the inexplicable until she had no choice but to surrender to it.

There were the women waiting for her at the store, apparently certain Frank could help them.

There was Pork Chop asking how she knew she couldn't if she didn't even try.

The evidence Frank wanted was that she was nobody special. She wanted the evidence to prove that she wasn't here to help anyone or solve any mysteries. She wanted the evidence to show that she was just an old cop licking her wounds.

And there was only one way to get that kind of evidence.

She would go to the store Saturday. She would prove to the ladies, Pete, Pork Chop, and Sal, that they were all wrong.

Frank stood, her muscles tight from the stress of the cliff trail. She stretched and the dogs copied her. She rode to the cliff trail and crossed with far less fear than before. If she was here for a reason—and she must have been, she reasoned, for why else had everything aligned so perfectly to put her here?— she didn't think that reason was to die by falling off the trail.

After giving Buttons a good rubdown and feeding everyone, Frank heated a can of soup. She took the pot out to the fire pit and drank from it, swabbing it with a slice of bread. The dogs splayed exhaustedly around her. Bone lifted his head when a chorus of coyotes sounded down by Pete's then let it drop with a solid thunk. Kook didn't even stir, trusting his pack to watch out for him.

One by one, she named the stars, but absently, by rote. She may have decided to prove everyone wrong about her, but there was still the matter of Sal's journal. She'd deliberately not thought of it all day. While she had to admit she was curious, she was also worried that if she delved into whatever mystery Sal had left for her she'd be committed to solving it. She'd spent thirty years solving mysteries and wasn't eager to solve one more.

Admiring the stars, she wondered if just this could be enough, witnessing each day and being a part of it. In the overall scheme of modern life it was nothing, what most would consider unproductive and a waste of time. Before being here she would have considered it a waste too. Now it felt like the most important work she'd ever done. And she didn't want to stop doing it to take care of Sal's unfinished business.

Maybe, she thought, she should have kicked the box into the creek after all.

CHAPTER 5

Rolled in her bedding with Bone against her back and Kook behind her knees, Frank let the morning unfold around her. First the pale gray leak of light back into the world, then the return of the colors. Every morning was a new amazement. The dogs rose and started their morning rassle. Bone was much rougher with the ranch dogs but he played down to Kook who was only a third his size. Having never had pets or animals Frank had never known their capacity for intelligence, devotion, and play. She'd always assumed that humans were the zenith of existence and that all other life existed on rungs far below them.

Now she wasn't so sure. From what she'd seen of humans and their insatiable needs, she was starting to think they had barely stepped onto the evolutionary ladder and that most other creatures were far more advanced. Like the *picogrueso* singing from the creek. She'd found it in the field guide (a black-headed grosbeak in English), verifying what Pork Chop had told her about their yearly migration back to almost the same spots they'd nested in the year before. How amazing was that? And that they were one of the few birds that could eat poisonous monarch butterflies, apparently indulging in eight-day cycles in order to give their bodies time to purge the toxins.

Listening to the male's chipper morning song she marveled that she couldn't fly to warmer or cooler places when the weather changed. She couldn't build a nursery in a couple days or even catch her own food, poisonous or not. The thought of food lured her from the warm bedroll. She noticed as the dogs followed her into the cabin that Bone was stiff and limping. Because he was all heart he'd be game for going anywhere today but she decided it'd be better to hang around the cabin so he and Buttons could rest.

After feeding the dogs she let the chickens loose, scattering feed for them in the yard. She sat on the steps with her coffee, absorbing the warm sun while watching the girls scratch and peck. Maybe later she would let them follow her down to the creek. They loved foraging in the leaf litter and along the damp banks but she wouldn't let them go alone. On wet winter days she'd thrown bird seed out into the yard and watched as quail gathered from the brush. They came by the dozens, sometimes a hundred of them, gorging placidly despite the onslaught of rain. More than once a gray fox had erupted from its concealment by the creek and dispersed the flock in a thunderous flurry of wings, all but the one that dangled from its mouth as it ran back to cover. Within half an hour the entire flock would reconvene around the seed, apparently with no concern for their missing member.

It was good, she thought, that their memory was so short. Would that hers was; Sal's box was where Frank had left it on the scarred dining table. She should put it somewhere else so she wouldn't be reminded of it every time she passed by. While it rankled that Sal had apparently left a mess for her to clean up Frank had to admit she was a little curious. The journal was her last link to Sal. Surely it would reveal more of the woman she knew so little about. Despite how Sal had killed her father and covered up his murder for forty years Frank had tremendous respect for her. She had paid for the crime by enduring a lifetime of guilt and isolation. Frank wondered if Sal would have been the recluse she was if it hadn't been for the dark burden she'd carried.

And if it hadn't been for that dark burden Frank probably

wouldn't be here.

She sighed and set her cup on the table. Frank might not like whatever Sal had left in the journal but like it or not she was indebted to the woman. Having justified her curiosity, Frank opened the box and extracted the notebook. She laid it in her lap, smoothed the cover.

But first, she thought, she should go down to the store and see if Sal's shack was serviceable for Saturday. While it still seemed silly to meet with the ladies Frank was pretty sure it would dispel any notions they had that she was a healer. Or psychic, or whatever it was they expected her to be. She was grudgingly willing to take on Sal's journals but not the additional responsibilities those women expected her to assume, and the sooner she could get rid of them, the sooner she could get back to enjoying her solitude.

The journal went back in its coffer.

After sharing toast with Kook and Bone, and reminding them again how spoiled they were, she loaded them into the truck. She drove to the store with the dogs hanging out the rear windows and left them in the shade of the oak. When Pete had told her they wouldn't jump out she hadn't believed him. The first couple times she took them anywhere she'd parked and spied on them. Bone always curled up in the back seat and Kook sat in hers, staring in the direction she'd gone. No matter how long she left them the little guy maintained his vigil. Not once had she seen either tempted by passing dogs or people. The only thing that had ever gotten a reaction was a nun in full habit. The poor woman had walked by the truck just as Frank was coming out of the store to see Bone lunge his head out, barking in full-throated fury. The nun had been startled but after Frank's profuse apologies she had laughed it off, admitting it wasn't the first time her bear-like outfit had frightened a dog.

Frank locked the truck, warning, "Stay. And don't bother any nuns."

Bone yawned and went to sleep. Kook stared solemnly after her.

Frank was grateful no one was in the store except the owner. Lolly was dusting but stopped when she saw Frank.

"You got no mail," she called.

"Hey, Lolly. I didn't come for that. I was wondering if you could let me into Sal's place out back."

The hefty woman frowned. "What do you want back there?"

Frank gave a sheepish grin. "Pete showed me the ladies that have been coming around and I thought I'd give it a go."

"Is that right?" Lolly put down her duster. "Can you do what Sal done?"

"Guess that depends on what you think she done."

"Well, I can't say she cured my arthritis but she sure made it feel better. Can you do that?"

"I don't know," Frank admitted, then surprised herself by adding, "but I'd be willing to give it a try."

"Oh, would you now?" Lolly squinted at her, sizing her up. "Tell you what." She came around from behind the counter and flipped the sign on the door from OPEN to CLOSED.

"Let's go and find out."

"Right now?"

"Why not? It'd sure be a relief to me if you could ease this a bit." She lifted a gnarled hand. "It's hurtin' something awful the last couple days. Come on."

Shoving open the back door, she pulled keys from her apron and found one. "Here we go."

She opened the shed, pushed aside a brightly colored curtain, and flicked on an overhead. "I keep it clean. Don't want the mice getting a hold in here. Have a seat. Let's see what you can do."

Frank started to sit in the chair closest to the door but Lolly said, "No, that's for the customers. You gotta sit on the other side of the table."

"Don't get your hopes up," Frank warned.

"I ain't but it can't hurt any worse for the trying."

Lolly sat with her arm on the worn card table and looked expectant. Frank asked her what she was supposed to do.

"Well." She thought a moment. "Sal just put her hands here."

29

She motioned for Frank's hands and placed her right wrist between them. "Like that. Now we just sit and you do your thing."

"And this is what Sal did?"

"Yep. Just like that. We'd chat a little sometimes but mostly we just sat. I asked her once what it felt like when she was doing it and she said it made her feel like she was giving people presents. That it was a good feeling. So do your thing, girl."

Lolly closed her eyes.

Frank had no idea what "her thing" was. She felt ridiculous but this had been Lolly's idea so she went with it. She closed her eyes and concentrated on Lolly's wrist in her hands. She waited to feel a tingling or vibration, something, but there was only the peaceful, steady silence. House finches squabbled in the eaves and a crow cawed. Another answered. A thin burble came from the old, mossy fountain behind the store. The shed was still and warm. Frank wanted to open her eyes and look around it, but she kept them closed, concentrating on the even pulse in Lolly's wrist. Eventually her head drooped. When she jerked it up Lolly was smiling at her. She took her hand away and rubbed it.

"You done good."

"Yeah?"

Lolly nodded. "Feels better."

"So that's it? That's all she did was hold people's hands?"

With a shrug, Lolly explained, "She told me once that there's a whole lot of energy in the world and we can use it for good or bad. She had the gift to be able to tap into that energy— she said most of us do, that it just takes practice and, and like . . . attention to harness it. She said it was like being next to a creek and laying a pipe in it and diverting the water where you wanted it. She was the pipe in all that energy and she directed it into her patients."

She got up. "I gotta get back. Stay if you like. I'll lock up later."

Frank still didn't get it. Sal definitely had had the touch— she'd seen it work firsthand, but it didn't explain how without

30

even meaning to Frank could do the same thing. Chalking it up to the power of suggestion and wishful thinking, she glanced around the shed. Thick workbenches to one side and along the back suggested the space had once been a workshop. She plugged in the white lights hanging on pegboards that lined the walls and the room took on a warm, cheery glow. A gypsy-like variety of cloths draped the workbenches. Deep shelves behind them held dusty vases, an impressive array of religious candles, and a couple cardboard boxes.

Frank pulled out a random box containing jars of salves and dried herbs. Each displayed an old-fashioned, hand-lettered label, *Generous Rose Hips, Magical Mugwort, Sniffles Blend, Hacking Hyssop.*

Frank smiled at the whimsical names and closed the box. Another one held bottles of oils and tinctures with the same waggish labels and carefully printed directions for use. A bigger box held an electric kettle and a couple of delicate teacups. Frank frowned; the cups were so unlike the thick, practical mugs Sal had at the cabin. She stashed the boxes and turned in the cramped space.

It was ridiculous to think she had helped Lolly's pain, but if Lolly thought she had, that was medicine enough. The Saturday ladies might think once or twice that she was helping them but eventually they'd realize she wasn't. Then their belief that she was a healer would dissolve and they could spend their time with someone who could actually help them.

She ducked through the low doorway and into the store. Lolly was behind the counter playing solitaire on her phone.

Frank asked, "You think I should bother coming Saturday?"

Lolly looked up over half-rim reading glasses. "Sure. Why not?"

"You really think it'd help?"

Lolly shrugged. "It helped me. I don't know what's wrong with those other ladies but you might help them too."

Frank nodded. "Okay, then. See you Saturday."

She shook her head all the way home.

CHAPTER 6

That evening fog blew down over the mountains. Wrapped in a blanket Frank watched it march in like an advancing army. When it finally got to the cabin she retreated inside and lit the logs she kept laid in the fireplace. The dogs were curled at either end of the couch and she settled between them, a cup of tea in one hand, Sal's journal in the other. It stayed on her lap while she sipped and watched the fire.

For almost a year Frank had been left in perfect solitude, alone at the cabin with barely any interference from the outside world. Now, in the same day, she had been shown the women and handed Sal's journal. She had to think the timing wasn't accidental. Maybe she just had to trust that like everything that had led her here, these next steps in her journey were unfolding as they were meant to. As Sal, and Frank's old friend Marguerite, had both warned, she had a tendency to let her head override her heart. She wanted to open the journal, to delve into what was inside, but so much had already changed since the morning Pete took her to the store. She was afraid once she opened the notebook even more would change.

Her head warned, *Don't open this. Just throw it away.* Her head's job was to protect Frank, to keep her safe. It was the cautious, hesitant organ.

Her heart, on the other hand, urged, *What are you waiting*

for? Open it up! Her heart laughed at caution and fear. Frank watched the flames dance. Had she come into these mountains to live or hide out? To be bold or be afraid? She sighed and opened the worn cover. The writing was tidy and small. Frank reached into the end table drawer and fished out Sal's battered cheater glasses.

> *I was looking for that stand of twinberry south of Pico Creek but found a fresh lion kill instead. That is the second deer in two months. It was a magnificent stag that must have been difficult to bring down unless it was injured. I didn't linger because the kill was still fresh and had some meat left on it but I did see a number of smaller lion prints, so the lion is a female with at least two cubs I should think, maybe more to push her to bring down such a big buck. This kill is closer to the calving pasture than the last but I hesitate to tell Pete. He would borrow J's dogs and hunt her down. I can't bear the thought of her cubs starving, so until she becomes a problem I will keep her a secret. Besides, as much as he hates it, it's not like he can't afford to lose a calf or two. Hopefully Pork Chop won't come across the carcass. That man sees everything.*

> *Worked on Pete. I really wish he'd go to a doctor but he's so damn stubborn. Such a man! No sense at all just pure, bull-headed will. I worry about him. He shouldn't be so short of breath and I don't like his color. Something is wrong with his lungs. There's a blockage there, something dense, worse in the left lobe than right.*

"Jesus," she muttered. "Pork Chop was right."

She felt like a spy. But still. Sal had bequeathed the journal for a reason. Frank put another log on the fire and continued.

33

It's so frustrating to see these things and not know what causes them! If I had a chance to live my life over, knowing what I do now, I'd have become a doctor. All I can do is point people in the right direction and hope they'll go. But I suppose doctors must feel the same way—just because they can diagnose a problem it doesn't mean a patient will follow their treatment.

Had lunch with the ladies. It's been months and W was nagging me to come. As much as W can nag! The food was delicious. R is such an amazing cook and such a gracious hostess. I envy her panache and generosity. It was good to see old faces. I'm terribly fond of my friends, and grateful that they always want to include me, I truly am, but as always I leave feeling so inferior. They're all so accomplished and have led such big full lives. I never feel like I have anything worthwhile to contribute. How to explain my hermetic existence? The peace and joy in my solitude? The mountains are my refuge. They always have been, but I've let them become my jail too. Nothing is free. Everything comes at a cost.

The days are dry and hot. We rode through a heady patch of vinegar weed this morning—the smell of high summer! I love it so! This time of year when everything is just hunkered down and waiting, waiting for the long cool rains. Soon they will come and I'll be grumpy I'm stuck inside all day so now I will soak up as much heat and sun as I can and hope it stokes me through the coming days. All the migrants have gone. It's been about a week since I've seen or heard the ash-throated flycatchers and the last of their chicks. The grosbeaks too.

Frank smiled.

There is nothing more comforting than the rhythms and cycles of the world. They are consistent and dependable. Unwavering. So unlike people with all our mercurial wants and needs and greeds. Goodness. I am such a misanthrope! No wonder I can't have lunch with normal people!

> *Only five people today.*
> *D, DD, JH - all limpias*
> *MA pregnant again. Bereft. Husband refuses any form of birth control because he wants to show how many babies he can make. Good grief! She and her children suffer while he drinks and whores around. Will sit with W.*
> *Dear C - I insisted she go to a doctor. There's something I don't like, a hard pull around her right breast.*

Just when I think I've made my peace with the past and the choices I made something comes along to stir it all up. Cassie showed up, sober for a couple days. Then she went on a bender and let me have it. She's not wrong. I was an awful mother. But she's wrong that I didn't love her. It was because I did so much that I let Mike raise her in town. What sort of life would she have had here with me? Yes, she has her problems, but what child doesn't? As hard as it was to do, I believed at the time and still do that giving Mike full custody was the wisest choice. And it wasn't like she never saw me, she did, often, but she still bears the wound of what she considers my abandonment. And in all honesty, she's a grown woman. She really needs to get over that. She apologized the next day but remained sullen and went home early. The past is over and done with. I can't change what I did.

Frank made a face and closed the journal. She hoped her own daughter wouldn't end up feeling that way about her. She put the cheaters back in the drawer and switched the lamp off. Firelight played around the room. The only sound was the steady hiss and snap of burning wood. Frank had wanted to know Sal better but now that she was getting an innermost glimpse she thought of the adage to be careful what you wished for.

While honored that Sal had trusted her with such intimate revelations, at the same time it felt almost like an obligation. Frank appreciated she was a rescuer. It was how she grew up, trying to rescue her mother from herself, from her grief over the loss of her murdered husband. It was probably what had pushed Frank into law enforcement, that need to be the one who could help, who could supply answers and solve mysteries. Sal's naked vulnerabilities tugged at Frank's desire to fix and mend. But Sal was beyond all that now. Wherever she was, hopefully she was in a deep peace. It seemed fair enough reward for the trauma of being human.

Frank drew a throw over herself. She stretched down into the couch, working herself around the dogs. At least, she thought before she fell asleep, nothing terrible had happened in the journal. Yet.

CHAPTER 7

Lolly had told Frank the women were usually at the store by eight, so on Saturday morning Frank got there a little earlier. Careful not to let the screen door bang behind her, she waited while Lolly finished with a customer.

"It's open," Lolly said. "I'll let 'em know you're here. Gotta give those old gals credit for patience. I thought they was nutso but here you are."

"Wish me luck," Frank called from the back door.

"You don't need it. You got the touch."

Frank propped open the shed door and pushed the curtain aside. She pulled out the candles and lit a few, plugged in the party lights, smoothed a clean cloth over the rickety table, and plunked a handful of wild roses into a jar of water. The effect was homey and Frank admired her rusty Martha Stewart skills. She took the seat facing the door and waited. Outside, jays shrieked at perceived slights and goldfinches twittered in the fountain. The fog was burning off but the room was still chilly. Frank blew into her fingers and rubbed her thighs. Still she waited. The birds quieted, and just as she was about to walk around to the front of the store, a gentle tap came.

"Come in!" she cried, chiding her nerves.

One of the old gals peeked around the curtain, clutching a purse and plastic bag. Frank scolded herself again for playing with these poor women.

"Hello," the woman said in accented English.

"Hello." Frank pulled out the other chair. "My name is…"

She caught herself about to say Lieutenant Franco. Then she thought to say Frank but it sounded too glib for the serious ladies, and her real name was foreign to her.

"Miss Frank," the woman said, scooting into her chair. "We know."

Frank smiled. A handful of men and women in South Central had called her that since she'd been a beat cop.

"That's right. And you are?"

"Isidria, but everyone call me Izzy."

"*Estoy feliz de conocerla.*"

"*Ah! ¿Habla español?*"

"*Un poco,*" Frank answered.

She confessed to Izzy that she had no idea what she was doing, and would it be okay if they continued in English for a while? Izzy agreed amiably and Frank asked how she might help.

"I come for my heart, to calm it. It go too fast."

"Have you seen a doctor for that?"

Izzy scowled and made a waving motion. "Too many pills. I don't like 'em. But La Señora Sal, she take my hand like this," Izzy grabbed both of Frank's, "and we sit, sometimes fifteen, twenty minute. Yes?"

"As you wish."

Izzy's hands were strong and rough. Frank didn't know what to do as they sat there so she imagined a heart beating slowly, evenly. She willed Izzy's heart to match her own steady rhythm. She wasn't sure how long they sat just quietly holding hands but at last the older woman pulled away with a calm smile.

"*¿Bien?*" Frank asked.

"*Si. Estoy bien tranquila.*"

"*Bueno.* I don't know what I did but I'm glad it helped."

"*Si.* I hate to tell my friend Dolores but she right. You have *el don.*"

Frank shook her head. "*No entiendo.*"

"*El don,*" Izzy frowned. "How to say? *La toca*, the touch. *Como curandera.*"

"No," Frank protested. "I'm nothing like that."

Izzy shrugged and lifted a plastic bag onto the table. "You like goat? I make *birria*. When I come back you give me bowl." She pushed her chair away and stood. "I see you, Miss Frank."

Frank opened her mouth, so many questions, but Izzy had swept from the room. Frank put the bag on the workbench and when she turned around the other old gal was standing in the open doorway.

Frank repeated her greeting. Apparently this was Izzy's friend Dolores. She made no attempt to speak English and Frank wondered if Sal had spoken Spanish. The woman sat with her bags in her lap, eyeing Frank shrewdly. She asked Dolores how she could help and as best as Frank could understand Dolores asked for a cleansing.

As with Izzy, she explained she wasn't sure what she was doing. Dolores nodded. Pulling closer to the table she laid her hands palms up on the table. Frank rested hers on top of them. Dolores closed her eyes and again they sat in silence. Frank kept waiting for something to happen but aside from feeling sleepy, nothing did. Dolores wanted a *limpia*, a cleansing, so Frank imagined herself as a vacuum, pulling everything dirty and unwanted from Dolores. After a while, Dolores removed her hands.

She nodded solemnly. In perfect English, she announced, "You have the touch."

Frank scowled, feeling as if she was the one being played with. "Why do you say that?"

"I can feel it. Can't you?"

"Not at all."

"Hm." Dolores eyed her coolly. "How long have you been using your gift?"

Frank laughed and looked at an imaginary watch. "Since about nine o'clock this morning."

Dolores thawed, smiling for the first time. "Then you'll just have to keep practicing."

"How did you know about me? I mean, *I* don't even know about me so how could you?"

"Sal told us you had *el don*."

Frank shook her head. "That doesn't make sense. Why would she say that?"

"She told us God had called you here and to look for you."

Frank was still incredulous. "She never mentioned God to me. Not once."

"Hm. To Sal the mountains and streams and trees were her god." Dolores quickly crossed herself.

There was no denying the land had called her, but Frank persisted. "How did you know I'd come?"

Dolores sighed impatiently. "She said if you came back here you might take her place. That you were gifted enough. But that you were stubborn too and might ignore it all."

Frank smirked at the recurring refrain.

Dolores stood. "Izzy told me she made stew for you so I brought tortillas." Passing Frank a bag full of them, she added, "They freeze good. I don't come every Saturday, but Izzy and I were certain that in time you would come. So now that you're here I'll be back soon."

"Wait." Frank's hope of discouraging the women was clearly failing. "I don't know that I'll be here every week."

Dolores measured her up and down with an almost disdainful eye. Then her mouth broke into a grin. "You'll be here."

CHAPTER 8

"That backfired," she muttered, driving up the mountain.

Much as she hated to, she closed the truck windows and turned the air on. Yesterday it had been spring and suddenly it was summer. She flinched at a sharp pain in her wrist when she got out to open the first gate. She'd noticed it a lot the last couple days, an excruciating stab that made her wince and stop whatever she was doing. It passed quickly but it was damn irritating and she didn't know what she'd done to cause it.

Glad when the last gate was closed she drove fast, grateful Pete wasn't out when she passed the ranch house. The dogs were barking joyously from their pen and when she let them loose Bone jumped on her and Kook raced in circles around the yard.

Hugging Bone, she laughed. "It's like you haven't seen me in a month."

She never tired of their pure, unmitigated delight in being with her. So unlike people. She wished she'd had dogs sooner but with her schedule it would have been an awful life for them. Better late than never, she reasoned, uncooping the chickens.

"Damn it!" Her wrist balked at the latch so she used her left hand instead. "What the hell?"

She thought about going for a ride but it was too hot. Besides, she was oddly tired and getting a naggy little headache. The thermometer in the truck had read 91 and Frank decided

41

she just needed to adjust to the heat. Los Angeles summers were hot but she'd at least had the luxury of going in and out of air-conditioning all day. The cabin barely had electricity let alone A/C.

She changed into shorts and a T-shirt and passed the journal on her way out. She paused in the doorway, then turned and picked it up. The dogs and chickens followed her to the creek where she sank into the smooth, knotted roots of an old sycamore. It felt good to not move. She pulled from the canteen wondering if maybe she was dehydrated. The dogs chased each other up and down the creek and the chickens made a racket looking for seeds and bugs. One of them found a grub and the other hens hurried to snatch it from her. The dogs came out of the creek and stood dripping in front of Frank. As if plotting against her they both shook at the same time.

"Hey!" she cried, the unexpected shower cold but refreshing. Bone rolled in dirt and leaves while Kook barked at him to get up and play some more.

"Kook," Frank warned, his shrill yaps like a pick in her brain.

He hushed and plunked next to Bone. The hens scraped some more but one by one they napped beside the dogs in the cool dirt. The creek gurgled and babbled. Soon they were all asleep.

The grosbeak warbling from the bridge woke Frank. She was shocked to see the sun hanging just over the mountains. The dogs were with her but the chickens had gone. She stood, aching from her cramped nap, and walked stiffly to the yard. Grateful the girls had put themselves to bed before the fox could grab them, Frank secured the coop. Scooping out dog food she realized that except for her piece of toast that morning she hadn't eaten all day.

No wonder she felt shitty.

She picked up Bone's dish but her wrist cramped and she dropped it. She frowned, massaging her arm as both dogs chased the scattered kibble. With her left hand she poured a token amount of Kook's kibble into Bone's dish and carried the stacked bowls outside. She left them to their dinner and gingerly opened the fridge. Not trusting her right hand she used her left to pull out Izzy's heavy bowl of stew. Her head was pounding and while she heated the *birria* her heart stuttered.

"What the fuck?" she growled.

Picking up the pot with both hands she carried it to the fire pit and dropped into her chair. She had to rest as a wave of light-headedness swamped her. Must be the heat, she thought. And no food. But that didn't explain the suddenly gimp wrist.

She dipped a tortilla into the pot and chewed. The stew was excellent and she gorged on it. If all her payments were going to be this good, it would be worth spending a couple hours playing witch doctor every Saturday. Tossing the dogs a shred of meat she warned herself not to get used to it. The novelty would soon fade and so would her visitors. She was pretty sure the women felt better after seeing her because they had willed themselves to feel better, not because Frank had done anything. They'd figure that out soon enough.

Pulling herself from the chair she carried the empty pot inside. She returned with bedroll and journal. After spreading the sheepskins out she smoked a cigarette. The sun had just fallen behind the toothy peaks and she watched dusk lay hold of the land. Shivering, she pulled a blanket into her lap. Kook looked up expectantly.

She shook her head and he put his head between his paws. But his brown eyes stayed reproachfully upon her as the journal took his place in her lap. She slid the lantern from the edge of the fire pit to the chair arm. Squinting to make out the fine print, Frank took up where she'd left off.

Three condors just sailed south over the cabin. It's still such a treat to see them! I ran in and got my binoculars just in time to catch their tag numbers before they flew out of sight. I will make sure to tell L as I know how they love tracking these magnificent birds. It's always such a delight to see

43

them, to think we almost wiped them out yet here
they are! Free and flying in all that blue. Oh what
I wouldn't give to fly like one, to see from such a
vantage point, mountain, sea and town all at once.
What freedom!

Frank looked up at the darkening ridge but all she saw was
Sal's graceful dive from the overlook. She wondered as she'd
leapt if Sal had thought of the *zopilote*, if in that instant she
had been able to see as a condor saw. She wondered about the
visions she herself had had, if that was what it had looked like
for Sal in her brief flight. She looked back at the entry. It was
accompanied by a pretty good sketch of three condors perched
on a boulder. Frank hadn't known Sal was an artist. Then again,
there was a lot about Sal she didn't know.

Such a wonderful morning, not hot yet and
so quiet. That deep summer silence when the birds
have finished their work and aren't singing all day
long over territory. That's a symphony I never tire of
yet this deep silence is its own symphony. The puppy
is settling in nicely, following Bone and Cicero, or
staying close by my side. Bone has taken him under
his wing like an old mother hen. Yesterday we rode
out to the old well and he did the whole trip on his
own. I think he will be a fine addition to the pack
and am so glad Pete rescued him.

Sat with W today for MA. She disappeared
into her extraordinary workshop and conjured up
two tinctures and a packet of herbs. She warned
me as always about side effects and efficacy but
unfortunately this isn't MAs first time using them.
Shared the tortillas and amazing bucket of pozole
MZ brought me. Such generosity for just easing
the poor dear's worries. I wish I could pay W for

her time, her craft, her loving attention to detail.
I at least take comfort that she loves her work and
would do it for free anyway.

I'm settled comfortably on the couch with Bone
and Cicero to either side and the puppy curled on
my lap. He is such a silly little thing and so delights
in playing with the big dogs that I have decided to
name him Kook.

"Hey," Frank said reaching down to stroke him. "You're in here."

Kook whapped his tail furiously and rolled onto his back for tummy scratches. She indulged him a moment then read on.

Fourteen women Saturday! I was there until
6! That's too much but I couldn't bear to turn anyone
away. There were four new women among them.
(Why is it always women who trust this type of
healing? Well, except for the men on the ranch.) At
any rate, I slept all day yesterday and have woken
fresh today.

Sal wrote out each woman's initials, their ailments, and sometimes treatments. The more Frank read the more impressed she grew with Sal's "knowing" and with "W's" use of plants.

Found a trapline yesterday, by the Canyon,
with a fawn in one of the traps. Still alive. I'm sure
D is setting them but Pete will do nothing about it
and I'm too cowardly to go over there alone. I let L
know. She'll take care of it somehow. She has her
own way of working in and out of the law. I'm so
grateful for her. Such passion and power packed into
such a tiny body! I wish I had half her courage. I am
making gumweed soap for her. She suffers terribly

after crawling through poison oak, but gods love
her she does so willingly and without complaint.
Per Ws instructions I've added mugwort to half the
soap, which may or may not help with the itch.

Frank reread the lines about the fawn and how Sal was too cowardly to do anything about it, how L, whoever she was, worked in and out of the law. Frank hoped this was the rough justice Sal had been talking about, that there was nothing worse.

Found a hoard of rose hips at old corral. W will
be happy!

Kook managed all the way to the overlook but
the little dear was dead tired so I let him ride on
the way home. He's as good as gold in the saddle
but I mustn't let Pete know how I'm spoiling him!
A hazy day I'm afraid, fog on the coast so I couldn't
see the ocean but still a beautiful ride. Despite all,
I am blessed.

Frank paused again. It pleased her to know how much Sal had loved the overlook and she couldn't help but admire her resolve in choosing to end her life there. Frank didn't know if she could ever take such a bold and final action. She hoped she'd never have to know.

Collected nettle for Pete then cooked it up with
pinto beans and chilies like I always do. After all
these years he still thinks I'm joking that it's nettle.
Silly dear fool.

Asked W if she can make a stronger balm for
NP's arthritis. I hate how she suffers but am sure
W can come up with something effective. Poor
NP fractured that ankle a couple times and never

saw a doctor. She's a tough old gal but now those improperly healed breaks are coming back to haunt her. I know some days she can't walk at all. Poor dear. But I have faith W can make an effective analgesic.

Frank smiled. Sal's deep warmth and affection were another surprise. She had, understandably in hindsight, been cool with Frank and reticent yet the journal revealed a generous, compassionate woman.

She flipped the page to a more reflective item.

Working with CP's stomach issues, encouraging her to talk about her daughter. I think she is coming around to the idea that her grief for her daughter's passing is the source of her continual problems. If she could only allow herself to fully grieve her loss I am certain this plague of GI ailments would stop, but she has literally swallowed her grief and it emerges as GI problems. I'd guess at least three quarters of the people I see have unresolved emotional pains emerging as physical pains, and why not? The physical pain is such an excellent distraction from the emotional. It's tangible, concrete, and far more manageable than untamed, wild grief. My dear ones think I have some magical healing gifts but mostly all I give them is an ear. Sometimes even just a touch is enough, a simple, quiet communion with no expectations or strings attached. Would that we could all have that.

Maybe that was why the women at the store were waiting for Frank—not because she had any particular talents but just because they were used to that special, one-on-one time with another person.

Frank marked her place with the letter and closed the

journal. She shut the lantern off and let her eyes adjust to the night. She called out the stars above the black line of mountains. Bone barked in his sleep. Kook looked up, decided everything was okay, and dropped his head again.

"Good idea," Frank said.

She took the journal inside, brushed her teeth, then slipped into her blankets. She was asleep almost before Kook and Bone had finished snuggling into her. She slept hard and through the night, surprised when she woke that the sun was up and already hot. She threw off the blankets and asked the dogs why they'd let her sleep so long. In answer they fell to wrestling.

"All right," she said rising. "Better join the day."

But before she could fully stand she was felled with dizziness. The dogs rushed in to lick her face and she pushed them away. Her heart skipped a couple beats. Swearing, she rose slowly from her knees. If this kept up she was going to have to see a doctor but what could she say? She was dizzy and her heart jumped the rails every now and then? It didn't seem like much to work with. It occurred to her it was already late in the morning and she hadn't eaten since early last night so maybe standing suddenly had just made her dizzy. It wasn't a big deal. But she was careful when feeding the dogs to carry their bowls with her left hand.

Cradling the journal and a bag of trail mix she took her coffee to the creek. She settled on the bridge while the dogs sniffed around and the chickens waddled to the water's edge for a cool drink. Though she couldn't see them amid the thick green she heard the chatter of the grosbeak, of bluebirds, song sparrows, wrens and magpies. The querulous *ank-ank* of a nuthatch reminded her of the winter, how night after night she'd played Sal's collection of Western Bird Song tapes on an old cassette player, stretched in front of the fire, a dog nestled under each arm.

Frank had drunk deeply of the cloistered nights and monastic days, the noisy peace of storms surging up from the Pacific to howl round the windows and pound on the roof. The electricity had gone out regularly and she found she preferred the gentle glow of firelight and carrying a lone candle around rather than switching on a lamp. Over-illumination was a holdout from living down below, a needless habit that impressed unnecessary details upon her; she didn't need a 75-watt glare to see her toothbrush or coffee pot, to roll back the bedsheets or fill the dog bowls. The excess had been symptomatic of most of her life—too much that wasn't needed, too little of what was.

Frank finished her coffee and opened the journal. She was determined to resolve whatever was inside so that she could return to what was truly important—nuthatches and sunsets, wind playing leaves, creek song, and above it all always, the long, brooding back of the mountains.

Sal's notes remained similar and uneventful. There were more anecdotes of weather, patients and treatments, what was growing where, and rough sketches of the land. They were interesting in that they gave Frank better insight into Sal, but she still couldn't see why she would have wanted anyone to read them, especially her. Frank was relieved that she was almost at the end of the journal and still hadn't found any great mystery to solve.

Until she read,

— came last week. It's taken me until now to even start to write about it. And at that I barely know where to start. I've never felt anything so strongly. Or shockingly. It gives me a jolt just remembering it. I've never felt anything like this before. It's taken a few days to even be able to think about it without my brain shutting down. I'm not sure what to do. How to help, if I even can. I wish I'd done something sooner, known more. I didn't see this coming. But then I never do. I can only react to what is. She hasn't come back and I'm afraid she won't. Even if she did, how can I help her? I can't stop comparing her situation to mine. We both reacted in the heat of the moment.

I think we'd both just had enough. I wanted to ask her about it, talk to her, but she left in such a hurry. She knows I saw something. Maybe I was mistaken? But I don't think so. Oh how horrid. How desperately sad. Is she justified? Was I? I don't think I was. I don't know that anything like this is ever justified. Certainly not in my case. We were adults, Cass and I. We had choices. — is an adult too and while maybe not justified, what recourse do the poor and underprivileged sometimes have but to take matters into their own hands? And here, with dear —, how can I possibly be judge and jury both? Is anyone capable of that tremendous power?

It's four in the morning. I've been up all night. Damn — has brought it all back to me. I have tried so hard to bury it all but of course it's never gone. It never will be, can be. I don't think of it much. I dream about it still but I thought I had made my peace with it and now — has stirred it all up. It's horrible. I can't sleep with all these old ghosts suddenly swirling around me. Bone knows how anxious I am and won't leave my side. Such a tender dear. I must deal with this if only for his sake. I don't know what to do about —. I hardly feel it's my place to do anything. How can I? What a hypocrite I'd be!

Sometimes I wonder why I keep doing this work but then I remember it is my penance. And even then it's not enough. Can it ever be? I think not. I can't get — out of my head. It's awful what she did yet I deeply sympathize. Anyone would who knew her situation and I probably know more than most. I can't possibly renounce her. I have to live with what she did just as I live with what I did.

50

Tonight there is one more ghost in my life.

Frank reread the passages then lowered the notebook. Sal must have "seen" something when she was working on whoever the dash stood for. She was writing in a private journal yet being deliberately vague. Frank assumed it was because she didn't want anyone to accidentally read what her client had done. Because Sal empathized so strongly with her, Frank surmised "Dash" had killed someone. Just like Sal had. She'd spent forty years hiding the fact so if Dash had killed someone in a fit of passion Sal would indeed be the last person to condemn her.

Frank sighed, sure this was what Sal had wanted her to see. She scanned the rest of the journal. There was nothing that seemed related until the very last item.

> *And now AS has killed her husband.*
> *Apparently she ran him over with his own very*
> *expensive pickup. It's tragic but there's a certain*
> *divine retribution in how violently and frequently*
> *he hurt her in that very same truck. I guess for her*
> *a life in prison, for that's what she will surely get*
> *no matter the abuse she suffered, will be better than*
> *one more day at his hands. I weep for her. She is*
> *such a talented woman who has suffered much in*
> *this life. A terrible thought, but maybe prison will*
> *be a relief for her. It's so unfair, after what she put*
> *up with from him. After all the cruelty he inflicted*
> *and which she endured. <u>Always</u> it's the women and*
> *children who suffer at the hands of grown men*
> *who should know better but because men make the*
> *laws they stand above them, or at the very least are*
> *invisible to justice. How can women be to blame*
> *when we take matters into our own hands after*
> *years of torment? And not just to ourselves, but to*
> *our children, our sisters, our mothers? How can we*
> *be any worse than those abusing us? I can't believe*

we are. I won't. It's a lawless justice, but justice, nonetheless. And where women are concerned, when have justice and the law ever been the same thing?

Frank winced. "Hard to argue with that."

> *There are things in this journal I have told no one, that I cannot tell for it is not my place to tell others' stories, no matter how horrific. Sometimes there is a rough justice in how things happen, in events that answer to a greater law than that made by men. It is not for me to say. I only try to help people, not wound them further. It is not my job to punish or dispense judgment. Those that come to me are usually women and their children. Often they seek physical comfort, but more often I think they seek a place to lay down heavy burdens, a place where men and their rigid laws cannot find them. Often my little shack is more confessional than doctor's office, and like priest and doctor, I am bound to secrecy. I am the repository where these women lay their burdens, and this is where I in turn relieve myself of these burdens, as much as one can. But I tire of their suffering. Thank all the gods I have these mountains to turn to. They remind me of my proper place, of how small and insignificant I am in the long run, how petty the worries of this oh so brief life. Here more than anywhere I lay my burdens.*

Frank closed the journal. The water swept by, unconcerned. Kook and Bone napped beside her, oblivious. The outline of the Santa Lucia range peeked through the canopy of trees, indifferent.

Frank rubbed her eyes. She was done with homicides.

And who knew, maybe whatever Dash had done wasn't even a homicide. But it didn't matter. This wasn't Frank's battle. What was done, was done. As Sal had said, a rough justice had been served. No stranger to rough justice, Frank was good with that. She would leave Dash and whatever she had done here in the mountains, just as Sal had.

She focused on the talk of the creek, its babble and gurgle. Picked out a raven squawking somewhere above the trees. Concentrated on the golden slant of sun. Finally she stood. Playful after their naps, the dogs gamboled back to the cabin. Frank trudged behind. She stopped at the corral and rattled the oat can for the horses. They trotted over and she fed them handfuls, scratching under their manes and along their chests. She rested her forehead against Buttons's neck, inhaling the sweet, grassy scent of horse. Grateful not to have missed this in her life, it niggled at her that she would have if it weren't for Sal. Sal who had given her so much, and until now, had asked nothing in return.

She took a deep breath and blew it out. Her head throbbed and her heart skipped a couple beats. She dragged a chair into the shade of the cabin and fell into a deep sleep. No dreams tugged at her. When she woke the headache was gone. The sun was near the rim of the mountains and the dogs danced around her chair to tell her it was dinnertime.

She'd slept another afternoon away. She called the dogs over and cuddled them, wondering what the hell was wrong with her. She got up, sore from the long nap at an awkward angle. After getting the hens to bed and feeding the dogs she watched the sun dip behind the ridge, then decided she should feed herself too. There was the last of the stew and tortillas but little else in the cupboards. She heated the tortillas in a skillet and carried the pot of stew into the yard. The sky had purpled and she ate while searching for the first stars. When she had wiped the pot clean she rolled a smoke. A baby owl begged loudly and a half dozen bats swooped overhead. From somewhere far to the south there came a faint chorus of coyotes. Bone and Kook joined in.

Her smoke rose into the air with their low and mournful howls. Frank ground out the butt and rose carefully. She went into the cabin and retrieved a piece of paper. It was the letter Sal had left her the night she killed herself. Switching on the lantern Frank smoothed the sheet on her knee. She took the cheaters from her pocket and balanced the crooked frames carefully on her nose.

> *I'm sorry it had to end this way. I know there will be trouble for you. I have asked Pete to let you stay but I don't know what he'll do. I've asked him not to be angry with you. What I did was not your fault. In a way it feels good to be free of it. I think for the first time in my life I feel at peace. I think you understand that I can't leave. This is far and away the best possible outcome for me. No matter where you end up, you have a deep gift for healing, for bringing peace. I hope you'll use it and I hope you get to stay here. You belong here. I think you know that. I will always be here. I promise to watch over you. I will take my place in the peaks, looking down, and watching over you, watching over the land. Be well, Frank. Wherever you end up, live from your heart, for it is a big one with much to offer.*

> —*Always, Sal*

Frank read the letter again. And again. Finally she folded the cheaters and put them back in her pocket. More stars appeared in the deepening dark.

Sal was certain she had a gift. Dolores was too. Izzy and Lolly confirmed it. Long ago, a lifetime ago back in LA, Marguerite had said she had it. Everyone could see it except Frank. Everyone said she was a healer but apparently Sal was also expecting her to take care of one more homicide. Frank couldn't wrap her head around either option.

There was a saying in AA: if you didn't know what to do, don't do anything. Meaning if you couldn't see a clear path, then wait for one to develop, trust that it would be shown you. So Frank clicked off the lantern. She looked up at the black peaks watching over her. She nodded, then named the stars, trusting them to light the way.

CHAPTER 9

Making coffee a few days later Frank realized she was down to her backup can.

"Uh-oh," she told the dogs. "Guess we better get to town."

She'd put it off because of the heat but running out of coffee wasn't an option. Plus, she'd eaten the last of the ladies' food and was down to frozen pig, a couple cans of soup and a heel of stale bread.

She loaded the dogs into the truck, and while she was at it man-handled a five-gallon bucket of water. Weeks ago she would have managed to heft the bucket in. Now she had to carefully accommodate her whinging wrist and lift it in stages, from an overturned bucket up to the tailgate. It was embarrassing to be so debilitated. She slammed the tailgate, glad no one had seen her struggling over such a simple task.

Passing the Celadores Store, it occurred to her that tomorrow was Saturday. Frank grimaced, wondering what insane impulse had made her tell Lolly she'd be back. Maybe no one would be there, maybe no one would be waiting on the bench. She took comfort in the thought and concentrated on the twisting road to town. It wasn't the tourists passing through to Carmel she had to watch out for but the locals like Pete who considered the road their personal Laguna Seca track.

Coming round a bend she stopped opposite a massive

rosebush sprinkled with dusty yellow blooms. It was about thirty feet up the slope and looked out over a wide, dry flood plain on the other side of the road. Sal had planted it there when her sister took the curve doing ninety. She had watered it ever since and now Frank did too, stopping every month to haul up the bucket of water.

Getting it out of the truck without dropping it was almost as hard as getting it in. Lugging it up the hill became an effort too. She stopped halfway to catch her breath.

"Something's not right," she panted, gazing out over the shimmering flood plain, heart bouncing in her chest. She grabbed the bucket with her good hand and forced herself the remaining way. Parting the overhanging rose branches she revealed a metal bucket staked beneath. Frank dumped the water in, waited until it began seeping out the stake hole, then clambered back to the road.

A faded red truck slowed as it approached her. It was one of the old guys that often volunteered the steering wheel salute, a quick wave in passing that made Frank feel ridiculously welcomed and accepted. The guy stuck his head out exclaiming, "That's how it stays alive! I've always wondered about that darn bush. I figured there must've been a tiny seep there or something."

Frank smiled at him. "It's a pretty tough plant. Might do okay without me but I don't want to find out."

"Is it there for a reason?"

"Yeah, it's like a *descanso*. You know, a roadside grave marker?"

"Oh, sure, sure. I'm sorry."

"No worries," she reassured. "Obviously a long time ago," she said indicating the overgrown plant. "I didn't know the person who crashed here. She was my friend's sister and my friend's gone now too." Frank shrugged. "Just thought it'd be nice to keep doing it for her."

"It is, indeed. It's lovely someone remembers. Now I will too." He extended a hand out the window. "I'm Kevin."

"Frank," she said, shaking cautiously.

"Where's your place?"

"My place," Frank mused. She wanted to jerk a thumb back toward the mountains. That was her place. "I'm at the Mazetti Ranch."

"Oh, yeah, I know it. It almost borders our place but we're separated by a lot of Forest Service land."

"Where are you at?"

"The hermitage on the other side."

"A hermitage," she repeated. "Forgive my ignorance but what's that?"

"Nothing to forgive," he chuckled. "It's not a common concept. It's basically a monastery—we're an order of monks—but instead of living all together under one roof we each have our own private cells. We come together for certain activities but mostly we live in solitude. It's open to the public," he added. "We have a great bookstore, lots of interesting locally made crafts; we sell our own breads and jams. You should come visit some time."

They both glanced toward the sound of an approaching car. Kevin laughed and said, "I better move before we need to plant another rosebush! It was nice to meet you."

"Likewise," Frank said. Getting back into the truck she glanced at the Lucias in the rearview mirror. "A monastery," she said to them. "All manner of mysteries going on up there." She edged back onto the road and cranked the air conditioning to high.

The library was her next stop. Leaving the dogs under a shade tree with the windows down, she gave them the ritual warning to stay and not scare any nuns. Finding an empty computer she signed in to her account. Her hand cramped over the keyboard and she winced. Shaking it out she scrolled through her emails. They were mostly junk except the ones from the property manager and Darcy. He delighted in telling her about their young daughter's exploits and she dutifully replied. He was such a great dad that Frank had never had a single moment's regret about not keeping their child born of a random, one-night fling. She'd had Destiny for him, knowing how much he had once loved another child who had died far too young.

She squinted at the pictures he'd attached. Destiny had her father's brown eyes and Frank's blonde hair, though technically Frank's was silver now. The kid was a beauty but her face in the picture was stern. Darcy wrote,

This might be the last picture for a while because while I was taking it Dez demanded, "No more pictures. Pictures steal your soul."

When I asked where she got that notion she said Gran'mama Pearl told her. Some kid, huh?

Someone stepped on Frank's grave; Destiny's Gran'mama Pearl had been dead for decades. That hadn't stopped Dez from casually mentioning, ever since she could talk, that Darcy's great grandmother had told her this or that.

"City?"

Frank turned, starting to smile. "Gomez. How are you?"

The women shook hands. Frank gritted her teeth at the flare in her wrist.

"I'm good, how about you? Heard you're living up to the Mazetti place."

"Yep. Pete's letting me stay in the cabin."

Gomez was wearing a skirt suit and at first Frank thought she was on her day off, then she noticed the bulge under her jacket. Frank lifted a brow.

"Are we Detective Gomez now?"

Gomez beamed. "We are."

"Congratulations. How you liking it?"

"It's different. I miss being on the street and I hate all the politics but it's an honor. And word on the street is you're working at the store like Sal. I didn't know you were into all that."

"Word on the street ain't always reliable, Gomez. I just did it last week for a couple of Sal's regulars. I'm pretty sure they'll get discouraged when they realize I'm about as special as a cow patty."

Gomez cocked her head. "Maybe. Maybe not. *Orale.* Come to dinner Sunday, meet my family. Everyone'll be there— brothers, sisters, nephews, nieces—it's a Mexican mosh pit around the dinner table."

"Geez, Gomez. You make it sound real inviting."

The cop laughed. "Nah, we have a good time. And the food, *ay Dios*, my grandmother's started cooking today. Everyone brings something but you would be my guest of honor so you're not allowed to bring anything. Come on, say you'll come. It'd be good for you to get down off that mountain."

"I don't know. I don't get out much."

"That's what I'm saying, City. But I guess I can't call you that no more. Come on. Trust me. You'll have a great time. I want you to meet my sister. You'll love her." Gomez rolled her eyes. "Everybody does. She walks into a room and it's like the sun's come out after years of rain. Ronnie's the sun and the rest of us just tag along in her shadow. I hate her."

Frank laughed and Gomez grinned. "See? You're already having a good time and it's just me." She pulled out her phone. "Still got the same number?"

"No. I don't even have a phone anymore."

"What? *¿Qué tipo de locura…?*"

Gomez fished around in her purse and pulled out a pen and notepad. "Here." She scratched out an address and handed it to Frank. "Three o'clock. Plenty early enough so you don't have to drive up there in the dark." Gomez shuddered. "I don't understand how you can live up there."

Frank smiled. She didn't understand how she couldn't.

"See you Sunday. It's casual, but don't wear shorts. My grandmami's old school and hates seeing women in shorts. And don't bring anything or you'll be in trouble."

Gomez turned and had a brief conversation with the librarian at the checkout desk. She gave her a pat on the cheek then ducked out a side door. Frank tucked the napkin in her pocket. She couldn't have refused dinner unless she chased Gomez down and tackled her.

CHAPTER 10

Saturday morning Frank woke exhausted. It was frustrating because she had no reason to be. She was sleeping long and well, getting plenty of exercise and fresh air. It didn't make sense. Despite the irritating fatigue she wanted to walk the dogs before penning them all day. It was an easy stroll to the ranch house, a flat couple miles, so they followed the jeep trail there. When they got close to the house Pete's dogs set up a holler and ran to greet them.

Pete glanced up from fixing a corral rail. "You going to the store, Chief?"

"Yep."

When she met Pete she'd corrected him, saying she was a lieutenant but he still delighted in calling her Chief, thinking it pissed her off. As far as she was concerned he could call her anything he wanted as long as he let her stay on his property.

"You can leave the dogs here if you want."

"Even Little Bo Peep?"

"Sure," he joked. "I'll let the real dogs herd him around all day."

She walked them over to Pete and refrained from telling them a sappy goodbye. He held their collars until she was well away and she realized how lonely she was without her best friends. Frank couldn't believe that before the ranch she had

61

been afraid of dogs—with good reason as the scars on her arm proved—but Bone had won her over, taken her under his wing just as he had Kook. After Sal died he and Kook had trotted up to the cabin one afternoon and never left. She couldn't imagine living there without them.

By the time she bounced past the ranch house in the Tacoma all the dogs were gone. Even Cicero, Sal's old golden retriever that spent most of his days asleep on the porch. She hoped Pete had been joking about letting them herd Kook around.

When she got to the store Frank was dismayed to see Izzy waiting on the bench. Beside her sat a younger woman and a girl. Frank frowned and parked. She'd been expecting to leave after confirming the bench was empty. She sat a moment, trying to decide whether to tell them they should go home and stay home, or humor them one more time.

Frank sighed. She really didn't have anything better to do than sit and watch the world turn, and while that seemed like important enough work for right now, she also had the feeling she ought to at least see what came of hanging with the women one more time.

Swinging out of the truck she lifted a hand to the women and said, "*Un momento.*"

Izzy nodded and called, "*Claro*, Miss Frank."

Frank smiled and walked into the store. "Morning, Lolly."

Lolly blew out a stream of smoke and laid her cigarette in an ashtray. She grinned. "Morning, *Miss Frank.*" Then added seriously, "You got time to work on me first? Hand's killing me this morning."

"Why not?" Frank answered, amused at Lolly's persistence.

"I already opened up for ya. I'll be there in a sec."

Lolly had turned the lights on in the shed and propped three calla lilies in a vase. Frank took a moment to appreciate the small space, the little touches that made it welcoming. She thought to light one of the many religious glass candles but couldn't decide which one. When Lolly came in she asked her if she wanted a particular candle lit.

"Sure," Lolly said sitting heavily. "Give me that Jesus one there. Couldn't hurt."

Frank put a match to the wick and on impulse lit the Virgin of Guadalupe candle beside it.

"Alrighty."

Lolly laid her hand on the table and Frank took it in both of hers, thinking, *in for a penny...*

The women sat with their eyes closed, and as before, Frank felt only a deep and gentle peace. She soaked up Lolly's pain, willing it away, taking it in. After a time she looked up to find Lolly eyeing her.

"What?"

Lolly frowned. "I don't know what the hell you do but by God you're good at it."

"Hm. I think it's the Jesus candle."

"Maybe," Lolly said, rising from her chair. "I'll send your ladies in."

Frank waited, relaxed and still. Izzy was next and as she took the chair across from Frank she said she liked that the candles were lit.

"*¿Tiene una preferencia?*" Frank asked.

"*Me gusta La Virgen.*" Izzy smiled shyly. "*Ella es mi favorita.*"

Frank put out her hands. "The same as last time?"

"*Por favor*, Miss Frank."

As they sat, Frank's heart skipped a couple beats, raced for a minute, then quieted. It had been years since she'd had a physical. Probably wouldn't hurt to find a doctor in town and get a full workup. On the other hand, she didn't really want to know if something was wrong. She slipped into a gentle doze and when she came out of it she saw Izzy's head was drooping too. Frank wiggled her fingers. Izzy looked up woozily, then broke into a radiant grin.

"*Doctora Frank*," she whispered, before withdrawing her hands and allowing a luxurious stretch.

"I see you next week," she said, depositing a bag on the table. Frank had remembered the Tupperware Izzy had left her and handed it back, thanking her profusely for the stew.

"No *birria* today. Tamales for you. *Pollo y pina.*"

"Together?" Frank asked and Izzy laughed. "*No-o, separados. Muchas gracias*, Miss Frank. I see you.*"

Frank picked up the bag then dropped it back on the table, grabbing at the pain in her wrist. She scowled at the offending area, massaging the pain to a dull ache. She decided if she still felt bad in a week or two, she'd find a doctor. She probably just had a bug. Maybe a side effect was what was making her wrist hurt.

A young woman, holding a girl's hand, peeked in the shed door. "Hello. Are you ready for us?"

"Please," Frank said, indicating the chair. Then she wavered. There were only the two seats. But the girl slid into the one across from Frank and the woman stood behind her.

"I'm Maya. This is my daughter, Viviana. Vivi."

Frank said hello to the girl. "I'm Miss Frank."

"Hi," the girl said huskily. She was about six or eight, with wide eyes and a serious expression. A dark-haired Dez. But she held her head at an awkward angle, twisting it to look up at Frank.

"What can I do for you?" she asked Vivi.

Her mother answered, "It's her neck. She gets these terrible pains, since she was little, and we can't figure out why. It's like there's nothing wrong with her but you can see how it bothers her."

Frank nodded. Treating grown women was one thing; practicing fraud on a child, another.

"You know I'm not a doctor. I can't tell you what's wrong with her and I can't cure her."

Maya snorted. "Well, the doctors can't do none of that either."

"You've taken her to doctors?"

"Lots of times and they all say the same thing—there's nothing wrong with her."

Frank frowned. The girl clearly seemed to be in pain. She

remembered Sal writing that sometimes her patients just needed a confessional, a warm body to sympathize with them.

"How did you hear about me?"

"Izzy. She's my mom's friend. She said you were great. I brought Vivi to see Sal one time but my mother found out and she forbid it." Maya admitted sheepishly, "She said Sal was doing the Devil's work."

Frank looked into Vivi's swimming brown eyes. "And did Miss Sal help?"

She nodded awkwardly.

"What did she do?"

"She put her hands around me like this." Vivi held the sides of her neck.

Frank looked doubtfully at Maya. "I know Izzy told you I was good, but I have to warn you not to expect anything."

"No, yeah, of course. I understand."

"Okay. Just so we're clear I'm not a doctor or anything like that."

"Yeah, I know. Neither was Sal."

"Right," Frank said dubiously, wondering just what the hell Sal had been.

She took Maya's place behind Vivi and asked, "Ready?"

Vivi nodded and Maya whispered, "I'll wait right outside."

Feeling like a snake oil salesman, Frank took a deep breath and put her hands on both sides of Vivi's slim neck. She shifted into a more comfortable stance and waited to see if anything different would happen with a kid. Nothing did, except Frank had the recurring urge to shift one of her hands over Vivi's eyes. She tried to visualize Vivi's neck being straight and supple but her hand kept wanting, almost itching, to move to the girl's eyes. Finally, she whispered, "I want to put my hand over your eyes. Would that be okay?"

The small head nodded and Frank repositioned herself.

There, she thought, that was much better.

"How's that feel?"

"Good," Vivi croaked.

Frank spoke gently, like she had as a detective when questioning a child. "I know you don't know me very well, but if there's anything you want to tell me, if there's anything you're afraid of, or that's hurting you, you can tell me and I promise I won't tell anyone else. Okay?"

Vivi nodded.

"Okay." Frank added, "You're safe in this room."

Vivi kept quiet and time passed as it did in the shed, peacefully and without notice. When it felt right, Frank took her hands away. "How was that?"

Vivi looked like she'd just woken from a long nap. "Good," she said, rubbing the right side of her neck. "It don't hurt no more."

"Good," Frank said, pleased and surprised. "I'm glad I could help."

Vivi scampered off her seat and turned to Maya coming in. Maya knelt to her. "How you feel, baby?"

Vivi's husky voice was louder and clearer when she said, "Good!"

Maya laughed and kissed her. She pulled a twenty-dollar bill from her purse and tried to give it to Frank. "I know it's not much, but I don't have time to cook like the other ladies, and even if I did it wouldn't be so good."

Frank backed away from the money. "Save it for cooking lessons. Really. I don't need it or want it. I'm just happy Vivi feels better."

Maya's face drooped. "Please take it. It's the only way I can think to pay you for what you done."

Frank realized it was important for Maya to pay. If she didn't take the money Frank would be giving her charity and she doubted Maya wanted that. Doubted too that she'd bring Vivi back if it was charity.

"Okay." She reached for the bill. "If you're sure."

Maya brightened. "I am, yes, of course. Thank you. You're as good as Izzy said you were."

Deflecting the compliment, Frank asked what the doctors

said about Vivi.

Maya threw her hands in the air. "They all say the same thing, that there's nothing wrong with her. But she gets these terrible pains in her neck and sometimes it's so bad she curls up in a little ball and cries her heart out. Eh, *mijita?*"

Vivi nodded gravely.

"They can't never find anything wrong but at least this seemed to help."

"How often does she get these pains?"

Maya hefted her shoulders. "No certain times. It comes and goes, it's really weird."

"Stress?" Frank guessed

"Yeah, maybe, who knows? It comes and goes. Don't make any sense, so I guess we'll just see you next time it's bad." Maya nudged her daughter. "What do you say to Miss Frank?"

"Thank you."

"You're welcome."

And she really was. Walking around to the front of the store under the shade of the gnarled old pepper trees, Frank was genuinely pleased she'd been able to help. Surprised too. She still thought it had to be mostly a placebo palliative effect, but she took note that she had wanted to move her hands to Vivi's eyes. It just felt right. It was the same when she ended a session; it just felt like it was time, usually about twenty or thirty minutes after starting. It was like the hunches she'd had while working. They were rarely prompted by anything rational or reasonable, just pure intuition, a gut instinct.

There was no one on the bench in front of the store so Frank closed the shed up and told Lolly she was done.

"See you next week then."

"Yeah," Frank said, looking forward to returning. "You will."

CHAPTER 11

Frank slept deeply that night but in the morning her fatigue was as bad as it had ever been. She spilled the dog food when she tried to pick up the bowls and after she rinsed her coffee cup she stood at the sink and rubbed at a tight kink in her neck.

"Must have slept funny," she told the dogs. They sat eagerly by her feet waiting to see what the morning's activity would be.

"Let's go saddle Buttons," she said and both dogs ran to the door. Sal had said that Bone understood a couple dozen words and Buttons was one of them because when she let them out he ran to the corral, Kook racing to catch up.

She was tired enough that she regretted agreeing to dinner at Gomez's yet at the same time was looking forward to it. For three quarters of a year Frank had been alone on the mountain. Ample time, solitude, and peace in which to lick her wounds. A lifetime of policing had left her with an instinctive suspicion of people but nothing in the world around her now had ulterior motives—everything a tree, a cow, a dog, or a lion did had a pure reason behind it. The natural world had no games or deceit. What it showed you was what it was, and while that was sometimes brutal and ugly, at least it was honest.

She ambled to a worn trail that crossed the lower mountain. It was going to be weird to face a roomful of people. But she genuinely liked Gomez and if nothing else she'd probably get a hell of a meal out of the afternoon. The cop had warned her not to bring anything but Frank rode to a section of the trail draped with yellow bush poppies. She cut a few long branches and on the way back added white manzanita bells and a couple purple lupine stems. Surely she couldn't get in trouble for bringing a bouquet.

After a real shower instead of just a dunk in the creek, Frank penned the dogs and made her way into town. She had an old-fashioned paper map in the truck and found Gomez' house easily.

The door flew open at her knock and Gomez greeted her, "Hello! Come in! I knew it had to be you because everyone else just pushes right in. I'm so glad you came! ¡Ay! Look at these pretty flowers! Come in, come in."

Gomez the woman was a one-eighty of Gomez the cop, with a frilly apron over a flowery dress replacing the drab skirt suit.

"Frank, this is my mother, Marta."

A small, neatly dressed woman with a dark head of hair took both Frank's hands.

"Hello! Welcome. We've heard so much about you."

Gomez nodded at a boy running by. "That's my wild nephew Martin."

He stopped long enough to ask, "Did you ever shoot anyone?"

"Martin!" his grandmother scolded. "What a question to ask!"

"What? Tia Carla has. Have you?" he persisted.

"Enough! Go outside with your cousins!" To Frank, she said, "I am sorry. Children!"

"No worries."

"Come," Gomez ordered and they followed Martin outside where Gomez continued with introductions—her husband, two brothers, two aunts, a brother-in-law, nieces and nephews, great nieces and nephews—more names than Frank could remember, and the librarian Gomez had patted on the cheek turned out to be her sister-in-law.

After herding Frank and her daughter back inside Marta disappeared into a kitchen from whence amazing smells issued.

"And this," Gomez said, "is my sister Ronnie."

A voluptuous woman, all generous curves and mounds, gave her a wide smile. "Ah, the famous cop from Los Angeles." She leaned to extend her hand, her swinging cleavage leading the way. "It's nice to finally meet you."

Ronnie's eyes held Frank's, sparkling as if they shared a delightful secret.

When Gomez introduced Frank to her grandmother the birdlike old woman clasped her hand and patted the space next to her on the couch.

"*Sientate, mijita.*"

Gomez raised a brow and smiled. "What can I get you to drink? Beer? Wine? Fresh horchata?"

"Horchata sounds great."

The old woman beamed and grabbed hold of Frank's hand. She appraised Frank with a benevolent eye, nodding all the while. Curled into an overstuffed chair Ronnie noted, "She likes you."

"*¿Qué hace ella?*" she asked her granddaughter, without looking away from Frank.

"*Fue policia, nana.*"

The old woman shook her head. "*No. Ella es algo mas.*"

Ronnie tucked her feet under herself, saying, "She says you're not a cop. You're something else."

"Not much of anything right now. Just retired."

"Living all alone up in the mountains?"

"Yes, ma'am."

Ronnie laughed. "*Ay*, don't ma'am me. It makes me feel like I'm back at work."

"What did you do?"

"I rose to the lofty height of assistant DA before I decided I'd had enough and packed it in."

"Monterey County?"

"*Sí.* I woke up one morning shortly after my fifty-fifth birthday—I call it my epiphany birthday—and realized I didn't want to be the District Attorney. It was the next logical career move but my heart wasn't in it anymore. That was four years ago and I haven't looked back once. Now my sister here," Ronnie swatted Gomez' rump as she handed Frank a tall glass, "is going to die with her badge on."

"Somebody has to keep us safe."

"That's you, *hermanita.*"

Ronnie squawked as Gomez mussed her hair in passing.

"*Traviesas,*" the old woman grumbled, clearly adoring her mischievous granddaughters.

"So tell us what brought you all the way up here from LA to the mountains?"

"Luck," Frank admitted. "The timing was right, the circumstances."

Ronnie nodded, seeming to glance all over Frank.

"I hear you're taking Sal's place at the store up there."

"I wouldn't say taking her place," Frank defended. "I don't think anyone can do that. But apparently some of the women that used to visit her think I can do what she did."

"And can you?"

Frank was about to answer but Gomez' husband and assorted brothers walked through the living room bearing platters of grilled meats and veggies. An auntie called all the children to the table and Ronnie uncurled from her chair to help her grandmother up. When Frank stood the old woman clutched her arm, steering Frank to the dining room. Aunts, uncles, grandmothers, kids, cousins, all talking at once, squeezed into chairs around the massive table. After helping the grandmother sit, Frank took a seat between her and Gomez. Luis, her husband, led them in a brief, hushed prayer, after which the babel immediately resumed. Gomez handed Frank a heavy platter and Frank hesitated, afraid she'd drop it.

"Would you mind holding it while I serve myself? I hurt my wrist somehow."

"*Claro*. Then help my nana, would you?"

"Of course." Huge platters of homemade tortillas and *pastor* and *asada* made the rounds with bottomless bowls of fragrant beans and rice and salsa.

The food was even better than it had smelled, and when Frank heartily chomped a grilled jalapeño the old woman patted Frank's leg, chuckling her approval. Frank fielded an occasional question but mostly tried to take in all the conversations at once, some in Spanish, some in English or a mix. A couple of times she felt Ronnie's keen ADA appraisal and turned to meet it. Each time Ronnie smiled, at ease with being caught out.

As the eating slowed and the kids were dismissed from the table she again caught Ronnie studying her. Ronnie toyed with the rim of her wineglass, full lips curved, and again they shared a look that almost begged a secret. Frank wouldn't have rubbed it in Gomez' face but she was bang on that her sister was intensely attractive. She had a gleam in her eye, a playfulness that was hard not to get caught up in.

The grandmother broke the spell, taking Frank's hand and declaring. "*Me gusta ella. Dile ella tiene que volver.*"

Not having let on that she understood any Spanish Frank let Ronnie translate that her grandmother insisted she return.

She lowered her gaze from Ronnie to the old woman. "Tell her the pleasure would be all mine."

She rose and tried to help clear the table but the old woman insisted Frank return with her to the couch. Frank settled her then turned to the two sisters.

"Gomez, thank you for the invite. You were absolutely right about the food. What a feast."

"I'm so glad you could come. Now that you know how good it is I hope you'll come again."

Curled back into the easy chair Ronnie waved a hand, commanding, "Sit, sit, sit. I'm dying to hear about what you do in the store. Tell us everything."

"Oh no, no." Gomez had been perched on the arm of Ronnie's chair but she jumped up. "Don't involve me in all that *brujeria* nonsense."

"It's not witchcraft!" Ronnie yelled after her sister. "*Ay,* that one. She's *so* superstitious. *Mira.* I hear you haven't been doing this long, is that so?"

"Where'd you hear that?"

"The Dolores that came to see you? She is one of my oldest, most cherished friends."

"Ah."

"She was impressed. And I'll tell you, Dolo does not impress easily." Ronnie eyed Frank with what she was positive was her old ADA look. "She said you were new at this."

"Yep. I just did it a couple times hoping I'd discourage everyone from wasting their Saturday mornings."

"But you haven't, have you?"

Frank shook her head. "Kinda the opposite."

"Um-hm." Ronnie's eyes were still bright and hard on her. Frank thought she would have hated to have been a defendant facing her. "Did Carly mention anything about me?"

"Just that you're like the sun after years of rain and everyone tags along in your shadow."

Ronnie threw back her head and belted out a laugh. "*Ay, mi hermana.* I love her. That's all she said?"

Frank grinned. "That's not enough?"

"It is!" Ronnie clapped her hands. "She didn't tell you I have my own little gift?"

"*El toque,*" Nana chirped, startling Frank. "*Ella tiene el don.*" Patting Frank's thigh she added, "*Esa lo tiene tambien.*"

"You speak English," Frank said to Nana. The old woman just shrugged. Ronnie said, "Don't let her fool you. She understands more than she speaks, *de vera, Nana?*"

The old woman shrugged again.

Frank was about to ask Ronnie about her gift but Ronnie said, "What's wrong with your wrist? I saw you favoring it at dinner."

"Oh, that. I don't know. I've just been getting these weird pains lately when I try to hold something."

73

"Um-hm. And your neck?"

"What about it?" Frank had just reached for the kink there and Ronnie said, "You've been doing that all day."

"Oh." Frank hadn't realized.

Gomez came in asking, "Do you two *brujas* still have your pointy little witch heads together?"

Ronnie sniggered. "Boil, boil, toil and trouble. Be nice to me or I'll make your brains bubble."

The sisters were fun to watch together but Frank didn't want to outstay her welcome. She rose, thanking the ladies for the wonderful meal and lively company. When she turned to say goodbye to Nana the old woman pulled her down and kissed her cheek. She said something Frank didn't catch but Ronnie translated, "She said you are welcome any time and that she hopes to see much more of you."

"*Gracias, señora.*"

"You have a good accent," Ronnie noted.

Frank winked. "Your nana's not the only one with secrets."

Gomez started to see Frank out but Ronnie said, "Sit, Carly. I'll see our guest out."

"*Bueno, jefa.* Good to see you again, City. Thanks for coming, and come back soon or Nana will be disappointed."

Ronnie led her out the front door where the sun was heading toward the rim of the Santa Lucias. Frank scanned the peaks. Her cabin was out there somewhere. As lovely as the afternoon had been, she couldn't wait to get back to the silence and her dogs, the birds twittering goodnight, the purple drape of night falling over the mountains.

Looking where Frank was Ronnie said, "We're a lot to handle all at once. I hope we didn't overwhelm you."

Frank grinned at her. "You did. But it was a nice overwhelm."

Ronnie hooked her arm through Frank's, the move as startling as it was pleasant. "Can I be blunt with you? Do you mind a little bluntness?"

Frank looked back at the peaks. "I was just thinking this morning that one of the reasons I love it up there so much is there's no artifice. Nothing lies to you."

"*Ay*, I'm sure that's refreshing after a career in law enforcement."

"Very."

"Come." Ronnie tugged her to a bench near the door. She smoothed her long, colorful skirt under her as she sat. "This gift of mine. I don't tell many people about it because one, it's none of their business. Two, it's hard to explain, and three, most people think it's *pura tonteria*, silly New Age nonsense. But I was watching you at dinner—"

"—I noticed."

Ronnie flashed a bright smile and Frank marveled that she really was like the sun after a storm. She was pretty sure they were flirting with each other and it was fun. Ronnie gave her shoulder a light swat.

"Listen. Long story short, your energy is all over the place. When you first got here, *ay, ay, ay.*"

She shot her hands out around her head. "It was spiky and shooting out everywhere, but it's better now. It's pulled in and smoothed out. I don't usually do this without asking permission first, but with you, *ay*, it's just *out* there, all over. Your neck and wrist—the *don* I have, the touch as Nana says—is I see colors. Not exactly see, like with my eyes because I can close them—" she did—"and still see them. There are blotches on your neck and wrist—your right one—that are dark like charcoal, and solid and dense and crumbly, like charcoal, and they suck in light like little black holes."

Frank popped her eyes open. It all sounded terribly bad but she almost laughed. Her life was suddenly in free fall—yucky black holes in her body, practicing medicine without a license, dinner with a roomful of strangers, and now this intriguingly handsome woman beside her.

"What are you smiling about? This is serious. You said yourself that you haven't been doing this long and I'm concerned you're doing it wrong, that you're going to hurt yourself."

The sounds of talking and kids' laughter drifted from the

backyard. Frank turned her gaze back to the mountains. "I'm sorry. Go on."

"This work you've done. I know Dolo asked for a *limpia*, and apparently you gave it to her. What else have you done?"

"Let's see. Someone's arthritis."

"Where was it?"

"Uh, in her wrist."

"Okay, who else?"

"Another person had heart trouble. Should I be telling you this?"

Ronnie flapped a hand.

"What was wrong with the heart?"

"Said it beat too fast."

"Um-hm. Anyone with a neck problem?"

Frank turned sharply. Ronnie had the ADA gaze all over her. "Are you getting the picture, *querida*?"

"Jesus." The fatigue, the erratic heartbeat, stabbing wrist pains, now this cramp in her neck. "Am I...I'm really doing something, aren't I?"

Ronnie laughed. "You really are, honey. Can't you tell?" "Not really. I was thinking yesterday that all it feels like is intuition. Like having a hunch about what to do. But other than that, it doesn't feel like I'm doing anything."

"Maybe that's all it is for you. But I think you might be going about it all wrong, and you say you've never done anything like this before?"

"Nope."

"Do you know about grounding?"

Frank shook her head.

"How about barriers, or filters?"

"Coffee, cigarette, or oil?"

"*Ay*, now you're making jokes. Fine."

Ronnie turned away from Frank to stare at the mountains. She crossed her arms over her ample chest and pouted.

Frank felt so comfortable with Ronnie, she blurted, "I think you're trying to be cross with me but you're totally adorable when you do that."

"And you are just being willfully ignorant," Ronnie snapped.

Frank laughed. "All right. Tell me about filters."

"No."

"Come on." She made an X over her heart. "I promise to behave."

"*Ay*, you're laughing now but keep doing what you're doing and we'll see how funny it is when you land in the hospital."

"Will you come to visit me?"

"No, because you're being too impossible."

"*Ay*, see? My heart's already broken. It's too late to save me."

Ronnie smiled and laid her head back against the sun-warmed wall. Frank did too. "Tell me about filters before I find myself dying all alone in some god-forsaken hospital."

"Only if you'll promise to come to lunch tomorrow."

They looked at each other.

Frank admitted, "I'd love to."

CHAPTER 12

Frank grinned all the way back up the mountain. She felt almost as excited as she had during that last drive to LA. Change was coming and though she didn't know what it was she was looking forward to it.

When she let Bone and Kook out of the pen she confided, "Helluva day, boys." And then, "I met a nice lady."

Easy on the eyes, Frank thought, then amended that to gorgeous, downright hot. Gomez had nailed it when she'd said Ronnie was like the sun after weeks of rain. She was so vibrant and vivacious it was a delight simply to be in the shade she cast. Without a doubt Frank had been instantly attracted to Ronnie, and while she was definitely sexy Frank considered that the allure felt more magnetic than sexual.

It was curious, as most of her past relationships had been driven by physical hunger. Except maybe for Maggie, so long, long ago, the sex was more important than the relationship. Sex was a way to be engaged with someone but not emotionally committed. Frank didn't think she'd have been capable of such a commitment while she was working, there was too much of her she had to hold back. To be an effective cop she'd kept a lid on her feelings, tried not to acknowledge them too much. That kind of blew up when she got sober, and now the lid wasn't necessary. She had no reason to hold back.

This attraction to Ronnie felt…it felt big. And whole. It felt complete, like she was attracted to the entire woman instead of her parts. She wondered if she'd ever liked anyone as much as she seemed to like Ronnie. She'd loved, she thought, as best she could at the time, but in retrospect her love was probably parsed, carefully doled out to prevent her from feeling too much.

"Curiouser and curiouser," she said to Bone and Kook. "But Mama's got a date tomorrow so more will be revealed."

But the date turned out to be lunch with three other women. Frank was disappointed and slightly embarrassed as Ronnie introduced her friends.

"Dolo you already know. And this is Winnie. Winnie is an herbalist. There's not a plant out there she doesn't know what to do with."

A fine-boned woman with freckles and a mousy bowl-cut gave her hand a light shake. "Hello," she said gently.

"We have lunch every couple weeks—"

"And Ronnie always cooks because she's the only one of us who can." A bald, eye-patched woman lurched from her chair and shook Frank's hand so hard she cringed. "I'm Char," she wheezed, one bright blue eye looking down on Frank.

"Pleasure," Frank managed, refraining from massaging her hand.

"There's a couple more of us, but whoever can make it comes, whoever can't, can't."

"I barely made it this week," Char said. "Chemo's kickin' my ass."

"Right now the dog is biting you, *querida*, but soon you're going to turn around and *bite the dog!*"

"You got that right," Char grumbled.

"Speaking of dogs." Ronnie pointed to five pint-sized beasts prancing around the living room. "I hope you're not allergic. There are cats around here somewhere, too. But now come, come, come. Let's eat before the flies carry it all away."

The house was an older bungalow and the women followed

Ronnie single file into a backyard twice the size of the house. Bushes and flowers and trees bloomed or fruited in every conceivable shade of the rainbow and tucked amid them half a dozen fountains splashed and burbled. Beneath a ramada covered in grapes Ronnie had set a simple yet elegant table. As the women pulled their seats out, she said, "No tomatoes yet, but the peaches are to die for, so fresh *queso fresco* I made myself, sliced peaches drizzled with a very old balsamic and a sprinkle of rosemary, and the bread is just out of the oven. Plain white for my *querida*, Char. I know that's about all you can stomach these days."

"Wouldn't you think I'd lose some of this weight on a diet of bread and water?" she asked Frank, patting the ample belly under her checked cowboy shirt.

Ronnie laid a warm hand on Frank's shoulder and pointed at a row of bottles. "My homemade blackberry brandy and a white wine from Winnie's own grapes, and of course water, with just a hint of watermelon and ginger. But I insist you try the wine with lunch."

Frank laid a palm over her glass. "Water will be fine."

"*Ay*, like Char, you are."

"Yep. This old gal went through all her booze tickets. Cashed 'em in twenty-one years ago March."

"You've got a lot of years on me," Frank admitted. Char broke into a toothy grin and they clashed glasses together.

The women served themselves with long reaches and ate heartily, except Char who nursed a single slice of bread and took nibbles from a peach slice. Frank asked how they all knew each other.

Dolores answered, "Ronnie and I grew up together, then we raised our kids together."

Kids, Frank thought, thinking she may have misread Ronnie's flirtatiousness. Then again, she'd had a kid...

"And I met Winnie through work," Ronnie said around a mouthful of peach. Winnie smiled but kept her eyes down. "Char's husband used to do farm irrigation where my ex works."

Kids and an ex. Frank had definitely been on the mountain too long.

The women started telling stories about each other, except Winnie, who even in her circle of friends seemed timid and uncertain. After they'd eaten their fill and emptied the wine, Ronnie went to the kitchen for dessert.

"So you're up at the Mazetti Ranch, is that right?" Char asked.

"Yep."

"I've never been up there, but it's where the Celadores Road ends, right? At the store there?"

"That's it."

Char nodded gravely. "I did have occasion to go next door once. Up Maldito Canyon. You know it?"

There was an unmarked road that yawed off south before the store and Frank asked if that was it.

"That's the one. They called me up there one day to do some dowsing for 'em. I don't like telling tales out of school, but there was some bad business up that canyon. Found their water and couldn't wait to hightail it outta there. That well apparently went dry—and it was a good one when I hit it—but they called me and asked me to come find another and I tell you what, I said, no thank you."

"Char," Ronnie chided, putting a casserole dish on the table. "Are you trying to scare poor Frank?"

"No, hon. Just telling it like it is. Now Celadores is fine, what's left of it. That store is quaint and cute as a button. But that canyon?"

Char made a noise and shook like a wet dog.

Ronnie dabbed a spoonful of dessert into the little bowl in front of Char's plate. "A brown sugar *crème anglaise*," Ronnie said to Char. "See if you can't eat a spoonful or two."

"Aw, sweetie, I wish you wouldn't go to so much trouble for me."

"*Querida*." Ronnie kissed the top of Char's bald head. "It's no trouble and it gives me a good excuse to cook. Now try a

81

little." She served everyone else much larger dollops and without asking poured brandy for Winnie and Dolores.

"You're a dowser," Frank said to Char.

"Was. I don't do it much anymore."

She was about to ask what her success rate was but Ronnie interrupted, "And that brings us to why I asked you here today."

She smiled sweetly at Frank, and Frank felt stupid, wondering how she had so badly misinterpreted Ronnie's intentions.

"You see, *querida, e*ach of us has a little special *don*. Char's is dowsing, mine is the colors, Winnie has a mysterious connection to anything with roots."

Winnie blushed and ducked her head, gazing into her lap.

"Oh, wait." Frank turned toward her. "Are those your herbs and potions in Sal's shed?"

The mousy woman suddenly came alive. "Yes! They're still there?"

Frank nodded, thinking Winnie was the "W" in Sal's journal.

Ronnie continued, "Dolo is, *pues…*"

"I see dead people," Dolores said with mock spookiness.

"She's a little clairvoyant," Ronnie agreed. "And you seem to have this touch. You know how I was *trying* to tell you yesterday about doing this work so that you don't hurt yourself? But then I thought it's kind of like telling someone what hobby to pursue. What works for me may be absolutely useless to you, so I asked the girls if they'd mind sharing how each of them works with their *don* without hurting themselves."

"Or others," Dolores added.

Startled, Frank asked, "Did I hurt you?"

"No. I think you helped a great deal. But these gifts we have, they're an energy just like electricity, and like electricity if they're not used correctly they can cause harm."

"And we—"

"Wait. Before we go any further. How did each of you know you had your gift?"

"My grandpa handed it down to me," Char piped up. Frank noticed her spot of dessert was untouched. "He taught me just to be quiet and stand still until I felt like moving in a certain direction. He'd say, 'Just wait 'til the good Lord tells your feet where they oughta go.' I was too impatient at first but gradually I learned to do like he said, and then it was easy after that. Some people say women can't be dowsers but I've got a paid mortgage on a ranch says that's bull. Most of the drillers in five counties have my name in their contacts."

Frank nodded, remembering how her hand had wanted to go in a certain direction when she was working on Vivi.

"Winnie?" Ronnie prodded gently.

Winnie shook her bangs at her plate. "Oh, I don't know." She reached for the brandy and filled her tiny, inlaid snifter. "I've just always felt like plants were my friends. I don't know. Maybe it's like how Ronnie knows what her dogs want. You just…feel it."

"I think dogs are a little more expressive than plants," Char argued.

"Not to me," Winnie insisted with sudden vehemence. Her cheeks were ruddy and Frank wondered if the wine and brandy were kicking in.

"When did you first notice?" Frank asked.

"When I was eight," she beamed. "I remember because I'd asked for a teddy bear for my birthday just like my sisters but instead my mother gave me a begonia. A wax begonia. I was so disappointed I threw it in the trash."

At least forty years later, Frank guessed, and she still looked ashamed at the memory.

"That night when we were getting ready for bed my sister teased me with her bear. She made me so mad I went outside and pulled my plant out of the trash. One of the flowers had broken off and a couple leaves were crushed but I brushed it off and carried it back into our room. I told her her dumb teddy bear wasn't even alive and that she'd never be given a plant because she was too stupid to keep one alive."

Dolores sniggered.

"After that, I *had* to keep the poor thing alive so I went to the library and checked out every book I could find that mentioned begonias. I fell in love with it," she said wistfully.

"What happened to it?" Frank asked.

"Oh, they don't live very long. But by then I had a whole collection of plants on our windowsill. Begonias, African violets, kalanchos. I loved them all and I just…"

She shook her bangs again, a tell when she was unsure.

"I just somehow knew how to take care of them. I could sense when they needed water or food, or more or less light. I don't know."

She finished off her snifter and Char said, "But she left out the best part. Not only can Winnie make anything grow, but she is also a truly gifted apothecary."

"I'm not." Winnie blushed and gave her signature head shake.

"You are. You make the most intuitive medicines. Tinctures and oils and ointments. I don't even know what all else, but I do know that whatever ails you, Winnie can find a treatment for it."

"She's a fine *yerbera*," Dolores said, patting her hand.

"That tea you make for me helps me sleep when nothing else does," Char attested.

Dolores added, "And don't forget Eddie's hemorrhoid cream." The women laughed. "He's going to sue Preparation H because their cream is such *shit* compared to yours."

This doubled them over and Frank grinned. So she'd misread Ronnie. It was still nice to be included in this group of obviously very devoted friends. When they were done laughing and drying their eyes, Dolo explained that she saw things before they happened.

"The first time was when my *yayo*, my grandfather, said to me that we'd go get ice cream tomorrow and I explained to my mother very loudly and clearly—I think I was seven at the time—"We can't get ice cream tomorrow because Yayo will be dead.' ¡*Ay*! She slapped me so hard it's a miracle my teeth didn't fly out of my head! But sure enough, he had a massive coronary in his sleep that night. You can be sure though I never said anything like that again."

"How did you know?" Frank pressed.

"I just did," Dolores said. "The picture popped in my mind. It's like when you've forgotten where you put something and then you think 'oh I'll go look here' and then there it is."

"Tell her about Yazi," Winnie begged. Even though it was warm out she rubbed her arms. "It still gives me chills."

"*Ay*, Yazi. My granddaughter. I was at work one regular day, I remember I was checking our pallet inventory, and I just had this sudden, *fuerte* urge to call my daughter. Mind you, I had a very important job and I didn't spend all day on the phone like people do now. I don't think I'd ever called during work to ask about any of the children or grandchildren, but I just couldn't shake the feeling."

Winnie hugged herself and shivered.

"It was like how a sneeze comes on and you just can't stop it. I tried to ignore it but it kept getting stronger and stronger so finally I just called my daughter. I woke her up. She'd fallen asleep on the couch and I said, 'Where's the baby?' She said, 'Right here.' But Yazi wasn't next to her. The next thing I hear is 'Oh my God, Mama, where is she? She was sleeping right next to me!' and she drops the phone. I hear her screaming for Yazi and then, 'Ohmygod, ohmygod.'"

Dolores crossed herself. "By then I'm screaming into the phone, 'What happened? What happened?' and finally my daughter comes on, she's crying hysterical-like and I think Yazi's dead and she says, 'Mama, she was behind the couch. She'd pulled the lamp plug out and was chewing on it, and Mama,'" Dolores paused and looked around the table. "'Mama,' my daughter said, 'she was just about to put her hand on the socket.'"

Dolores sat back with a satisfied expression. She pointed a finger at the roof of the ramada.

"Mary," she said.

"Mary? The Virgin Mary?" Frank asked. "She told you?"

"No, of course she didn't *tell* me," Dolores scoffed. "But she's the one who put the idea in my head to call. It's always God that does this. Not me. It's nothing I can control. It's all," she lifted her eyes and pointed again.

"You?" Frank said to Ronnie.

"Oh, I was a late bloomer. For me it started the same time I started the menopause. Someone would walk into the room and I could tell where they were emotionally—it was the most interesting thing—I mean obviously when someone walks into a courtroom they're going to be stressed but I started noticing, not exactly feeling and not exactly seeing but a kind of combination of the two, so I just call it sensing, like an extra sense.

"I started sensing this compactness I was telling you about, kind of like a black hole around people who were hiding something. Not that everyone was always guilty of what they were there for because all of us are hiding something, right? But I started noticing the more someone was hiding things, the darker and denser they felt to me. And not just parts of them but like they were covered in a dark, wet blanket. But then sometimes people had a lightness around them, a clear and breezy kind of feel to them, but they're both pretty rare. Most people are a mix. At least in my experience.

"At first it just seemed kind of fun and harmless, but then I started feeling bad. I thought I was coming down with one of those vague autoimmune diseases that just leave you frazzled and achy all the time. I went to doctor after doctor, and no one could find anything wrong with me. Then Dolo said I should go see Sal. She took one look at me and said, 'My gods. What have you been doing?'"

Frank smiled. Sal had always pluralized her god.

"She explained I'd been so busy sticking my nose into other people's business that I hadn't thought to take care of my own. She worked on me for half an hour and by *todos santos* if I didn't start to feel better *immediately*! I felt like a *teenager* the rest of the day and that night I slept all the way through for the first time in months. After that, I never ached again. She showed me how to keep sensing *and* take care of myself. Like I was trying to explain to you yesterday but you were being *tonta.*"

"Like I said," Dolores picked up. "It's just like electricity. Some is so scattered and so diluted you can barely feel it, but then some of it is so concentrated in one place—"

"Like lightning!" Winnie blurted. She had finished a third snifter of brandy and Frank had seen Ronnie quietly stopper the bottle and put it on a table behind her.

"*Exacto*. You know how houses have those grounding rods so they can—" She waved her hand. "What's the word?"

"Dissipate? Diffuse?" Ronnie supplied.

"*Si*! So they can dissipate the energy. Your body has to do the same thing. Too much energy and boom! You explode. Let me ask you," she said to Frank. "When you worked on us what were you thinking of?"

"Uh." Frank pursed her lips. "Not much really. I was just trying to absorb whatever—"

"Absorb?" Winnie said. "You can't *absorb* anything. Oh my gosh. I need to make you some bath salts right away."

"See?" Ronnie lifted a brow. "I told you."

Dolores was wagging her bunned gray head. "Winnie is right. What happens if the house tries to hold the lightning?"

"Boom?" Frank suggested.

"*Big* boom," Ronnie said. "You have to let the energy, the electricity if you will, move *through* you, not *into* you. I was doing the same thing. I was looking at people and taking all that nasty energy in instead of just observing it and letting it move on. You have to be the grounding rod. In your case you have to take the energy that's coming into you and let it move *through* you and into the patient you're treating."

"Through them, too," Dolores added, "and down into the ground where it *dissipates*." She winked at Ronnie.

"Speaking of the ground. This is something else Sal told me." Frank looked around the table. "Did you all know Sal?"

Each head nodded. Each woman looked at Frank knowing she was the last person to have seen their friend alive. She wondered if they believed what had happened to Sal or if they had doubts.

"She would come on Mondays when she could."

"I think she coulda come a lot, but Sal was private like that. Not much for socializing."

"But when she did come I think she enjoyed herself," Winnie ventured.

"Anyway." Ronnie flapped a hand through the air. "Sal told me before you start putting your nose into anyone else's business that you have to ground yourself. You have to connect yourself to something bigger and larger than yourself. For me, I think of all my ancestors, and my lineage, their spirits above me and their bodies returned to the earth. Everyone has their own way of doing it. You have to find your own thing. Winnie, I bet you think of a tree."

"Yes!" she cried, eyes bright. "How did you know?"

Everyone chuckled.

"I imagine myself as a great big oak with my branches high in a warm blue sky and my roots down deep, deep, deep in the cool earth. I love that feeling."

"Char?"

"Well, I just go down to the water. I know it's under there somewhere and I just try to imagine it in its bed, just waiting for me to come find it. Dolores, when these visions come on you the way they do, do you even have time to prepare yourself for 'em?"

"Oh, right away I make the sign of the cross and ask Mary's protection and for her help to do what she wants me to. I didn't used to, but now I slow down enough to do that."

Ronnie put her hand on Frank's. "*Pobrecita*. Are we making you crazy with all this talk of lightning and trees? Oh but you know," she said suddenly, "it's like Dolo said about asking for Mary's protection. That's the filter I was trying to tell you about. That you allow in what needs to come in but make a barrier, a filter for anything that's unwelcome or not necessary."

"*Ay*," Dolores agreed. "There are things out there you definitely don't want coming in."

"Like what?"

"Enough!" Ronnie clapped her hands and Winnie jumped,

looking for the brandy bottle. "Who wants more dessert?"

"I reckon I'm done in," Char said.

Her friends gathered around to hug her and see her to the door. Ronnie dropped back to ask Frank if she could stay after everyone had left and she agreed. When she thanked the ladies for sharing their stories with a complete stranger Dolores pulled her into a hug and said, "You're not a stranger anymore. I expect to see you here every Monday."

"Thank you," Frank answered, surprisingly touched.

"It was nice to meet you," Winnie said. She stood by Ronnie, clearly waiting for Frank to leave, but Ronnie kissed her friend's cheek and said, "Drive carefully, *mijita.*"

"Oh." Winnie was startled, then resigned. "Oh, okay."

As they watched Winnie leave, Frank asked, "Is she okay to drive?"

"She'll be fine. She's only a few blocks away."

Ronnie closed the door and leaned against it. "Did you enjoy lunch?"

"Very much. Thanks for having me. I like your friends."

"They're your friends now, too. Come," she ordered, moving to the sofa and patting beside her. "Sit. Do you have a little time?"

Frank grinned. "For you? Eons."

"*Ay, que bueno.* I was hoping we could get to know each other a little better. Just the two of us."

"I'd like that. A lot. Now tell me about your kids."

"*¡Ay,* the loves of my life! My daughter and her husband live in San Francisco. I hate she's so far away but I'm glad she didn't settle here and didn't get stuck making a living in commercial ag. I know I sound ungrateful because my father made an excellent living for us doing exactly that, and Carly's husband too, but how we grow food here? With all the pesticides and herbicides and gasses? *Ay!* I know we feed the nation and to produce food on that scale you need all those chemicals and processes but it's so sad, and everything tastes," she shuddered, "like nothing. That's why I *adore* my little garden that's *real* food. You can taste the love and sun and good old-fashioned *manure* in what

I grow, and I don't grow it just for me but *mi familia tambien*."
She laughed. "My *abuelita* won't cook with anything that's not from my garden or fresh from the farmers market. Don't tell my father."

Frank smiled, dazzled by Ronnie's passion, her zeal.

"*Pero* anyway, they both have careers that are more important to them than children, so no grand-babies for me. Yet."

Ronnie put a hand on her heart.

"My son." She sighed. "He's in and out of prison. I love him. I always will, but by all rights he should be dead." She ticked off on her fingers. "Meth, heroin, coke, crack, pills. He can't stay clean. I won't see him anymore. Neither will his sister. I used to try and help him but he doesn't want help. Just money to put in his arm or up his nose. I wait every day for the phone call that tells me he's OD'd or been stabbed or shot. Something. And such a sweet baby, such a sweet boy. One's greatest loves are also one's greatest sorrows."

"I'm sorry. His father see him?"

"*¡Ay*, don't get me started!" Ronnie shook her head. "He can't say no to him. He's his only son. He's *tonto* with him, he's always spoiled him."

Ronnie made a clear effort to shrug off her grief. "Now tell me about you, *querida*? Any *niños*?"

"One. A girl. She's almost seven."

"*Ay*," Ronnie cried, "she's little! Is she up there with you? How old is she? And her father, where's he?"

Frank chuckled at Ronnie's whirl of questions.

"She actually lives in Louisiana with her father. It's a long story but we hooked up one night, it was a completely random thing. I can't say I'm a Gold Star Lesbian—"

"*¿Que es eso?*"

"A lesbian who's never been with a man."

"*¡Ay que rico!*" Ronnie laughed. "Go on."

"So right away the odds of sleeping with him were pretty slim, but one night it was just the perfect storm for both of us. It never occurred to me I could get pregnant. My periods were pretty erratic by then. Thought I was in menopause. Imagine my surprise when my gynecologist told me I was pregnant. I never wanted kids. I wouldn't be a good parent, so I told Darcy that unless he wanted the kid I was going to abort it. He's a good man. Said it was 100 percent my decision, but that he would love to raise it if I was willing to have it. He'd lost a daughter to cystic fibrosis so he was pretty excited. He never pressured me. Never pushed. But it seemed kind of fated. Both of us coming together that one time, and me a lesbian, an *old* lesbian at that. I knew he'd be a great dad. So I had her. He retired and moved back to be with his people in Louisiana."

"*¡Ay*, that's so far away! Don't you miss her?"

"It was harder to let her go than I thought it'd be but I knew that was mostly the hormones kicking in. Like I said, I never wanted kids. Never understood 'em. Maybe because I never was one. Had to be an adult early on. So it was relatively easy to let her go and I could never in a million years raise her as well as Darcy is. She has lots of family around. She's got friends her age. She's healthy and adored."

"How often do you see her?"

"Never. She hasn't shown any interest in meeting me and Darcy doesn't want to force her. He said someday she will and I'm fine with waiting. He sends pictures every week and keeps me updated."

"And that's enough?"

"Yep."

"*Pues*, what about the rest of your people?" Ronnie asked, "Where are they?"

"Dez is my only people. There is no one else."

"*Ay, querida.* That sounds so lonely!"

"I suppose it sounds that way but it doesn't feel that way." Frank guessed, "Maybe because I grew up an only child? I'm used to being alone, being my own best company."

"Are you saying I'm not good company?" Ronnie sulked.

"I would never say that. You're the best I've had in a very long time."

Not willing to beat around the bush anymore Frank parroted Ronnie. "Can I be blunt with you? Do you mind a little bluntness?"

Ronnie tossed back her head and laughed. Frank already knew she loved making Ronnie laugh. "*Ay, ay, ay.* What have I set myself up for?"

Frank smiled. "Nothing terrible. This may sound ridiculous, and it's the butt of many a lesbian joke, but it seems that after barely knowing you twenty-four hours I really like you. I think maybe you feel the same. Am I right or wrong?"

Ronnie was smiling at her. "I would say you were..." She toyed with Frank, biting her lower lip. "Right."

"*Que bueno.*"

"*Sí.* What do you think we should we do about this?"

"Well. Life is short and getting shorter by the minute. Let me show you what I think."

Leaning in, she showed Ronnie what they should do. Ronnie must have agreed for they kept kissing.

"Crazy," Frank said, sitting back. "I barely know you."

"But life is short," Ronnie reminded.

"It is." Frank laughed. "I've never kissed anyone on the first date."

"Technically it's our second. But *querida*, we have to get back to you and this business of absorbing other people's energies."

"Must we?" Frank let her lips trail Ronnie's. After a moment Ronnie said, "Yes. We must. This isn't good for you, all this . . . *energía mala.* And I don't want it to rub off on me!"

"Really? It can do that?"

"I don't know, but I don't want to find out! We need to find someone who can give you a *limpia. Ay*, I wish Sal were here."

"Me too."

Ronnie's gaze turned into that of the ADA. "You were with her when it happened?"

Frank nodded. She'd been waiting for one of the women to ask her about Sal. She told it true to Ronnie, just as it had happened. Ronnie took her hand. "Such a shame."

They were quiet until Ronnie said briskly. "*Mira!* I have a friend in Salinas. Tammy. She does wonderful massages and body work. I think she could help dispel some of the bad juju in you. Shall I call her?"

Frank couldn't help but be enchanted. "Yes. You shall."

Ronnie rose to find her phone and Frank petted one of the three dogs wedged with them on the sofa.

"You have dogs up there?" Ronnie asked. She'd put on glasses and was working her phone.

"Two of Sal's."

"Are they friendly?"

Ronnie flumped her considerable heft down next to Frank.

"Most definitely."

"You should bring them next time."

"There'll be a next time?"

"There better be." Ronnie whipped off her glasses and kissed Frank. "I could do this all day."

"I'm in."

Ronnie laughed. "I feel like a kid."

Beats feeling like an old woman, Frank thought. "Let's call your friend."

"Yes. The sooner we get you cleaned up the better."

"This is so weird. You know I just started seeing those women at the store in the hope that they'd go away. I didn't for a sec think I could help 'em. And it still sounds too far-fetched to be real."

"But your pain is real, yes?"

"Oh, yes. And you can still see all the dark spots?"

Ronnie appraised her. "*Absolutamente.* At least now I think we know what's causing them, and honestly, I really don't see the colors much anymore, but, *ay,* with you they were everywhere! I couldn't not see them!" Ronnie held the phone to her ear. It rang a while then she said, "Tam, hi. It's Ronnie. I have a friend who *desperately* needs to see you. Give me a call when you can. I'd love to schedule an appointment for her."

Frank grinned. "Desperate, huh?"

They chatted a lot, necking gently. Both jumped when the phone rang.

Ronnie held her phone far away to see it without her glasses. "It's Tammy!" She answered, "*Querida!* How are you?"

Frank almost laughed at her slight jealousy that Ronnie called everyone *querida*. Christ, she thought, what am I diving into?

"*Ay*, hold on." She told Frank, "She can see you in an hour."

Then Frank did laugh. "Sure. Why not?"

Her free fall continued.

CHAPTER 13

Ronnie offered to drive Frank to Tammy's and Frank consented, glad to have an excuse to spend more time with her. As they buckled up for the half-hour trip Ronnie asked what she had been doing since she moved up to the cabin.

"You'll think I'm crazy," Frank said.

"Oh, *yo se* from crazy. Try me."

"I spent the first couple months just trying to learn everything around me. I'm a city girl, born and bred, so it was like I'd been dropped off on a strange planet. I didn't go anywhere without a bunch of field guides. And I've learned so much. I had no idea how much life there was out there, how much diversity. A bird was just a bird and a bush was just a bush. Nothing unique or special about any of 'em."

She waved a hand at the Santa Lucias rolling by the window.

"I've learned a lot but there's still so much I don't know. I'm getting a good feel for the ranch. I've been pretty much everywhere—canyons, hills, fields. It's gorgeous country. Again, who knew? And it changes with every season, every hour of the day. I just love it. Can't get enough."

Ronnie glanced from the road to smile at her. "I hear. What about when the sun goes down, what do you do then?"

"So much. First I sit and watch it go down and watch the stars come out. I watch the owls feed their babies in the sycamore tree. I watch the bats swooping around me."

"*¡Ay*, bats! Are you crazy?"

Frank laughed. "They're no more dangerous than a bird flying around you. Plus they eat all the gnats and mosquitos. But you never hear 'em. Just see their stealthy flight. I listen for the coyotes, and foxes, the treefrogs at the creek. I'm pretty sure I heard a lion one night. Crazy. Sounded just like a woman screaming, just like everyone says.

"I read a lot of natural history books—so much I want to learn about this place—and a lot of poetry. There's one who claims that life isn't about anything but devotion, and that devotion is just pure attention—to the ant at your foot, the bee in the flower, the bat in the air. I love that. I've always paid attention to the world around me, but it's always been with an eye to see where the danger was, where the next problem or crisis would come from. Trying to sniff out who was lying to me and who was telling the truth. I've been devoted to death and trauma and crisis management, but never to life. Now I just sit in my chair and watch the day unfold like a miracle. It's like I'm making up for lost time, for all I've missed."

"What made you decide to pull the trigger? Ha! So to speak."

"It was Sal. There was a day I was working on her case—the day I realized she'd been lying to me the whole time—and I knew I was done." Frank snapped her fingers. "Just like that. I couldn't do it anymore. The lies, the cruelty, the senselessness, the politics. Put in my papers and didn't look back."

Ronnie was nodding.

"Same for you?"

"It took me a little longer to decide but I had a trial that pushed me over the edge. And I think I understand how you feel. My house, the garden, my kitchen, they became my refuge, my sanctuary. But I did the opposite when I retired. I took on too much. It was a way of forgetting everything and starting fresh. After a couple years I cut back on commitments and now I only do two things I really love—immigrant advocacy and the animal shelter. The rest of my time is for me and my family and friends. Chauffeuring crazy *gabachas* to bodyworkers."

Frank grinned. "It's appreciated."

"The pleasure is all mine."

They took a couple turns out of Salinas and ended up in front of a ranchette.

"Does Tammy go to your lunches?"

"No. I'm ashamed to say we're a little cliquish about the company we keep."

"How so? What's the criteria for entry to your club?"

Ronnie hefted a meaty shoulder. "I'm not sure. Age maybe? We're all older women. We've all done our time with kids and family. We know a little, we've put in our work. And you definitely need a sense of humor. I'm very fond of Tammy but I don't know that I'd enjoy her company outside of what she does. You'll see. She's very business-like."

"I'm honored to have been included," Frank said, getting out.

Ronnie laughed. "You should be. I had to assure everyone you would fit in. And you did," she said.

Grabbing Frank's hand and swinging it Ronnie walked toward two little granny units set away from the house. The door to one swung open before Ronnie could knock.

"Tam," she cried, to a slim, youngish woman with cascading dark hair. Before the woman could say anything Ronnie took her in a firm hug. "It's so good to see you. Thanks for accommodating us on such short notice."

"It was perfect timing. My three thirty cancelled so I was happy to fill the slot."

Tammy closed the door behind her and led them to the second, adjoining unit. It was enclosed by a low fence hedge of what Frank recognized as gooseberry and fuchsias and manzanitas. A small pond bubbled quietly in front of the tiny cottage.

As they stepped through an arbored gate covered in wisteria Tammy asked Ronnie if she was staying.

"I was thinking of running back to town to do a little shopping."

"That's a good idea." She looked Frank up and down sternly.

"I think this might take a while."

"When should I come back?"

"Are either of you in a hurry?"

They both shook their heads and Tammy answered, "Give me at least an hour and a half, but probably two."

Frank raised a brow, asking how much it was going to cost.

"I charge ninety dollars an hour, one hundred and twenty for an hour and a half. No more than that so if we go over it's on me. I want to be able to work on everything that needs it. Is that okay?"

"As long as you take a check or card."

Tammy nodded and dismissed Ronnie with instructions to make herself comfortable in the yard if she got back before they were done. She told Frank to leave her shoes outside then ushered her into the dim, candlelit cottage. It was dominated by a plush massage table but Tammy indicated a hard-backed chair against the end of the room. Frank sat, taking in the soft music, the aroma of oils and incense, a row of singing bowls. Tammy sat in the chair beside her, asking what brought Frank. Frank explained how she'd been working on people and Tammy's grave expression grew graver.

"You can really hurt yourself doing that," she admonished.

"So I've found out. Ronnie and some of her friends gave me an earful about it. I was just trying to help," she added weakly.

When Tammy asked Frank exactly what she had been doing Frank explained again. Tammy scowled at the floor and shook her head. Almost verbatim, she repeated the lessons Ronnie and her friends had given Frank, about filters and grounding and letting the energy move through her, not into her.

"I heard," Frank allowed with a sheepish nod.

"Okay, then," Tammy said. "Let's get you on the table and see what we can do. Take all your clothes off and leave them on the chair. Lie face down on the table." She opened the door. "I'll be back in a moment."

Feeling like an errant schoolgirl Frank did as she was told. The room was cool but the table had warm sheets on it. Frank burrowed in like a little animal.

"How's the temperature?" Tammy asked, stepping in softly.

"Perfect."

"Okay. I start by feeling what's going on with your body, where the energy is moving and where it's not."

Frank heard Tammy rubbing her hands over her back.

"Wow," Tammy breathed.

With her face in the face holder Frank asked the floor, "Good wow or bad wow?"

"Hard to tell. You have *a lot* of energy which is good, but it's all tangled up. It's like a high speed freeway pileup."

Frank started to say that didn't sound good but Tammy *sh'*d her. "Let me work a bit. You just relax. Let yourself sink into the table like it's a big puffy cloud."

She did as she was told, wondering if Tammy was ever going to touch her. When she did Frank mumbled into the face holder, "What do you feel when you do this? Is there some sort of physical sensation for you?"

"Oh definitely. But we'll talk after. Right now I need to concentrate and you need to relax. The more relaxed you are, the easier it is for me to work."

Frank wanted to know more, right now, but she fought her impatience and gave in to Tammy's touch. There seemed to be some massage, but it wasn't exactly that. It was much lighter than any massage Frank had ever had. Tammy made lots of sweeping motions or held her hands in a given spot for a while. Kind of like Frank had with Vivi's eyes. Frank wondered if she should be doing that with her other…patients? Clients?

She nodded off trying to decide what she should call her vistors. She woke to Tammy's gentle hands on her shoulders, instructing her to scoot down and turn over. For a second Frank didn't know where she was but after flipping over she drifted right back into a dreamy doze. The next time she woke Tammy was whispering in her ear that they were finished and she should take her time getting off the table.

"I'll be right outside."

CHAPTER 14

Ronnie and Tammy were talking quietly by the pond when Frank stumbled from the cottage. She felt like an overcooked noodle. But for the first time in weeks nothing hurt.

"There she is," Ronnie said, and laughed. "You look like you were worked over pretty good, *querida*."

"I feel like it," Frank said, surprised to see evening coming on. "How long was it?"

"About two and a half hours," Tammy said.

She rose from her chair and perched on a nearby stump, motioning Frank to take her seat. She held out a glass to her.

"Swallow this down."

"What is it?" Frank asked.

"Just water. You need to drink a lot for the rest of the day. I did intense work on you and that will help flush your system."

Frank drained the glass and set it on the chair arm.

"How do you feel?" Tammy asked.

"Stupid," Frank grinned. "Like Rip van Winkle."

Tammy allowed a slight smile. "You were down pretty deep. Which is good. It made it easier to work on you."

"Yeah. So about that. What happens to you when you're doing that?"

"For me it's very physical. I experience heat in places where the energy's stuck. The greater the blockage the greater the heat."

"Where do you feel it?"

"In my hands."

"Okay. Then what do you do?"

"I stay very present. That's why when you talk I get distracted. I need to concentrate to tap into the energy around me. I call it the greater energy. Everybody calls it something different. God, Higher Power, Love. It doesn't matter. It's all the same thing."

"And it's a heat for you."

"Yes. That's not uncommon, but I have a colleague who feels energy kind of like a humming. She says it feels like humming with your hand covering your mouth. Without the noise, of course. She says sometimes it's loud, sometimes faint."

"What did I feel like to you?"

Ronnie and Frank both startled when Tammy laughed. "Like parts of you were on fire. I had to stop so much and shake off your heat and reground. You were very intense, and all over the place. You were super strong hot where you were blocked but then really cool, barely any heat at all where your energy wasn't flowing. It's like a log jam in a river. The water crashes into the log jam, then trickles around the sides, so the flow downstream is very faint. If you'd like we can go inside and I'll tell you what I worked on."

"It's nice out. Can you tell me here?"

Tammy glanced at Ronnie. "If you'd like."

Frank nodded consent and Tammy drew in a deep breath. "You were so messed up it took me a while to figure out where to even start."

"Sorry."

"No, don't be. I'm glad Ronnie had the good sense to call me. And once you settled down you were very easy to work on. Your energy's very accessible. There was just a lot to do. I started at your heart. It was hot in there. Lots of fire. I smoothed that all out and kept grounding you. You ground very easily and once I got your heart energy smoothed out it cleared a path to untangle the rest of you. It took me a while to work on your head, your neck really. There was definitely energy stuck in your neck."

"That hot, too?"

"Yes." She hesitated. "But lumpy, too. Knobby. That needed some good old-fashioned massage. How does it feel now?"

Frank swiveled her head around. "Amazing."

Tammy nodded. "It felt like you were stuck there but while I was working there I kept feeling like I should be working on your eyes. It was weird."

A prickle went up Frank's spine.

"Okay," she said, "that *is* weird. I was working on a little girl with neck pain and I kept wanting to go to her eyes. I finally did and that seemed to help her."

Tammy leaned forward. "How old is she?"

Frank shrugged. "Nine? Ten?"

"I wonder if she saw something. Children don't always have the verbal or the emotional intelligence to express trauma so it often shows up as a physical complaint, an illness or a chronic pain."

Frank nodded. "I had a woman walk into the station one day twenty-three years after she'd seen her father kill her mother. She'd been watching something on TV that triggered the memory. She hadn't remembered it until that show brought it all back to her. Bang."

Tammy nodded. "I'm not saying that's what's wrong with your girl but it's something to consider. Now, your left side, your arm and torso were all off-kilter, too, like you've been guarding or protecting that side."

Frank thought of her wrist. Bone had barely brushed his head against it and the pain had been excruciating. She'd been cradling the hand ever since.

"And what did that feel like?"

"A lot like your neck. Hot, with lots of knobs and bumps. But the rest of you was very strong. Once I got it untangled your energy flows very easily. Do you meditate a lot or do any intense physical activity?"

Frank smiled. "Since I retired life's one long meditation."

"That's good. Do you plan on continuing to treat people?"

Frank's gaze drifted to a scrub jay working at something on the ground. She watched it, asking, "Do you think I should?"

"That's not up to me. But it might be a natural outlet for all your energy. I don't know. But if you plan on continuing I have some good books I'd be willing to loan you. They might give you some insight as to what you're doing and how to do it more effectively so you don't jack yourself up again."

The jay flew off into a eucalyptus and Frank turned to Tammy. "I wouldn't mind helping people, but is it safe? I mean, I'm doing Christ knows what to a little girl. I don't want to hurt anybody."

Tammy shook her head. "No, of course not. And to be honest, a lot of New Age stuff is crap and nonsense which *does* harm people. What I'm talking about, and what I think you can offer, is the type of healing that's been done everywhere in the world since there were people. Modern doctors act like health begins and ends with Hippocrates."

She snorted. "What they don't want us to know is that we're each responsible for our health. That often what's wrong with us is caused by and controlled by us. Not that modern medicine doesn't have its place. It definitely does. But what I do, what I think you do, goes much deeper than that. We are going in blind and tapping into something far greater and older than modern medicine. It's primitive medicine, the very first. It was practiced long before men took over medicine. And just because they can't quantify what we do they say it doesn't exist."

Tammy scoffed, "They used to think washing our hands in wine or rubbing them with lemon juice had nothing to do with preventing disease. Then they discovered bacteria. They used to think there was no such thing as electromagnetic fields until a man named Hertz proved there was. They laughed when people said we'd have phones someday where you could see who you were talking to, or that we'd be able to fly in the air like birds. Just because of existing limitations on technology and imagination they claim the energy work we practice doesn't exist. It's all quackery and nonsense until some man proves it isn't and then it will be sanctioned and embraced as the Holy Grail."

Tammy flashed an apologetic grin. "I'm sorry. I get pretty emotional about this."

"We can tell," Ronnie said with a generous smile.

Frank asked, "Did you know Sal?"

"Casually," Tammy offered. "I saw her a couple times."

"Did she help?"

"Very much so. She had a real talent for healing."

"She told me it's nothing supernatural. That what we're doing, these talents"—Frank made quote marks in the air—"are all natural but that we've removed ourselves so far from nature and have cocooned ourselves in such artificial worlds that what was once normal and taken for granted now seems unreal. That what was once ordinary is now considered extraordinary and what was once natural is now supernatural."

"Exactly," Tammy agreed. "That's it exactly. We all have talents and gifts but only certain ones are sanctioned. The ones that don't rock the boat. The ones that don't threaten the established cultural order. What would happen to the medical industry if people took more responsibility for their health instead of abdicating to pills or the knife? Good God, what would happen to churches if we acknowledged that everyone could tap into the energy of the universe and not just priests or rabbis? That we are each a discrete and direct conduit to a greater energy?"

Ronnie answered, "There'd be chaos. They'd have to start burning the women again. It'd be the Inquisition redux."

"You're right. If anything, we should be called *pre-ordinary*. What we do is what people have done for millennia. Before Western medicine people had always healed through touch and energy and herbs. It was wisdom passed down from mother to daughter as surely as a doctor's stethoscope to his son. It was the way of all healing before men decided women couldn't be doctors anymore. Then the Inquisition came along and put a period, full stop to any kind of healing not sanctioned by men with power. And what were women supposed to do? If they got caught healing they were labeled witches and slaughtered, so of course the old ways went underground. There are people today who will still say that anything not sanctioned by a Western doctor is the Devil's work. But the old ways persist. They're in our DNA. They're a gift in our blood and bone. We can't help but be healers. What's extraordinary is that we keep denying these gifts. It's such a waste, such a shame."

Frank interrupted, "What's to say what we do isn't all placebo effect?"

Tammy argued, "So what if it is? Between 50-70% of all medical complaints are psychosomatic. If the illness isn't real why should the cure be? And if it helps, what difference does it make if it's a placebo effect? And that's the point: to help. Which gets back to your little girl. Has she seen Western doctors?"

"Loads of 'em, apparently."

"Then there you have it. In this society people like us are usually a last resort. If we were the first resort we wouldn't have such a bloated medical industry and doctors would be able to focus on really fixing things instead of wasting their time holding our hands."

"That's what we do," Frank guessed.

"In part. I think that's a lot of it. And it's huge. Sometimes it's all that's needed."

"Tell her about Paco," Ronnie urged.

A slight smile creased Tammy's face. "You tell her."

"My old chihuahua, the one between us on the couch this afternoon?"

Frank nodded.

"*Pues*, one day he comes up lame. I take him to the vet and he says, 'Oh, it looks like he's torn his ACL. We can operate but it's expensive and he'll be in a cast for months, no exercise.' *Ay*, what a decision I have to make. But I have this thought: let's take him to Tam. So she works on him for what, twenty minutes, a half hour?"

Tammy nodded.

"And I take him home and he's worse that night. Can barely

move. Next morning? He's running around the house with the other dogs, dancing on his bad leg asking for breakfast. He's like a puppy!"

Ronnie sat back with satisfaction. "Now tell me how *that's* a placebo effect!"

"True?" Frank asked Tammy.

"True. What Ronnie didn't tell you was that the week before or something, he'd gotten out with one of her other dogs, and the other dog got run over. And that was his buddy, right?"

"His brother. From the same litter," Ronnie said grimly.

"What I felt in his leg was a great ball of grief. Loss for his brother. That was where he was holding it. Like it paralyzed him. I helped move the grief through and out. That was all."

"That was all," Ronnie said, amazed. "I was about ready to put him to sleep. You saved his life!"

Tammy stood. "Let me get those books for you. Mind you, they're none of them the Holy Grail. It's been my experience that we each have our own unique ways of healing. No one book or teacher can cover them all. But there are a lot of common areas, like grounding and creating filters. Those are pretty standard. After that, the sky's the limit. Each to her own abilities and ways, so take what you like from them and leave what you don't."

She went into the other cottage and returned lugging a full canvas bag. "I want them back," she warned, "but take your time. I don't need them."

Frank promised and reached for the bag.

"No," Tammy said, "You relax." She carried the books to the car and when Ronnie gave her a big hug, she stiffly returned it. Frank thought to shake her hand but it seemed so formal after such intimacy. Instead she offered sincere thanks.

"It was my pleasure. I'm glad Ronnie brought you. If you have any questions about anything I'll be happy to help."

"Thanks. I might take you up on that."

"Anytime. And just remember—you can't do any harm if you ground, filter, and move energy *through*. Got it?"

"Got it. Oh wait. What do I owe you?"

"It was one-twenty. But Ronnie got it."

Frank slid into the car, still feeling boneless. She asked Ronnie if she could write her a check.

"*Claro.* I thought you might be a little out of it so I took care of it while we were waiting. I hope that was okay."

"Yeah, thanks. I appreciate it." As Ronnie steered toward the freeway, Frank laughed. "This has been a helluva first date. Sure you want a second?"

Ronnie put a hand on Frank's thigh. "*Sin duda,* querida. Without a doubt. I'm so glad she had time for you today. And you know, I have a bunch of books you can borrow too. I didn't want to give them to you because I wanted you to find your own way. Like Tam said, what's true for one person is not necessarily right or true for another. *Por ejemplo,* when I started seeing colors I immediately researched everything I could about auras and chakras and what they *should* look like, but none of them matched my own experience. The books said calm was supposed to look like shades of blue, but to me it's yellow. To me sad people look blue. I saw it all the time in court. Anger's supposed to be red but to me it comes off like glinting armor or swords, hard and grey, metallic. I had to learn to trust my perceptions over other people's. So maybe what you are doing isn't written anywhere. It doesn't mean you're not doing it, you're just doing it your own way."

Frank liked Ronnie's hand where it was and covered it with her own. "So far it doesn't feel like I'm doing anything. I just sit with someone for a while and then they tell me they feel better."

Ronnie squeezed her leg. "Then maybe that's all there is for you to do."

"Maybe. That's true though, what Tammy said about kids and trauma. I talked to a lot of 'em who'd seen things but couldn't verbalize what they saw. Sometimes we could get 'em to draw the events but not always."

Ronnie nodded. "You said the pain's in her neck?"

"Yeah." Frank wondered wryly about patient confidentiality but decided she hadn't used any names so it was okay to talk about Vivi. "I wonder if I could ask her to draw what the pain looks like."

"Oh, that's a good idea! Maybe she saw somebody hang himself, or get strangled. Who knows?"

"Sal would have. She could see things. Apparently the girl's mother brought her once but then *her* mother found out and forbade her to come back. Like Tam said, thought she was doing the Devil's work."

"*Ay*, if we kept the Devil as busy as they claim we do he wouldn't have enough time for all this mischief! Now Sal, that woman, she had the touch for sure. But you can't compare yourself to her. As far as I know Sal had been using her gift since she was young. You're only just starting, so be patient."

"*Si, mami.*"

Ronnie laughed, "*Ay*, only our first date and already we're like an old married couple."

Frank grinned and undid her seatbelt. She scooted next to Ronnie and kissed her beneath her ear. Ronnie was giggling and Frank whispered, "Do old married couples do this?"

"*¡Ay*, I hope so!"

She slapped at Frank playfully. "*Quitate, niña.* Put your seatbelt on."

Frank fastened it so it would stop beeping but stayed where she was, Ronnie's free hand entwined with hers. When they pulled into Ronnie's garage she cut the engine and took Frank's face in her hands, her lips devouring Frank's.

"*Ay*," she finally said, "I've wanted to do that for *miles*."

"When do I get to see you again?" Frank asked.

Ronnie took a deep, satisfied breath. "Thursday? I'll come up to you, you can show me that land you love so much."

"No." Frank shook her head. "Not yet."

Ronnie lifted a brow. "Not yet, what?"

Frank shifted away, looking out at the tidy garage. "Don't take this personally, but I'm not ready to share it. I just, I can't imagine anyone else there."

She turned back to Ronnie. "This'll sound stupid, but it's

like . . . it's sacred up there. Like how the old landowners in Europe used to have their own private chapels. Up there is like one big private chapel to me. It's my alone place. There's no one but me and the dogs and the chickens and the wild things, and I'm not ready to share it with another human. Not even a human as special as you."

"*Querida*," Ronnie said brushing her cheek. "I think you're in love with another woman."

"I am."

"How can I compete?"

"Down here there's no competition. So how 'bout I come see you Thursday?"

"*Bueno*. It's a date. And bring your little dogs. I'd love to meet them."

"Ronnie," Frank purred. "A woman after my own heart."

CHAPTER 15

Frank was packing to spend the night at Ronnie's when her eyes landed on Sal's journal. Between Ronnie and all the books Tammy had leant her Frank hadn't given much thought to it. Truth be told she hadn't wanted to. Whatever the business was with Dash, it was at least five years old. If it was what she thought, that Dash had killed someone, surely Soledad PD or the Sheriff's Office was on to it by now. It wasn't Frank's job to look into it, not anymore.

After hefting a five-gallon bucket of water into the truck, and appreciating that nothing hurt, she tossed her pack in the truck and loaded the dogs.

"Got a surprise for you," she told them, jouncing down the mountain. "Hope you like it."

Ronnie had suggested they meet at the park so they could introduce the dogs on neutral territory. Sal must never have used leashes so Frank hooked the dogs to sections of rope before letting them jump from the truck. Bone looked offended but accepted the restraint with his usual dignity and forbearance. Kook leapt like a fish on a hook and pulled to get to Ronnie's dogs.

After much sniffing and tail wagging the younger dogs chased each other around while Bone and Paco seemed to enjoy watching over them. Ronnie had somehow managed to bring not only her five dogs to the park but a picnic basket too. They spread a blanket on the grass and made all the dogs settle down while they ate cold chicken, jalapeño potato salad and homemade pickled vegetables. Ronnie had lived in town her whole life so it wasn't surprising when at least half a dozen passersby greeted her by name. Frank enjoyed watching how friendly they were with her, how warm and approachable she was. When Frank mentioned that being an ADA didn't seem to have hardened her, Ronnie professed, "*Ay, querida*, but it did. It was one of the things that pushed my ex away. I was too hard. Too focused on work. Too cut off."

"But you're not now."

Ronnie stretched out on the picnic blanket with a disarming lack of self-consciousness. Frank copied her and all the dogs wiggled for space between them.

"I don't need to be now. I have all this. The rest of my life is for softness, for ease. I spent too much of it being hard and cold. I'm done with all that, it takes too much energy, energy I'd rather spend doing this."

"Me, too."

Ronnie was intelligent, funny and kind. Frank liked being near her, liked caressing and nuzzling, yet her desire for Ronnie still wasn't sexual so much as companionable. Maybe the sex would come. She scolded herself that it was only their third date.

"What are you thinking, *querida?*"

"How much I like you."

Ronnie rolled onto her stomach to face Frank.

"*De vera?*"

"Truth."

"Are we silly? I feel like we're two schoolgirls crushed out on each other."

"Maybe it's silly. But all I know is I want to hang around a while."

Ronnie grinned. "*Yo tambien.* It's funny because there hasn't been anyone since, *pues,* in a long time, that I've wanted to be with. There were some itches I scratched here and there but they were just that. *Pero*, you, *querida*, with your blue eyes and mountain heart, and wild soul, you're something different. You're someone I want to spend time with. And I don't say that about a lot of people. *Ay*, I love my family, and my cherished friends, but I'm always ready to return to my quiet little home and my plants and animals. But you? You're someone I think I want to spend *a lot* of time with."

"Are you going to tell your family?"

Ronnie rolled onto her back and smiled at the leaves above her head. "*Ay, ay, ay.* Sixty-something and I should worry what my family thinks."

She turned back onto her side with a serious look for Frank. "You're serious, *amor*? This isn't just a game? I should bother telling them?"

Frank ran a finger along Ronnie's arm. "It's not a game to me. Is that what it feels like to you?"

"*Pues no*, not at all. I like you *mucho*. I'd like my family to like you *mucho tambien*. At this age I think we have a pretty good idea what we like and what we don't. So yes, I'll tell them. But only if you're not going to go running up into those mountains and never come down again."

"Oh, I'll be back."

She ran a finger against Ronnie's cheek, marveling at the softness.

"There's probably someone watching right now who's going to report to them before I can tell them myself."

"Should I kiss you? Make it official?"

"No, *querida*. For their sakes let's maintain at least an illusion of decorum."

"Fair enough." Frank grinned. "I can wait 'til I get you alone."

"Come to dinner Sunday?"

"I'd love to."

"*Bueno*. I want them to fall even more in love with you before I tell them."

"Who do you think will be most upset?"

Ronnie chewed her lip. "Probably Carly and my mom."

"Not your *abuela*?"

"She'll make noises but honestly, she's lived through so much there's very little that rattles her anymore. Mami and Carly are the good Catholics. They'll be the ones most offended."

"What about you, are you a good Catholic?"

"*Ay*, I'm the worst type of Catholic, the lapsed. I usually go to church on Sunday with the family but for me it's purely social, it's a community thing."

"Have you ever brought a woman home to your family?"

"Except for my ex I've never brought anyone home. There's never been anyone I cared enough about to bring home. Like I said, all itches that went away after a good scratch."

"I'm honored."

"You should be. It's not just anyone who can capture the heart of Doña Veronica."

Frank laughed and slid her hand into Ronnie's warm grip. After romping the dogs a little in the cool grass they packed up and returned to Ronnie's.

"Come," she said taking Frank's hand, leading her to the sofa. "Show me what you wanted to do to me at the park."

"*Con gusto*," Frank agreed. They kissed and touched, stroked and explored, gently, without urgency. Until Ronnie pushed away and looked seriously at Frank.

"*Querida*. I have to tell you something."

Steeling herself for disappointment Frank said, "Okay. I'm listening."

"I like all this very much, *mucho mucho mucho*, the kissing and touching and being close to you, but I have to tell you, I'm not much interested in *sex*. And it's not you! I just have zero sex drive. I used to *love* sex but since the menopause…" Ronnie gave a thumbs up sign then twisted it toward the floor. "I think I've lost all the hormones that make me want to rip your clothes off and take advantage of you."

Frank laughed. "Is that what you have to tell me?"

"It's funny?"

"Not funny." Frank searched the low ceiling. "Maybe a relief.

I love this too, I really do, and I keep waiting for that zing, that desire to ravage you to kick in, but it's not. Doing this, like we are, it's like being next to a warm fire after having been out freezing in the cold all night. It's amazing. I keep waiting for an urge to flare up too but it's not."

"*Ay*, what a relief! And *amor*, I don't mean never, of course not; I think I'm just a very slow-burning flame right now. Does that make sense?"

"Totally. I think you are amazingly sexy Doña Veronica, but sexy doesn't always have to involve screaming orgasms."

"*Ay, mijita.*" Ronnie fanned herself. "You make me blush. What about you, *bambina*, are you through the change?"

"I think so," Frank mused. "I haven't had a period in….at least a year and a half. And I went through hot flashes. Not bad, just irritating. Couldn't sleep well. And like you said," Frank made a plane with her hand and crashed it toward the ground, "pretty much zero sex drive."

She curled onto her shoulder to face Ronnie.

"If you think about it from a biological standpoint, why would women our age be having sex anyway? We can't procreate anymore so why would we need a sex drive? Doesn't it make sense we'd be helping raise grandkids and wouldn't want sex as much as cuddling and closeness and touch?"

"*Ay.*" Ronnie spooned into her. "I think we're supposed to want it because men *always* want sex and in a monogamous culture what's a wife supposed to do but be as interested as possible? I think this, what we're doing. is really what we want, but men want more so we have to pretend we do too. *Pero*, honestly? I couldn't care less."

"Do you take anything?" Frank asked. "For menopause?"

"No, no, no. Winnie made me some salves and potions but other than that, nothing. I want to live *a la natura*. That's why all this." She fluffed the silver strands in her thick, unruly hair. "And these," she added, stroking the downy hairs on her chin. "I have more hair here than down there!"

They cackled together like the aging women they were,

sanguine, unpretentious, at home in their own skins.

"Was it hard for you? Going through it? I think I got off pretty easy."

"*¡Ay, Dios,* did you ever!" Ronnie fanned herself again. "I used to have to take two or three outfits with me to work, I'd soak them through. And my memory? For *shit!* Sometimes I'd have to take a recess just so I could look up the name of a prosecutor I'd been working with for twenty years! But it passed, and now I'm just as lazy and content as an old cat with a bowl of cream. *Ay, cariña,* I'm so *relieved!* I thought I was going to scare you off for sure!"

Frank chuckled. "Take a lot more than that to scare me off. Come here, my apostate." She pulled Ronnie on top of her. "Let's just keep doing what we're doing. If anything changes we talk about it."

Ronnie screwed up her face. "*¿Qué es* apostate?"

"You're an apostate—a backslider, a recreant. One who has turned her back on her faith."

"*Ay.*" Ronnie laughed. "So many big words! I'll have to buy a dictionary if I keep dating you."

"If?"

"Okay, okay," Ronnie relented. "I guess I'm going to have to buy a damn dictionary."

She kissed Frank, calling her Mrs. Webster. Then she smacked her on the chest and cried, "*Ay,* I'm necking with you like a pimple-faced kid and I don't even know your real name!"

"You don't want to know."

"I do." She gave her a little whack again. "Tell me, or no more kisses."

"*Ay,*" Frank imitated her. "But you can't laugh."

She ran her lips along the tender skin at Ronnie's throat, nibbled her ear and whispered her name.

Ronnie doubled over. "You're kidding me!"

"*Te juro.*" Frank made an *X* over her heart. "My mom had a new religion every month. Unfortunately she was in her Wiccan phase when I was born. Thought it would be a powerful name."

"*¡Ay Dios!*" Ronnie was still laughing, but she snorted out, "Lucifera Angelina. I feel like I'm invoking Satan."

"Hey, now. It's a nice name. Lucifer means light bringer, Angelina's angel. Light-bringing angel. What's wrong with that?"

"Oh, yes, what's wrong with that?" Ronnie said wiping her eyes. "Have you ever once in your life used that name?"

"Not once." Frank grinned. "Even my dad wouldn't. He always called me Little Frank or Frankie, and after a while my mother did too."

"*Ay*, Frankie. That's so cute," Ronnie said, gently pinching her cheek. "The apostate and the light conjurer, what a pair."

Ronnie snuggled into Frank, a hand comfortably exploring the length of her. Frank gave her a squeeze. "I could get used to this."

"I hope so."

"But I should probably get going."

"No," Ronnie protested. "I wish you could spend the night. I'd love to fall asleep wrapped around you."

"That could be arranged."

"*De vera?*"

"Honestly," Frank affirmed. "How about Sunday? Wake up together and have all day Monday."

"I'd love that!"

"Then it's done."

They untangled themselves and Frank asked if she could bring something Sunday.

"Just you." Ronnie kissed her.

"Is it gonna look weird, you bringing me?"

Ronnie shrugged. "Maybe. But that'll be their first clue, yes?"

"It's a good one," Frank agreed.

After some delicious goodbye necking at the door Frank made her way up the mountain reflecting how easy it was to be with Ronnie. So comfortable she didn't even miss the cabin. But it was good to get home with an evening still long enough to take Buttons and the dogs for a quick ride. They went to a favorite watering hole where Frank shucked her clothes and jumped in. She scrubbed herself with handfuls of gravel then shook herself like the dogs. She dressed wet but was dry by the time they got back to the cabin. Ronnie had pressed the picnic fixings on her so for the second time that day she had a feast.

Munching by the fire pit she told the watching dogs, "Gotta stay with that woman if for nothing but the food."

Kook swept his tail in the dirt. "Yeah, you like her, too. That's good. You're gonna be seeing a lot of her."

She gave them each a bite of chicken and then rolled a cigarette. The stars came out and the bats swooped for insects. A pair of great horned owls hooted as she admired the stark black ridgeline. Frank tried to think if she'd ever been so content. Her life felt fuller and richer than ever. Heavy with wonders. And whatever Tammy had done to her, it had gotten rid of the wrist pain, the crink in her neck, the funky heartbeats and fatigue. She remembered Ronnie saying she felt like a teenager after Sal had worked on her and thought it a fair analogy. Except for the raging hormones, which Frank missed not at all.

Switching on the lantern she got up and retrieved Tammy's books from the cabin. Like Ronnie and her circle of friends, each book had a unique perspective but the one thing they all agreed on was the necessity to get oneself grounded before doing any kind of work. Most instructed the reader to ground herself by imagining a rod running the length of her body into the earth or to visualize being a tree with her roots spreading underground. Frank had dutifully tried, sitting outside in her chair, bare feet squared on the ground. Each time she felt ridiculous, but eventually she had hit on a technique she actually liked.

She clicked off the lantern and searched out the tallest peak. She studied it a while then sat up straight. Closing her eyes, she imagined her head was the tip of the peak, high in the sky, almost touching the stars. Her feet were solid bedrock, miles below the surface, connected to the whole continent, touching tectonic plates around the entire globe. The image calmed and steadied her. She hoped this was what the books and the ladies meant when they talked about grounding.

The books had also suggested breathing techniques that Frank found equally troublesome. They were supposed to quiet the chatter in her head but so far they had just frustrated her or made her hyperventilate. But diligently she tried one that didn't seem too odious.

Breathing at her own pace, she silently counted "Breath one in" on her inhale, and "Breathe one out" on the exhale. Then Breathe two in, Breathe two out, and so on. If she forgot where she was she had to start all over again at one. Sitting in the dark, Frank got to sixty-one before she realized she'd stopped counting. She'd stopped doing anything. It was like she'd been asleep yet was keenly awake.

Frank's face split into a smile only the stars could see. She wasn't sure how long she'd had a reprieve from her thoughts but it was a start. She wiggled down into the chair and called Kook into her lap. She kissed the top of his curly head and said, "Your mommy's a goddamn Buddha. Whaddaya think about that?"

He licked her chin.

Frank tilted her head to the sky. The stars twinkled prettily but impersonally. She was sure they were unimpressed with her. That pleased Frank just fine. She was impressed enough with herself. As she stargazed she remembered how she used to take her murder books home and spread the contents on the dining room table. She'd turn the phone off, put on some mellow jazz, then circle the table, letting her mind skip and wander over reports and photographs, notes and forms. With distractions eliminated, and the chatter in her brain stilled, she'd slide into a kind of meditation. Hushing her rational mind had allowed her intuition to take over and she often saw things she hadn't seen with her conscious, logical mind.

Maybe her touch, *el don*, was like a shy, quiet kid that needed coaxing to speak in front of the class. It was just as smart as, or smarter than everyone else but it had a hard time being heard over the clamor of the more insistent kids. She just needed to give it an environment to thrive in, and where better than here?

She rolled out her bed, brushed her teeth, and crawled under a blanket of stars. She gave a little shiver, not from the cool evening, but in anticipation of who would show up at the store on Saturday.

CHAPTER 16

Frank walked the dogs to the ranch house for a little exercise before penning them. Like the last Saturday, Pete was outside and greeted her, "Off to the store, Chief?"

"Yep."

"Leave 'em here," he said, motioning his head at Kook and Bone romping with his dogs. "They'll have more fun and I won't have to hear 'em barking."

"Okay."

He grabbed their collars and she turned to go.

"You been in town a lot."

"Yep." She decided he'd hear about Ronnie sooner or later so she told him, "Got a lady friend."

"Is that so?" He busied himself with scratching the dogs. "Brought her here yet?"

Frank had always had a light hand with people and she acknowledged, "It's your place, Pete. I wouldn't bring anyone here without asking you first."

He nodded and she left it at that, walking away. He called, "Anyone I know?"

She answered slyly over her shoulder, "Guess you have to meet her to find out."

She was at the store early, ready to try her new tricks on Lolly first. But Lolly was busy as Frank walked through the store. She called around a customer, "It's open."

"Thanks. Catch you before I go?"

"The old hands would appreciate it."

Frank smiled. Lolly had turned the lights on and set a huge yellow rose on the table. Its candy-like scent filled the tiny room. Frank lit a couple candles and sat down. She practiced her breathing then pictured herself as steady and solid as the mountains. She'd remembered last night as she was falling asleep that she needed to create a filter, too, a sort of energetic shield that would allow in only the energy of whoever she was working on.

There'd been a day with Sal—Frank still wondered if it had really happened or if it had just been part of all the dreamlike days with Sal—when she took Frank up a treacherous slope across the mountain to a cave where there lived an impossibly old woman. It was so improbable—an old, blind woman surviving up there alone—that Frank could barely conjure the memory, and what had happened to her there only added to the mistiness and muddle. Nonetheless, the cave was clear in her mind, a redoubt of ancient boulders with a long, narrow entrance. Like a womb, Frank had thought, sliding deep into sleep.

She'd decided to use the cave as her filter, protected all around by venerable stone that permitted only the energy of her patient seated at the entrance. So rapt was she in picturing her cave that she jumped when there was a tap on the door.

"Come in."

To her surprise it was Vivi again. Her head was cocked almost to her shoulder and tears soaked her sleeve on that side.

Maya looked helpless. "She's been like this since Wednesday. I tried everything—I even took her to the ER—but she kept saying she wanted to see you."

"Okay," Frank crooned, guiding Vivi into the chair. "Okay. Let's see what we can do."

Maya backed out, mouthing *thank you.*

"Okay. Shh." Frank brought her chair around to Vivi's. "Let's start here."

She cupped the exposed side of Vivi's neck. "How's that?"

"Good," Vivi hiccuped.

"Okay. I've got you. You're safe. Nothing bad happens here. Everything's okay."

The reassuring words and lulling tones came automatically after a career spent dealing with traumatized people but Frank realized she had only fleetingly, if ever, touched anyone except her lovers. This "laying on of hands," or whatever she was doing, was completely outside her ken yet it seemed to come naturally, easily. She remembered how Lolly had told her that Sal said it felt like giving a present, and indeed it did. A very much needed present. Frank smiled to herself. It felt good to be able to help, to be in a position to do so even if she didn't understand the mechanics of what she was doing. It seemed she didn't have to understand. All she had to do was be there.

Tam had said she focused and stayed present so Frank returned her thoughts to the cave, pictured Vivi at the entrance, happy and healthy. She slowed her breath, imagining the great bowl of the cave feeding her energy. She passed that energy through Vivi back into the ground, down into the sleeping bones of the earth. Without thinking, she covered Vivi's eyes with one hand, keeping her other on the girl's neck. Frank didn't notice when Vivi stopped crying or when her head eased up to a normal position.

"Better?" Frank finally whispered.

Vivi blinked sleepily and nodded.

"Good job," Frank encouraged.

Vivi yawned and Frank asked her if she'd like to try something. She shrugged.

"Do you have crayons at home?"

Vivi nodded.

"Okay. If you drew me a picture of what the pain in your neck looks like that might help me make it go away longer. Could you do that?"

"Yeah."

Maya stepped in. "How's it going?"

"Good. I was asking Vivi if she could draw me a picture of

what the pain in her neck looks like. It might help make it stay away longer."

"Oh, that'd be good," Maya said. "I bet she could do that, huh, baby?"

Vivi nodded, chirping, "I'm a good drawer."

"You are." Maya hugged her daughter and pulled a twenty from her purse. "God bless you, Miss Frank."

"It's my pleasure. I'm glad I can help."

"So are we. This is so stupid, that no one can figure out what's wrong with her. It makes me so mad."

Frank ventured, "Sometimes things that make us sick aren't physical."

Maya rounded, "You think she's making it up? You seen her."

"No, no, no. The pain is absolutely real. But what causes it isn't always physical. Sometimes it's emotional."

"Vivi, wait outside. I'll be right there. Go play by the fountain."

The girl skipped out and Maya said, "So you're saying it's like that psychosomatic thing, where you make yourself sick."

Borrowing Tammy's number Frank explained, "They say about 50-70 percent of people see doctors because of a psychosomatic illness. Sometimes it's easier to express something scary or uncomfortable as a physical thing instead of talking about it. Especially with kids because they don't always have the words or the vocabulary to talk about what's bothering them."

"You think something's bothering her? Like I'm a bad parent or something?"

"Maya," Frank soothed. "I see how much you love Vivi. You're a great mom. I'm not saying you did anything bad at all. But maybe something's happened to her, or maybe she's seen something that she hasn't told you about, and for whatever reason it's coming out as pain in her neck. And mind you, I'm not a doctor. I'm not pretending to be. I'm just thinking out loud that that might be what's going on with her."

Maya was biting her lip, thinking hard. "She tells me everything. She's shy here, but at home she never shuts up."

"Just for the heck of it, see if you can't get her to draw the pain. Maybe it'll help. I don't know. I'm just throwing out ideas to see which ones stick."

"Okay. We'll try it."

"Can't hurt, right? And don't push if she doesn't want to. It'll either come naturally or not at all."

"Okay." Maya grinned ruefully. "I got a pain in my shoulder. Maybe if I draw that she'll want to draw the pain in her neck."

"Yeah, try that. And I'd be happy to work on your shoulder, if you like."

"Oh, okay, yeah, maybe next time. Miss Sal worked on it a couple times. I broke it when I was sixteen. Riding around on the hood of a car and fell off." She grinned and smacked her head. "Such a dumb kid. I was lucky that was all I done."

"Did Miss Sal help it?"

"Oh, yeah, for sure. She even saw me falling off the car. Spooky, huh?"

"She was gifted."

"Yeah, she had the touch. You got it too. Vivi didn't want to go to no doctors, only Miss Frank. See you next week."

Frank took a deep breath and tried to get ready for whoever would be coming in after Vivi. She liked the quiet, healing part of the work. Such gentleness compared to policing. What tender moments there were had been sandwiched between hard events and ugly facts. Frank gave her head a shake. She focused on breathing and being the mountain until a woman she didn't know peeked into the shed.

"Hi," she said shyly. "Are you Miss Frank?"

"I am. Come in." Frank stood and pulled out the other chair.

"My name's Lydia. I'm friends with Maya. She said you really helped Vivi so I was hoping you might be able to help me."

The woman looked about Maya's age, but she was puffy and pale. Frank guessed chemo and hoped the woman didn't think she could cure cancer.

"Happy to if I can. What's going on?"

She'd guessed right; Lydia was undergoing treatment for

an aggressive stage IV lung cancer. She explained that she was working with as much natural healing as she could in conjunction with the chemotherapy, to help the drugs work as effectively and easily as possible.

"I'm kind of a mess." She flicked a smile and ticked off the noxious side effects. The list was overwhelming but all Frank could do was try. She nodded with a false confidence and said, "Okay. Let me ask, before we get started, if you'd like any of these lit."

She indicated the row of glass candles behind her.

"Oh, I don't know if I believe in all that. But," she added, "I kinda like that one."

"This one?" Frank reached for one picturing a beatific Madonna.

Lydia nodded. Frank lit it and set it between them, then for some reason asked about Lydia's mother.

"She died when she was a couple years older than I am now," she admitted.

"Okay." Frank held out her hands. Taking Lydia's thin bones in hers she found herself confessing, "My mom died early too. But even when she was alive she was pretty ill so I never had much mothering. I think that's why I'm so drawn to the mountains, to this area. It feels very...fertile here. Very nurturing. The mountains are like a huge, giant mother. Oh, they can take life too, but it's part of the deal. The Mother gives and she takes. Births and buries. All part of the normal order. I find comfort in being part of the cycle."

"I never thought of it like that."

"Jeez, I'm rambling," Frank apologized. "Forgive me. Now how about you close your eyes and we'll just sit a while. Try and breathe as easy as you can."

She gave Lydia's hands a gentle squeeze. "For the next twenty minutes or so, you're fine. You're safe in here. So just relax into that."

Frank closed her eyes wondering where all those instructions had come from and the talk about the mountains being like a mother. She almost laughed at herself for sounding like she knew what the hell she was doing. Lydia let out a huge sigh and her hands, light as feathers, settled into Frank's. Frank concentrated on the mountains, the ocean pushing at their feet on the other side, the *zopilote* piloting the air in between. She went into her dozy, almost sleeping place that wasn't quite awake but wasn't asleep either. When she opened her eyes Lydia's chin was on her chest. Unwilling to interrupt her peace, Frank waited patiently until she lifted her head.

"Hi." Frank smiled at her.

"Hi." Lydia returned the smile. She was still poorly colored but her face had lost its rigidity. "Guess I fell asleep."

"That's good."

Frank was curious how she felt but didn't want to coerce an answer. Lydia fumbled in her purse and giggled. "I feel dopey. Like I'm high, or something."

"Did you drive yourself?"

"No, thank God. Maya's waiting for me."

"Good. Maybe take it easy the rest of the day, if you can."

"As easy as one can with three kids." She grimaced. Placing two twenties on the table, she asked if that was enough.

"That's really too much. I don't think accepting cash for what I do is either legal or in my particular case, ethical."

"Oh. Maya said she paid cash."

"She did," Frank agreed, "and I'm going to have to figure something out because I'm really uncomfortable taking it, but I know people want to pay, too." Sliding the money toward Lydia she told her to hang on to it until she could figure out a better system. "Brownies are always good," she winked. "But let's wait until we get you solidly on your feet again."

"Do you think that'll happen?"

Lydia was slinging her purse over her shoulder but paused to search Frank's face.

"I can't say. I hope so."

"Me, too." Lydia nodded. "After all, I owe you a pan of brownies."

She left with a genuine thank you and was followed by Izzy with her same gentle complaint. When she left Lolly came in.

"I'm your last one," she grunted, settling into the chair. "Are you up for it? You've had a busy day."

"A record. So much for discouraging everyone."

Lolly grinned and put her hands out. "I don't see that happenin' any time soon."

The women closed their eyes. The shed was stuffy with the day's heat. Frank's stomach announced its hunger. Outside, a lone raven quorked from somewhere far over the mountains. A dry breeze swished the pepper trees. A quail called. Lolly pulled away, rubbing her wrist and nodding.

"Good?" Frank asked.

Lolly sighed. "I don't reckon I'll ever be good again, but I'm definitely better." She pulled her bulk out of the chair and said, "I'll make you a sandwich while you close up. I thought there was a bear snoring under the table."

Frank blew out the candles, unplugged the lights, and leaned into the door until the latch caught. Lolly was waiting on a greasy fellow she clearly disliked. When he left she shuddered and turned to slap a ham and cheese sandwich together.

"Who was that?" Frank asked, leaning against the counter.

"No one you want to know. He's one of them no-goods up at the end of Maldito Canyon."

Frank frowned. "You're the third person with nothin' good to say about that place."

"Yeah, well, good luck findin' someone with anything' good to say."

"What goes on up there?"

"Christ knows, but he ain't tellin' and you don't want to know. Trust me. There's just bad juju up to that place. Always has been, always will be. You want a pickle?"

"Sure."

Frank wanted to know more but she gathered from the set of Lolly's square shoulders not to push it.

"I appreciate the sandwich, Lolly."

"My pleasure. You do good work. I'm glad to benefit from it." A woman clanged the door open and Lolly said, "See ya next week," before turning to greet her customer.

Frank walked out onto the creaky wooden porch and ate her sandwich on the empty bench. Studying the mountains beyond the old oak, she pondered that she'd spent her whole adult life in the same neighborhood, same job, yet had never felt more at home than she had after being in Celadores less than a year. She was settled here in a way she'd never been anywhere else, as if her bones were part of the land, her skin the thin cover of grass and soil, her breath the wind that came and went. LA and its environs were as familiar to her as her own face in the mirror, but in hindsight she'd never belonged there. Her city life had been superficial, always skimming her surroundings but never immersing herself in them as she had the mountains. It was weird to feel so at home but it was good, too. Wiping her fingers on the hem of her jeans, she amended good to *very* good.

CHAPTER 17

On Sunday Frank was at Ronnie's well before three. They sat in her lush garden and watched the dogs romp around like puppies, except Paco and Bone who looked on with grave dignity. Like old lovers, the women held hands and nuzzled, telling about their lives since they last saw each other. Frank described working with Vivi and asked Ronnie if she could see things from far away.

"No, I'm not that good. I suppose I could work harder at it but honestly it's more a curiosity to me, I haven't enough interest to pursue it. *Pero* you seem to."

"Yeah. I've been thinking about that. Fixing things seems to be what I do."

She explained about taking care of her mentally ill mother, especially after her father was killed, then becoming a cop and trying to fix other people's traumas and tragedies.

"Thought I was done with that but maybe it was all just prep for this, for a deeper type of fixing and healing. I don't know. Seems that's what's next for me. You ever wonder why you're here? Why you're taking up oxygen?"

"*Ay, cariña*, not too often. I like the mystery of life! I think there's a reason, a purpose for each of us but that's not for me to know. All I can do is take care of my little corner of the world and try to be the most decent person I can, and believe me, some days that is work enough! But let me ask you this—do you like what you're doing or is it a bother, like something you have to do, or should do?"

"Surprised to say, Ronnie, I like it. I really seem to be helping people."

"And you like that." Ronnie said it as a fact, not a question.

"I do. And I'm really starting to think there's a reason I'm here. Just the way everything happened with Sal and now all the healing stuff. It feels good to do it and it comes naturally. Even though I don't know how or why. But it feels like it's what I'm supposed to be doing right now. Like I'm meant to be here on the ranch, at the store, with you. It's just all unfolding so…"

Frank rolled her hands in search of the right word. Ronnie supplied, "Naturally?"

"Yeah. People, places, situations—they all just keep getting dropped in my lap."

"*Pues*, it seems to me like you have your answer."

"I guess."

"What, you need an explanation in triplicate from God?"

Frank laughed. "Okay, so you can't see someone's energy from far away. How about this close?"

She kissed the soft down of Ronnie's cheek.

"*Ay, arina.*" Ronnie closed her eyes. "You have smoothed out *completamente* since the first time I met you. Those dark spots are all gone and now you're…you're golden, like a beautiful yellow sun." She opened her eyes and smiled at Frank. "I love being near you. That yellow was there the first time I met you but the spikiness and all the dark spots were like interference, like static."

"If you were close to my little girl could you see her colors?"

"Probably, but *querida* this is your avocation, not mine. I'd do it this once for you but don't make it a habit."

"No, that's okay. I was just curious. Hey," Frank changed the subject, "shouldn't we get going?"

Ronnie stretched languidly and sighed. "I suppose so, *pero* this is heaven, being here with you and the dogs and all my lovely *plantas* and fountains."

Frank admired the verdant garden. "I'm looking forward to coming back to all this."

"I know, I'm so happy!" Ronnie turned into her for one more cuddle then they gave the dogs their stern warning and went to her folks' house. The greeting was as warm as the last time and again her *abuela* insisted Frank sit next to her. The old woman grabbed Frank's hand and kept it between hers. Ronnie teased that she was hogging Frank and the old woman agreed but said that of everyone there she probably had the least amount of time left to spend with anyone.

Frank asked the *abuela* how many years she had and the old woman lifted her bony shoulders. "*Quién sabe?*"

Her parents had never recorded her birth or celebrated their children's birthdays so she guessed she was anywhere between ninety and one hundred years old. But some days she felt two hundred. She said that was why she liked sitting near Frank. Because of her *don,* she added with a tight squeeze to Frank's hand.

A week ago Frank would have flinched but now the old woman's grip merely amused her. She wondered if she could get Tammy to see Vivi but as she half listened to one of the aunties telling a story it occurred to her that Vivi was Maya's responsibility. It wasn't Frank's job to arrange visits to other healers. She'd mention Tammy to Maya and if she was interested she'd call Tammy and let her arrange a meeting. Frank checked a smile—a year ago she wanted nothing to do with people. Now, she had to keep herself from getting too involved.

Gomez interrupted her thoughts, plunking herself down beside Frank on the free end of the couch.

She said beneath her aunt's conversation, "I hear you and Ronnie had a picnic."

Frank nodded. "She said the whole town would know about it."

"Um-hm. I also heard you two looked pretty cozy."

Gomez was flinty-eyed. She was looking for information

Frank didn't feel it was her place to offer.

"Your sister's a pretty cozy gal."

"Is there something I should know?"

"If there is shouldn't you be asking Ronnie?"

One of the aunties laughed and Gomez leaned closer. "I'm asking you."

"Gomez. I like your sister. She's fun. You were right—she's pretty remarkable."

The cop rolled her eyes and sat back.

"Hey, listen." Frank again deftly switched topics. "Let me ask you something. I've got a little girl who's been coming to see me Saturdays for really bad neck pain. Apparently she's been to a bunch of doctors but they can't find anything wrong with her and I'm wondering if it might be psychosomatic."

"Now you're practicing psychiatry without a license?"

"Yeah, I know. I worry about that. But I warn everyone I'm not a doctor. And I'm not dispensing medicine or anything."

"I'm just kidding," Gomez said. "Kind of."

"No, I hear you. That's a line I absolutely do not want to cross. I always ask if they've sought real treatment. Anyway, this poor kid's in chronic pain and her mom's at her wits' end. I figure it can't hurt to explore the psychosomatic angle. I keep feeling like the neck pain is related to her eyes, like maybe she's seen something really traumatic. I was wondering if you could think of anything off the top of your head, like any hangings or strangulations? Slashed throats? Maybe about five, six years ago? I know it's a stretch."

Gomez puffed her cheeks and blew out a loud breath. "I couldn't tell you. I can think of a couple suicides, not sure when. Found a guy in a ditch with his throat cut but that was years ago. How old is she?"

"Eight."

Gomez shook her head. "And you're thinking that far back because she'd be too little to talk about it?"

"Exactly."

"Hm. I can run a search and maybe get some ideas. But even

if I did, what would you do with the information?"

Frank sat back and looked up at the ceiling. "Track down if there was any relationship between the girl and the victim?"

"And then what? Show her a picture from the scene and say, 'Hey, recognize this?'"

"Yeah, okay."

"Tell you what. I can get you the number of a good child psychologist. Why don't you give it to the mother and let a professional take care of this kid."

"Yeah." Frank nodded. "You're right."

The cop eyed Frank shrewdly. "You don't have a phone but you and Ronnie seem pretty tight so if I gave her the number you'd get it?"

"That'd be great."

Ronnie breezed into the room and Frank marveled how she was sunshine to Gomez's shadow.

"What have I missed?"

"Not much," Gomez said, lifting herself off the couch. "Just persuading your girlfriend not to play doctor."

Ronnie cocked her head at Frank with a mischievous smile. "My girlfriend?"

Gomez studied them both then left after an exaggerated sigh. Ronnie sat down next to Frank and hugged her arm. "What did you tell her?"

"Nothing. But she heard we were cozy at the picnic."

"Ha! I told you. I'm sure I'll hear all about it! *Ay, pues.* Are you ready to go home, *querida*?"

"Lovely as this has been, yes. More than ready."

The dogs were hysterical at their return, making Frank and Ronnie laugh with their histrionic dancing, wagging and wiggling. Ronnie played tag with them around the garden until she fell breathlessly into the swing beside Frank.

"I don't know if it's more fun watching you or the dogs."

Ronnie squeezed Frank's thigh. "Me, *querida*, but they're a close second."

Paco jumped onto her lap and two of the others wedged

between them. Kook looked at Frank, wagging expectantly.

"All right." She patted her lap and he leapt into it.

Ronnie chuckled. "I think we were made for each other."

"Yeah, but the funny thing is a year ago I didn't even like dogs."

"*De vera?* What happened?"

Frank heaved a shoulder. "Damned if I know. Bone scared the crap outta me first time I saw him. Thought he was gonna eat me up until I realized how gentle he was. And for whatever reason he took a liking to me."

"I know Sal loved them. Didn't she have a golden retriever too?"

"Yeah, Cicero. He likes being with Pete and I think Pete likes having him. But when I moved into the cabin these two migrated up from the ranch house for some reason and never left."

"Maybe they knew you needed them."

Frank scratched under Kook's chin. "That's possible," she admitted. "I think they're both smarter than I am."

"Speaking of smart. You think Carly knows about us?"

"Oh, yeah. No doubt."

Ronnie shrugged. "*Ay pues.* It's probably best to ease her into us. I'll talk to her this week."

"Will she tell the rest of the family for you?"

"Oh, no. Not Carly. She's very close-mouthed. My sister has her faults but she's not a gossip."

They chatted the late afternoon away, cuddling in the swing, watching the shadows stretch over the garden. Before the sun dipped all the way down they took the dogs for a walk, stopping often to chat with neighbors. On the way home Frank observed, "You are much beloved in this town."

"This is my home," Ronnie said simply. "These are my people." Before opening the front door, she turned and asked, "Is that going to be a problem?"

"Why would it be?"

"I don't know. My ex always complained we had no private

life, that everyone knew our business."

"I would assume that's how it is in a small town. Especially when you've spent your whole life here."

"It is." She bent to unhook the dogs. "I love it. I just don't know that you will."

"Ronnie." Frank waited until she'd straightened and was looking at her. "To be clear. My life is up there." She gestured backward toward the mountains. "I love spending time here with you but I'm not moving in. We're clear on that, right?"

Ronnie burst into a loud laugh. "*Ay, querida,* we are *so* clear. I'm too old to have anyone move in with me! And just because I'm not a hermit on a mountaintop it doesn't mean I don't need my quiet time. I just meant that when you're with me you're really with me, my family, and my whole community. I'm the entire package and for some people that's too much."

Frank rested her hands on Ronnie's broad hips. "I'm good with that. As long as I get you all to myself in the bedroom."

"*Ay,* what are you going to do to me in there?"

Frank laughed. "Probably nothing, but I still want to do nothing to you all by myself."

They pressed into each other with the practiced ease of old lovers, arms entwined, torsos joined. A knock on the door pulled them apart.

Ronnie glanced through the peephole. "It's Winnie." She glanced apologetically at Frank. "Part of the whole community."

Frank grinned.

Ronnie cried her name as she opened the door and greeted her friend. "Come in, come in, come in."

Winnie stepped through excitedly, but froze when she saw Frank. "Oh! I didn't know you had company."

"Hi, Winnie."

The woman ducked her head shyly. "Hello."

She turned awkwardly between Frank and Ronnie. Looking at neither she extended a little gift bag.

"I-I actually brought this for you." She swung the bag toward Frank. "I had to do a little research, but, um, I think it might help get rid of that energy you pulled into yourself. I don't know." She shook her bangs in serious self-deprecation.

Frank accepted the package. "Thank you, Winnie. I really appreciate that."

"*Ay querida*, you are so thoughtful, that is so sweet. What magic potions have you concocted?"

"Well," Winnie said warming to her subject, but still nervous as a lookout caught between cop cars. "I made a bath salt of eucalyptus, vetiver, and sage. I hope you have a bathtub. If you don't you can just rub it all over yourself and let it sit for just a minute before you get into the shower. I also made a spray with that and some sage. I hope it helps."

"I'm sure it will," Frank said gently, thanking her again.

"I should get going. I didn't mean to interrupt."

"You're not, *querida*, we were just relaxing in the garden. Come have a drink."

Winnie shook her head hard. "I can't stay." She fumbled for the door and slipped through before Ronnie could stop her.

"*Pobrecita*," she said, leaning against the closed door.

"Would I be safe in saying she has a little crush on you?"

"You would. We were a *thing*, years ago, for about a minute. Let's just say there was much alcohol involved."

"Years ago and she's still holding out hope?"

"No, *querida*, I've made it abundantly clear that there is nothing between us but friendship even though she may wish for more."

Frank nodded. She was amused to catch herself wondering jealously how many others Ronnie had had a *thing* with. She peered into the bag.

"That was kind of her to go to all that trouble."

"She's a darling woman. She's had much trouble in her life, raised by wolves basically, and a brutal marriage. She's come far since I first met her but I don't know that she will ever be confident with anyone or anything but plants. Would you like me to run you a bath, so you can use your salts?"

"No, that's okay. I know we got great rain up at the ranch but aren't you in a drought down here? Kind of in the rain shadow?"

Ronnie made a face. "*Si*. It's bad. It never used to be like this but every year we get less and less rain and more and more people needing water."

Frank nodded. "I'll save it for a shower."

"I could rub it all over you," Ronnie offered, nuzzling against Frank. "Then we could shower together."

Securing her arms around Ronnie, she murmured, "I like the shower together part. Saves water."

They kissed until Ronnie pushed away. "Let's get all the *niños* settled for the night and lock up."

Frank helped and then in Ronnie's dim bedroom, with a bored four-legged audience, they slowly, slowly slipped each other's clothes off.

"Come on," Ronnie ordered, pulling Frank to the bathroom. Three of the dogs started to follow but Ronnie warned, "Ah-ah-ah" and shut the door on them. "This is for Mommies only," she said, running a finger between Frank's breasts.

Ronnie rubbed the salts on Frank while she lathered Ronnie. Their hands wandered appreciatively over folds, mounds and creases. They shared a deep contentment in not being young and nubile and satiny. They were older women who had lived well and hard and they carried their triumphs, and their sorrows, proudly in their flesh. There was slow arousal without burning passion, glowing coals instead of a conflagration.

Ronnie laughed. "The drought! Plus, my water bill's going to be *exorbitant*."

"I'll help you pay it," Frank said. She was reluctant to leave until Ronnie turned off the hot water.

Frank jumped out of the shower, grabbing both towels. "That'll teach you," she said.

"*Ay!* " Ronnie squealed, "Give it here! I'm freezing!"

Relenting, Frank wrapped her up and pulled her close. They continued where they'd left off.

"Hmm, *cariña*, you're all goose-bumpy. Let's get you into bed."

They opened the door, laughing at all the dogs arranged in front of it. "It's like a kennel in here."

Ronnie threw her towel on the pillow and dove into the sheets, all her dogs piling on top of her.

"Hurry," she warned, "before they take your spot! They're not used to sharing!"

Frank covered her pillow too and squirmed in. She patted the bed and Kook jumped into the fray but Bone looked on.

"If a dog could frown he'd be frowning," Frank said.

Ronnie laughed, her hands flashing among the fur. "He's the only one in this room with any sense! He has the whole floor to himself."

She rolled into Frank, her skin shockingly cool. Frank chattered her teeth. Ronnie threw a leg over her. Resting her head close to Frank's she purred, "*Cariña*, this is so perfect."

Then she looked up seriously, cupping Frank's cheek. "But if it changes, do you promise you'll tell me? It would be my great honor to pleasure you however I can."

"I swear, my beauty. And ditto. You promise, too?"

"*Por la vida de mi madre.*"

They sealed their vow with a kiss and Frank brushed the back of her hand against Ronnie's breast.

Ronnie groaned. "Keep doing that and things may change quickly."

Lowering her mouth to the nipple, Frank swore, "I'm yours to command as you wish."

Frank's reward was Ronnie's laugh and then her kiss. They talked, hands roaming, lips close, until they fell asleep curled together like puppies.

CHAPTER 18

Heading home the next day after a sexy, lazy brunch in bed Frank saw the old red pickup parked on the side of the road. Kevin leaned against the driver's door.

"You okay?"

"The darn gas gauge in this thing has been broken for years. I thought I'd have just enough to get into town but I didn't." He shrugged a shoulder. "Don't happen to carry an extra can, do you?"

"Nope. Sorry."

"You wouldn't need to in a beauty like this," he said, admiring the Tacoma.

"Got a hose? We could siphon some."

He gave a rueful shake of his head. "I usually do but I know right where I left it when I swept the bed out yesterday."

"Hop in," Frank said. "I'll give you a lift to town."

"No, no, no," he answered. "That's the opposite way you're going. There'll be someone along soon enough."

"It's no trouble," she said and made a U-turn. He stowed an empty gas can behind the cab and climbed in, exclaiming, "This is terribly kind of you."

"Happy to do it." She got a better look at him as he buckled up. He was portly, probably sixty-something, and when he turned to look at the dogs there was a twinkle in his eye that made him look like a scruffy Santa Claus.

"Who are your friends?" he asked, twisting to let them sniff his hand.

"The little one's Kook. The big one's Bone."

"Well, hello Kook," he said, rubbing their ears, "and Bone. You two have unique names."

"Can't take the credit," Frank admitted, steering back onto the road. "I kind of inherited them. How's the hermitage?"

"Busy as ever. Never enough hours in the day."

"What exactly do you do in a hermitage?"

"*Ora et labora.*" He laughed and his belly shook "like a bowlful of jelly.

"We pray and we work, that's the short answer. The long answer is, everything that needs to be done in a monastery, from contemplation and prayer to toilet cleaning and gardening. Throw in a little cooking, some carpentry and plumbing, and that's pretty much what I do."

"I assume you're a Catholic order?"

"Indeed we are. Camaldolese Benedictines."

She smiled at him. "I got no idea what that means."

"We're an offshoot that follows the teaching—the rule—of St. Benedict, which is basically a life dedicated to prayer and contemplation."

"That sounds pretty intense."

Kevin gave his hearty laugh. "Quite the opposite." He swept a hand toward the windshield. "All this down here is intense. I don't know how folks do it."

"I hear you."

Frank found herself telling Kevin how she'd retired from the LAPD and holed up in the mountains, how she was just now, cautiously, returning to "down here."

"Our Benedictine sisters are always looking for a few good women," he offered.

Frank chuckled. "I doubt I'd be good religious material."

"You might surprise yourself," he said taking in the view. "In my experience some of the best nuns and monks are the older ones who've seen a lot of life. There are far fewer worldly mysteries to tempt them; hence they're much more interested in spiritual mysteries than corporeal."

"Duly noted."

Kevin laughed. "Look at me! Proselytizing to a poor stranger kind enough to give a daft old man a lift into town."

Frank grinned. "It's good to know someone would want me."

They chatted easily on the way to town and as they came back, with a full gas can, Kevin thanked her. "I hope you'll visit the hermitage sometime and let me at least feed you lunch."

"Can you do that? Are women allowed there?"

"Of course." He laughed. "We're not Carthusians!"

Frank shook her head indicating she didn't understand but he waved away the reference. "We're actually a retreat center. We welcome everyone, of all or no faiths. You must come visit."

"I will," she said.

"You know," he admitted, suddenly sheepish, "I write mysteries. They're cozies, silly little things, but people seem to like them. And they sell well enough that my boss encourages me to write them, which I greatly enjoy. I was wondering though, I hate to ask." He looked as bashful as a schoolboy asking a girl out for the first time. "I like to get the little details straight but I don't know any police or detectives, and if it wouldn't be too much of an imposition, might you be willing to share an email or phone number with me?"

"Don't have either one."

"A miracle!" he exclaimed. "You see? You're just a hop, skip, and a jump away from a nunnery!"

Frank laughed. "Slow your roll, Padre. If you're willing to correspond by snail mail I'll give you my address."

"Oh, marvelous! You're sure you wouldn't mind? I promise not to be an imposition!"

"No worries."

"I think this will actually work better." He looked abashed again. "I don't have a phone, either. We use the monastery's."

"Vow of poverty kinda thing?"

"Exactly. The monastery furnishes all our corporeal needs so we haven't need of our own income or things."

"Fascinating."

"It's different," Kevin allowed. "It's one more way of eliminating distractions in order to better fulfill our commitments."

"To prayer and contemplation."

"Indeed."

U-turning to park behind Kevin's truck Frank said, "I think I get it. Kinda why I'm up there with no phone or internet. No TV. No people. Mostly just books and nature."

"Exactly!" He wagged his finger again. "I'm telling you, you have the makings of a fine Benedictine."

"And you're preaching again." Frank scratched out her address on a napkin.

"Ah," he crossed himself playfully, "*mea culpa.*"

He pocketed the napkin and lifted the can out of the bed. Pausing at her window he warned, "I'm going to hold you to that visit."

"Deal," she answered.

Frank was glad she'd helped the old priest and while her overnight at Ronnie's had been heavenly she was glad to be finally home. She'd missed the solitude, the noise of birds instead of cars and wind over machines. Most of all she had missed the dark, steady presence of her mountains, the way each peak and crag held her fast. Ronnie's touch was warm and wondrous, but the mountains had a deeper hold on her.

It was too hot to ride or walk so she grabbed a slim volume of Joy Harjo and headed for the creek. The chickens followed noisily, happy to be free of their coop. Frank took her spot in the bowl of sycamore roots. The book remained closed. Watching the dogs splash and wrestle was entertainment enough. When the dogs finally rested the chickens amused her, scratching and pecking amid the dry leaves. Eventually they too tired and ranged themselves sleepily amid Frank and the dogs. Then the only sound was the water splashing from mountain to sea. Frank read then reread a poem, savoring its wild flavor, its carnal love of earth and water, fire and sky. Her eyes gently closed.

She had jumbled dreams of a little girl and someone getting stabbed in the neck, and blood, far too much blood. Then as dreams do she was riding a horse in the mountains but she couldn't control it. The horse raced faster and faster down a steep hillside, about to break a foreleg and toss her over a cliff. A condor winged over them. Frank was certain she and the horse would be its next meal.

Bone and Kook woke her shaking their collars. They stepped up and licked her cheek.

"Thanks," she said. "Didn't care to see the *zopilote* eat me."

She petted them, recalling the bloody dream. She couldn't see who was getting stabbed but a knife was clearly deep in the side of a neck, spurting blood everywhere. The little girl was amorphous—maybe Vivi, maybe not. No telling. Frank stretched and stood. Bone and Kook trotted ahead to the cabin. She trailed with the chickens, not leaving them lest the fox make a dash for them. Not likely in the heat of broad day but she'd hate to lose one of the girls.

She put a couple of their eggs on to boil and found Sal's journal. She had neglected but not forgotten it, and while she was curious enough to keep Dash in the back of her brain she wasn't going to make a crusade of solving Dash's mystery. She would let it come to her or not, as everything seemed to since moving to the ranch. Sitting on the shaded cabin steps she leafed again through the notebook:

Worked on C's back today. She's spent too many years bouncing around in that old jeep of hers! Cassie is sober again and came for a few days. I okayed it with Pete – he's fiercely protective of me and remembers what happened last time. But this was a good visit. The girls even invited us to lunch and she read the cards for everyone. Of course Ronnie drew the Empress and we all laughed when my card was the Hermit!

The first time Frank had read the entry she'd had no idea who Ronnie was. Now she stood up and scanned one of Sal's bookshelves. She was pretty sure she'd seen a couple tarot books and because Sal had kept her books well organized Frank found them quickly. She stood muttering the Empress card's description.

"Often a lush, full-figured woman . . . sensual, creative, nurturing . . . deeply connected to nature . . . signifies comfort and abundance."

With a laugh she shelved the book and plunged the cooked eggs into cold water. She returned to the journal.

> *She's a gifted reader. I know she makes a fair living at it when she can stay off the sauce. She's so much like her grandfather. It scares me. She was remorseful and apologetic, just like he always was afterwards. She was sweet and attentive this visit (just like him). I can't help but wonder if she'd have become an alcoholic if I had been a better mother.*
>
> *I can't blame her for being angry with me. I didn't do a very good job with her.*

The entry was accompanied by a sketch of an attractive middle-aged woman. Frank had met Cassie twice while investigating her grandfather's murder, and if memory served, it was a pretty accurate likeness.

> *Worked on Pete's sciatica. Ranching is rough on a body! Wrestling calves, breaking colts, getting thrown, digging ditches and postholes, in every kind of weather. It's a miracle he's as healthy as he is! Of course I'd never hear about it from him and I only know the sciatica is acting up because he can't hide the limp.*

Among a list of patients seen on a Saturday was:

*- JH - just a cleanse. Always the guilt with her. I
can soothe it, maybe even make it go away for a
while but it always comes back. Don't I know that.
I so wish I could do more for her.. She's never told
me in so many words. She doesn't have to and
I've never pushed her about what I think it is. We
women endure what we have to and our reasons
are our own.
– D - lovely to see her today. Aways a pleasure to
work on her. I think she heals me more than I heal
her! She's retiring in a year! I am so happy for her!
– RK - a new patient. Char sent her, lupus—
easy to work with that energy—gave her W's
autoimmune blend.*

Still waters, Frank thought, touched again by the compassion
and exuberance beneath Sal's stolid exterior. She had an idea and
flipped back to the beginning of the journal. After skimming
partway through it she went in and scrounged around for pen
and paper. Settling back with the journal she took note of how
many times she saw the same initials. Only a select few people
like Ronnie, Pete, and Sal's daughter Cassie were named. Frank
was guessing she named friends and family but gave her patients
anonymity.

No initials or entries matched Vivi or her complaint though
it wasn't likely there would have been from five years ago as
the girl's pain seemed more recent. Frank wondered what Sal
had done with all her other journals. If the one she'd left Frank
was any indication she had kept them regularly. There should
have been a huge collection somewhere. Maybe she'd disposed
of them, maybe burned them or dropped them down a steep
cliff when she had realized her time was almost up. What Frank
wouldn't have given to see those last entries.

She closed the journal and fed the dogs. As they gulped their food she peeled eggs on the step and rolled them in a plate of salt and pepper. They were warm and delicious. She couldn't eat store-bought eggs since she'd been eating fresh ones.

"Thanks, girls," she said as they hunted by her feet.

Because Pork Chop had told her to feed them their shells for calcium she scattered broken bits and watched as they snatched them up. Their red wattles caught her eye and she flashed on the dream image of the bloody neck wound. Gomez was probably right—she should just give Maya the name of a good psychologist and quit fretting about Vivi. It wasn't her place to probe or press the etiology of Vivi's pain, just to assuage it as best she could. And she seemed to be doing that. Even as she told herself that, she knew she wouldn't let it go. She loved a good mystery, the hunt for answers and explanations, causes and reasons.

That, plus an inherent appreciation for justice. Not necessarily of the legal variety, but one of fairness and balance. It was no wonder she'd ended up here. What greater arbiter of justice than wind and sun, fang and claw, rain and rock? Where better to sink into the bones of mystery than upon an ancient land under deathless stars?

The cabin's shadow had crept past the chair by the fire pit and the chickens were wending their way to the coop. She encouraged them with a handful of bird seed then sank into the twilit chair. After a lean diet of dry range and scrub Ronnie's yard was a feast for the eyes but Frank had missed the stark, scrubby mountains, their plain and humble honesty. Rolling her evening cigarette, she glanced at them and smiled. A coyote interrupted the silence. It yipped from somewhere on the hill behind the cabin. Another answered from the east. It may have just been the two of them or others may have joined in but they set up a howling that made Bone sit up and add his voice. Kook chimed in with a high-pitched yap and Frank lifted her head, pulling a long, low cry up from her belly. The songs faded and they were left well pleased with their efforts. Kook jumped gleefully into her lap and Bone presented his flank for scratching.

"Good boys."

Finding the first eager stars she wondered when she would, if she would, ever share all this with Ronnie. The ranch was so private. It didn't invite scrutiny or comment. Ronnie would bring loud opinions, good or bad, and Frank didn't want them coloring her view. She loved the land exactly as it was and that love needed neither commentary nor judgment. That could all stay down below as the background noise of town and people. Here, only the opinion of owl and coyote mattered. Even Frank's little thoughts were broken on the unyielding spine of the mountains.

Lighting her cigarette, she decided she'd ask Gomez if she could track down any neck slashings. It might be a waste of time but if the Soledad PD had access to decent databases it shouldn't take more than a few searches. She couldn't shake the hunch that Vivi had seen something ugly, something traumatic, and because she'd had a pretty good track record trusting her hunches as a cop, why not as a healer?

CHAPTER 19

On Saturday morning Frank's hunch was confirmed. When Vivi stepped into the shack she proudly handed Frank a sheet of paper. It was completely covered, edge to edge, in dark red crayon. In the middle she had scrawled a hard black line.

Frank hid her excitement. "That's great, Vivi. Do you know why it looks like this? What makes it so red?"

"I don't know. That's just the way it feels like."

"Excellent." Frank propped the paper on the workbench. "How did it feel to draw it?"

Vivi shrugged. "I don't know."

Frank nodded. "It looks like your neck feels better."

Maya answered, "Yeah, it does, but she wanted to give you this and I thought as long as we were here maybe you could work on my shoulder?"

"Sure."

"Okay." Maya turned to her daughter. "You go back to the front of the store and wait with Tia Lydia."

Vivi skipped out and both women watched, smiling.

"I'm glad she feels better."

"Yeah, that was a good idea to get her to draw what it looked like. I think it helped."

Maya pulled the chair out and Frank sat opposite her. "Before we get started, can I ask you something that may or may not have anything to do with Vivi?"

"Yeah, sure."

"This is a hard question," Frank started delicately, "but do you know if she could have ever been around anyone that was stabbed?"

Maya blanched. "My father was stabbed."

Frank sat back. She'd swung at the ball and hit it out of the park.

"Could Vivi have possibly seen it happen?"

"Oh my God." Maya put her hand to her heart. "Oh my God."

Frank leaned across the table. "What is it?"

"She was there. The day it happened, she was only, she was only…she couldn't have been more than three. Like two and a half. Oh my God."

She looked at Frank with horror. "If she saw it why didn't she say nothing, why didn't she tell me?"

"Kids don't always have the vocabulary for something that traumatic. Their little minds can't make sense of it. And they're— they don't know better so a lot of times they get things mixed up in their heads. Things happen that they think are their fault and they feel responsible for things that have nothing to do with them. Sometimes traumas are just too scary, too overwhelming for them to express."

Frank reached for Maya's hands. She was pale and looked like she was in shock, but Frank focused her.

"Maya. Was she different after your father died?"

"I don't know. We was all so upset. I don't know that she was different. I remember thinking it was hard for her because you know, all our normal things were different, our routines were upset. Everyone around her was upset. Oh my God."

"Maya, can you tell me about that day?"

She shook her head. "I don't like to talk about it."

Frank waited her out.

"He got stabbed at home. The police thought that someone followed him home to rob him and got scared."

"Did they ever catch the guy that did it?"

"No, he's still out there somewhere." Maya rubbed her arms.

"Can I ask where on his body he was stabbed?"

"Right here," she said, raising her hand to the side of her neck. Her mouth and eyes widened. "Right where Vivi's pain is. Oh my God. What do I do?"

"The first thing is Vivi's okay right this second. What happened to her—what may have happened—was a long time ago, but now we can help her. Okay?"

Maya nodded.

"I can get you the name of a good child therapist and maybe we can get to the bottom of this. And Maya?" Frank got her full attention. "She might *not* have seen anything. It might not have anything to do with her neck pain."

"She was there that day. When I got there one of the neighbors was with her. She was crying, I remember that, but we were all upset. She was with my mother, they were watching TV when it happened. My mother went into the kitchen when she heard the noise. I just thought Vivi would stay watching TV but of course she would have heard my mother crying. The neighbor called the police, she was crying so loud. Vivi would have followed her into the kitchen. She would have seen. Why didn't I think of this before?"

Taking her hands, Frank consoled, "Your father had just been murdered."

It occurred to her that she and Maya had the bloody murders of their fathers in common. But the difference was Frank had the comfort of knowing who had killed her father.

"Vivi was safe. She wasn't in any danger. And right after your father died you would have been focused on his murder and your mother and all the consequences of his dying. You had no reason to worry about Vivi. And maybe you still don't."

"What should I do?"

"Relax, for one thing. For her sake. There's no reason for her to see you so upset. And like I said, I can get you some phone numbers. There are professionals who can help you figure out what to do next. But right now, I'd just let it be. What's happened has happened. It's over. And now that we know what *might* be causing her neck pain we can go from there."

"Yeah, okay." Maya struggled to regain some control. "Okay."

"Good. I'll have the numbers for you by next Saturday. Until then, nothing's changed. Vivi's fine. Now how about we work on you."

"Okay. I guess so."

"Your shoulder or just everything in general?"

"Oh, I think now I need everything. What my mother would call a *limpia*."

Before Frank reached across the table she asked, "You said your mother used to see Sal."

"Yeah, she used to come a lot."

"When did she stop?"

"Oh, I don't know. Maybe... oh I do know. It was right after my father died. She came home furious and said Sal was a witch, and that was when she told me never to go near her."

There was a reason they called hunches "gut instinct." It really was a visceral feeling. Frank had had a lot of them over the years, that sensation of something suddenly dropping perfectly into place. Maya's mother stopped seeing Sal right after her father died—because Sal had seen something. Frank couldn't help but wonder if Maya's mother might be Dash.

Frank smiled. "Sal could be pretty scary. She could see things people didn't always want her to see."

"You think she saw something bad about my mom?"

"I don't know if it was bad. I know she saw things about me I'd rather she hadn't. She was pretty amazing like that. Hey. What was your father's name?"

"Augustin Hernandez. Why?"

"Just curious. I used to be a cop. Thought I might have heard about him."

Fortunately Maya was too preoccupied to wonder why a cop from LA would have heard about a murder in Soledad. A familiar surge of excitement coursed through Frank: the retired

151

but not forgotten thrill of the hunt. She willed herself to focus on the mountains, the cave, Maya at the entrance. She pictured a shelf just over the door where everything else could wait.

Frank slid into the slipstream of calm, pleased when they both opened their eyes that Maya seemed much more at ease. Assuring her she needn't worry about Vivi any more than she already did, Frank promised to get her the contact for that child psychologist.

"I'd appreciate that." She fished a twenty from her pocket and laid it on the table.

Frank frowned at the bill. She wished Maya could cook her something like the other ladies. But all thoughts of Maya fled when Lydia limped into the shed.

"Hi," Frank said, helping her into the chair.

"Hi. 'Fraid the heat's done me in."

"Can I get you some cold water?"

Lydia shook her head. "The lady that runs the store gave me a bottle. I'm okay."

She put her hands out on the table, ready for Frank.

"Let me light your candle," Frank said. She struck a match to the Madonna candle. "I'll leave it over here. Little cooler. I should get a fan."

"That'd be nice," Lydia agreed.

Taking her hands, Frank observed, "Looks like it cost you a lot to come this morning."

"Yeah. Rough week. But I really wanted to see you. I felt great for a couple days. Well, great by my standards. I have a pretty low bar these days but I wasn't as tired or nauseous. I think you really helped."

"Good. Then let's do that again."

Lydia gave a business-like nod and shut her eyes. She straightened in her chair as if making an effort to absorb as much healing as she could. Frank suspected she was an orderly, take-charge type of woman and that even sick she ran her home like a well-organized military unit.

"You can relax," Frank whispered. "There's nothing for you

to do right now but that. Just relax." Then she added, "I've got you."

Lydia's shoulders dropped. Her hands grew heavier in Frank's. She breathed a deep sigh. Frank closed her eyes. Felt the mountain beneath her feet, the cave of old, old rock surrounding her. Saw Lydia standing relaxed and healthy at the entrance. Frank let the magic run through her.

When they were done, Lydia said quietly, "Thank you. I owe you another batch of brownies."

"You do." Frank smiled and squeezed her hands before letting go. Watching Lydia gather her purse and leave, Frank really hoped she'd get them someday.

Driving back to the cabin that afternoon Frank struggled as she often had to figure why some people got to live long and healthy lives while others died so young. No one was owed a long life. It wasn't like there was a biological guarantee, your money back if you didn't get to at least fifty, so was it all just a genetic or environmental crap shoot?

She used to believe it was just bad luck, wrong place at the wrong time kind of thing. More and more she was less convinced. Since being on the ranch life felt more purposeful than it had before and though she couldn't even begin to tease out the purpose or who decreed said purpose, she just had a mounting sense that there was a reason for everything. She was starting to think that a lot more went on 'twixt heaven and earth than mere mortals could explain. Not that she needed or wanted an explanation. There was a beauty and richness to living in this new unknown, in allowing each day to unfold with whatever mystery it may or may not present.

Thinking of mysteries got her thinking of the journal. After she picked up the dogs from Pete she spent the afternoon scanning for references that could possibly have been related to Dash. Like she'd done with a murder book, Frank read and reread the journal hoping to spot something she hadn't before. And as often happened with an old murder book, she found nothing new. At least not this time.

153

She slapped the ledger shut. Bone bolted upright.

"Sorry, old man."

She stroked his flank and he settled back to the ground. If she was still a cop she'd have found Maya and talked to her but as a civilian she had to wait until Saturday and hope Maya came to the store. She'd have questioned Vivi too, but now she didn't dare. She had no authority to risk upsetting her with questions about an event she likely didn't remember. And couldn't elucidate even if she did.

Frank rose and paced around the fire pit. Kook lifted his head and wagged his tail. Bone eyed her cautiously. Frank ticked off the circumstantial evidence as she paced round the pit.

Someone, Dash, did something very bad, possibly a homicide.

Vivi's grandfather, Augustin Hernandez, was killed by persons(s) unknown at approximately the same time as Dash did whatever bad thing she did.

Vivi was there with her grandmother when her grandfather was killed. She may or may not have seen who did it. But *if* Dash was her grandmother, if Dash did indeed kill her husband, that would be an even more serious trauma for a little kid, which may well have manifested as a physical illness.

Immediately after her husband's death, the grandmother saw Sal like she had for presumably years, then abruptly stopped seeing her and called her a witch.

"Because you saw what she did?" Frank asked the air. "You saw this woman, Vivi's grandmother? Stab her husband? And because of your situation you were in no position to say anything? Is that it?"

The pieces fit—the timeframe, the players, Sal's opaque hints—but Frank needed more. She needed the glue that would hold the pieces together, glue that might be found in the Hernandez file. Frank wondered what the odds were that Gomez would let her look at it. There was only one way to find out but Frank couldn't do that until Sunday.

Splaying her hands open above the ground, she announced,

"Lettin' it go."

Long experience had taught her that the mind was a devious, selfish organ. If one forced it to look at something it often balked, refusing to see. But if you happened to look away from the problem, pretended you didn't care about it, then the mind *wanted* to look. The more you averted your gaze, the more lures and temptations the mind would pitch out, tempting breadcrumbs filched from a subconscious larder.

Frank did her few chores around the cabin. After, she strolled up the hill behind and smoked, waiting for the stars. A half-moon stood at attention directly overhead. Sparrows tittered goodnight. Crickets and treefrogs began their evening chorus. Not a leaf stirred. The sky became an orange stripe between darkening dusk and land. A Rothko not even he could have painted. No, Frank thought, studying the soft lines, more like an O'Keeffe. The one with the black cross in the foreground. Frank shook her head, so glad she hadn't missed any of this. Once the sun was well and set the moon lit her way back to the cabin. Crawling into her bedroll, refusing to think about Vivi, Dash or anything in the journal, she concentrated instead on Ronnie.

Frank fell asleep smiling.

CHAPTER 20

When she knocked at Ronnie's door on Sunday afternoon, she heard her yell, "Who is it?"

"Frank!"

"Come in!"

Ronnie's pack went into a frenzy greeting Kook and Bone. Frank stepped around them, following the sound of Ronnie talking in the kitchen.

"I know, *mijita*. But I'd get it in writing. They want to have all these children but they have no idea the work involved."

Ronnie was a flurry of activity, on the phone, stirring something in a bowl, presenting a cheek for Frank to kiss.

"My daughter," she whispered. Frank nodded and squatted to love on the dogs.

"*Pues, yo se*! It was the same with your father. He wanted you both desperately but his only expectation for fatherhood was to provide for you and protect you. Nothing about changing diapers or washing dishes or feedings at three in the morning. That was all still on me even though I was working over forty hours a week. *Ay Dios*, how did I do that? And you know I love your father but that was just how he was raised. He thought I'd drop my career once we started raising a family and expected me to quit when I got pregnant with you. I always argued with him that if it was so important to have a full-time parent then he could quit and I'd be the sole provider. *Ha! That* was never an option."

She listened, running a finger inside the bowl and presenting it for Frank to lick. Frank took the tip of her finger just inside her mouth and sucked it. Ronnie covered the phone to whisper, "*Diabla!*" and kiss her.

"*Pero claro*, of course I'm here! But I should go, baby. I've got to frost Martin's cake and get to dinner. I will. I love you *mucho mucho mucho*. Bye."

She put down the phone and turned to Frank. "*Amor.*"

They embraced, refamiliarizing themselves with each other's lips and feel and smell. Ronnie pushed abruptly away.

"Enough of that! I still have to ice the cake."

"What is it?" Frank asked, watching Ronnie slide it from a pan to a platter.

"*Tres leches* for Martin's birthday."

"Delicious. Like the cook."

Frank wrapped her arms around Ronnie as she smoothly spread the frosting .

"How's your daughter?"

"*Ay*, disturbed. Her husband's making the baby talk and she's not ready. But it's a good sign I might be a grandmother soon, eh?"

"*Claro*. She know about us?"

"Not yet. I'm curious how she'll take it. I think she'll be okay, but I want to tell her in person. 'Oh, by the way, your mother's a lesbian' isn't the kind of news you tell over the phone. *Pero* speaking of which, I told Mami and Carly about us."

"Ah. You think they've fallen in love with me enough?"

"We'll see, eh? I was telling them you were coming to dinner and they were all happy about that so I said how good that was because they were going to be seeing a lot more of you."

"How'd they take it?"

Turning to circle her arms around Frank, she said, "I was surprised how disappointed my father was. I didn't think he'd care *un dirrecion o el otro*, but he wants me to find a nice man who'll take care of me in my old age, someone strong. I didn't have the heart to argue that the women in our family usually outlive their husbands and the last thing I wanted was to push some 200-pound man around in a wheelchair and change his bedpan."

Frank laughed.

"Carly was predictably upset, *pero* Mami surprised me too. She was more resigned than anything. She said, '*Ay, mijita salvaje.* It's not a surprise. You were always my wildest—the first to walk, the first to talk, to get pregnant, to finish college, the first to divorce, and now first to...'" Ronnie waved a hand. "She said all she can hope is that you make me happy. Can you do that?"

"I don't know. How'm I doing so far?"

"*Ay, excelente!*"

They smooched a little more and then Ronnie whipped off her apron and asked Frank if she could carry the cake to the car. She gave all the dogs little dog bones, kissed each one, and told them to be good. As she drove the few blocks to her parents' house, chattering all the way, Frank looked out the window and shook her head.

"What? Why are you shaking your head?"

They'd pulled into her folks' driveway and Frank admitted, "I'm nervous. I want your family to like me."

Ronnie leaned over and hugged her arm. "They *do*. Don't pay their moods any mind. They'll get over it in time."

"Yeah, I know. It's just funny. It's been a long time since I cared enough about anyone to care what they thought about me." She smiled at Ronnie. "I just want it to be easy for you."

"*Querida.* When is life ever easy?"

"*De vera,*" Frank agreed.

Balancing the birthday cake she trailed Ronnie into the house. As usual, the men and children were all in the backyard, and the women mostly in the kitchen. Ronnie's mother greeted them cordially but not as effusively as last time. All Frank got from Gomez was a cool nod, dampening her hopes of sneaking a peek at the Hernandez file. They left the cake in the kitchen while the *tias* fussed around it and Ronnie pulled Frank into the living room. Her *abuela* was enthroned on her couch and after Ronnie kissed her Frank gently shook her hand.

The old woman patted the empty space next to her. Ronnie went to help in the kitchen and Frank was left with a handful of nieces and aunties who made small talk and no doubt wanted to see what this *lesbiana* dating their Ronnie was like. They were all called into the dining room after the men tromped through with their platters. The old woman let Frank support her as she shuffled in to dinner. Frank helped her sit then took the chair beside her. Ronnie claimed the seat opposite and winked at her as Gomez pulled out the chair on Frank's other side.

The food was again delicious and Frank felt guilty she had contributed nothing more than another bouquet of wildflowers. She noted that last time they had been placed on the table; this time they'd been left in the kitchen. A subtle snub or maybe an oversight in the tumult of getting dinner out? It didn't matter. Ronnie looked radiant, commandeering the conversation as she and her brother argued heatedly with their father and Gomez' husband about local politics.

While everyone murmured support or disagreement, the Nana startled Frank, pulling on her arm. Frank bent towards her and the old woman whispered in her ear. Frank nodded, gravely replying, "*Claro, Doña Ester.*"

Ronnie caught her eye and raised a brow. Frank offered a slight smile. Cutting into a *chile relleno* Frank asked Gomez how work was going.

She shrugged, but focusing on her plate, she said *sotto voce*, "Really, Frank? My own sister?"

"What can I say? I didn't intend for this to happen," Frank defended. "But you warned me—everyone loves her."

Gomez shook her head and made a disgusted noise.

As dinner went on around them Frank hoped she wouldn't be buttonholed by anyone else and was grateful when Ronnie finally grabbed her to help with dishes.

"What did Nana say to you? You two looked very serious."

"I'm not sure, but I think the drift was that she'll have monkeys beat me from the inside out if I hurt you."

Ronnie cracked up over the sink. "*Ay,* welcome to the Gutierrez family," she finally said. "I hope it's worth it!"

"So far." Frank grinned.

Ronnie excused herself to find candles for Martin's cake and Frank started washing. Gomez plunked a half dozen dirty glasses next to her.

"Hey. 'Member you said you could get me the name of a child psychologist?"

Gomez nodded curtly.

"Could I get it?"

"I'll look it up at work tomorrow."

"That'd be great. I could drop by the station and pick it up."

Gomez didn't answer and Frank pushed her luck. "And you remember that search we talked about last week? I have a name for you now. Pretty sure it's one of your unsolveds."

"Jesus, Mary, and her husband Joe. You got some *huevos,* you know that? First you seduce my sister; now you come sniffing around asking me for help with your..." she threw up her hands, "your *brujeria* or whatever it is you do up there."

Undeterred, Frank countered, "It's not for me, Gomez. It's for a little girl."

"Oh, so that makes it okay for *me* to spend all my time helping *you?*"

"All right. Never mind. I didn't mean to bother you."

"You don't mean to do a lot of things, Frank, yet you seem to do 'em anyway."

Ronnie interrupted, "What's going on here?"

"Nothing," Frank answered.

"You two," Gomez huffed and stalked out.

Ronnie hugged Frank's arm. "Give her some time. She'll cool down. She's like a dog with a bone, once she's worried all the meat off she'll forget about it."

"Hope so. I like your sister."

"Come on. It's time to sing Martin happy birthday. In Spanish." She winked.

They lingered after the cake but were happy to get home and be alone together. Snuggled in the garden, content with their animals and the coming dusk, Ronnie asked, "Will you stay for lunch tomorrow? It's only Char and Dolo this time."

"No Winnie?"

Ronnie frowned and shook her thick waves. "I think her nose is still bent out of joint. Have you used those salts again?"

"No. Tammy helped so much I don't feel like I really need to. How often do you see her?"

"I don't know. Maybe every other month or so? Not as much since I retired. *Ay*, when I was working I saw her practically every week! So yes to lunch?"

"Sure. They're lovely women."

"Good." Ronnie hugged her arm. "I'm going to make a nice frittata for Char and just some fruit. Simple and hopefully appetizing for her."

While Ronnie talked about another friend who might join them Frank's thoughts strayed to Gomez. She clearly wasn't going to hand over the murder book now, not without considerable wooing. Even then she probably wouldn't. But if the Hernandez case was an unsolved, like Maya said, she might be able to pique Gomez' interest. Unless she was completely barking up the wrong tree and Gomez had a solid suspect already.

"*Amor*, where are you? You're not worried about today are you?"

"No. Sorry. But I do want to talk to your sister before I go home tomorrow. She's gonna get me the name of a child psychologist for my girl with the neck pain. She offered to run a search for me last week but got kinda pissed when I asked her about it. That's what you came in on."

"A search for what?"

"I'd originally asked for any incidents involving neck injuries but I've got it narrowed down to an actual name."

"And what will you do with this information?"

Frank pulled Ronnie closer. "*Ay*, you're such an ADA."

She was reluctant to divulge Sal's journal. It was too private, too intimate.

"Between you, me, and the dogs, *amor?*"

"*Claro.*"

"Cross your heart?" Frank took Ronnie's hand and lazily drew a cross upon the swell of her breast.

"*Lo juro por mi madre.*"

"Okay. I think the girl's grandmother might have had something to do with her grandfather's murder. Nothing conclusive mind you, just lots of circumstantial stuff so I want to talk to Carly about it."

"*Neta!*" Ronnie whistled.

"Who knew this healing business was so nefarious?"

"Well, the kid's got nothing to do with it. Just some odd coincidences her mom's mentioned around her neck pain." Frank was dismissive. "It's probably nothing but still worth running to ground."

"*Ay*, still a detective, you are."

"Seems so." Steering Ronnie from further questions she asked, "Was it easy for you to let go of work?"

"*Ay!* Like dropping a stone down a deep, deep well! All this," Ronnie swept a hand around the garden, "I started years ago when the kids were little. All the things that are so big now I had my husband plant years ago, the bougainvillea and grapes. All the trees." She pointed. "I've got banana, lime, orange, lemon, plum, guava—I put them all along the fence so the kids could have the yard to play in. I didn't do much gardening back then except for simple things like tomatoes and peppers, squash. But then when I retired I had Julian—my brother-in-law? You met him—he made all the planters for me, *ay*, and that was when I *really* blossomed."

"Pun intended?"

"Yes!" Ronnie clapped her hands. "You know, the menopause, it's *such* an amazing time for a woman if she listens to her heart instead of all the horror stories they tell us about it. We *bloom* in old age into *ourselves* because we finally start taking care of ourselves instead of everyone else. The kids were on their own and I'd already divorced Henry, and as I was going through the menopause I remember thinking, *what am I doing?* I knew I didn't want to be the ADA anymore, and I didn't want to be the District Attorney even though it would have been the next logical step for me. What I wanted in my heart was quiet. I wanted to spend time in my garden with my animals. I wanted to be with people I loved and to help people that really needed me. That was how I got in so over my head when I first retired—there were so many good causes I finally had time to help with and I took on too many all at once. But I learned. It's a big transition and it's so underestimated. Other than having children, I think it's the most sacred time in a woman's life. She's finally giving birth to *herself*. For me it was magic. It still is. I love my life. I wish things were different in it, like my son, and I'd love to have grand-babies, which may yet come. And my son may yet straighten out. Who knows? It's all in God's hands."

Frank took Ronnie's. "I was just thinking that yesterday. Just the beauty of not struggling to control the day and letting life happen as it will. A woman in AA used to call it 'living life on the natch.' I never knew what she meant until I moved up here. I was always so busy plotting, and planning, trying to make shit happen."

Ronnie nodded. "*Claro*, I think there's an acceptance that comes with age. We realize looking back there was so little we could control and looking forward, *pues*, that just as much is out of our hands."

They sat in simple silence, rocking together, until Ronnie's phone rang. She glanced at the name and ended it.

"Speak of the devil. My daughter again. I'll call her back later. I want to *savor* you while I can."

Ronnie pressed into her, hugging her arm.

"Sure?"

"*Absolutamente*. We talk all the time. If it's important she'll keep calling until I answer."

"Thanks. That's one of the reasons I don't want to get a phone again. They're just one more distraction in a world full of distractions. I wouldn't want to miss this. Or that hummingbird there. Or the dogs padding around. I've missed enough life. I don't want to miss any more."

"I hear you, *querida*. But it would be nice to talk to you sometimes when you're not here."

"Just have to *savor* me while I'm here."

Ronnie gave a dramatic sigh. "I suppose." Then she cupped Frank's face in both hands. "How about we get naked and savor each other in bed?"

"My god," Frank laughed. "How was I lucky enough to find you?"

They rose and headed inside, seven dogs in tow.

CHAPTER 21

Frank was used to rising with the sun. Ronnie not so much, so Frank tiptoed out of bed and got the coffee started. As the dogs followed her into the kitchen she knelt to greet each one. One by one they flapped out the dog door. Frank poured a cup for Ronnie and perched next to her. She kissed her cheek, her neck, her collarbone.

"*Ay*. That's not Paco."

"No. Better than Paco."

"I don't know," Ronnie smiled, eyes still closed. "I love my *viejo*."

"Yeah, but does that old man bring you coffee in bed?"

"*Ay*, you didn't?"

"I did. Sweet, creamy, and strong enough to plant a flagpole in."

Ronnie laughed. "Okay, you win. I'm sorry, Paco."

She sat up, fluffing a pillow behind her. "Where is he?"

"They're all out back peeing on everything. You shoulda got more girl dogs."

"They chose me, *querida*, not the other way around." Ronnie held the mug with two hands and slurped. "I'll hose everything down after you leave. What time is it?"

"Early. Six."

"*Ay!*"

"Let's take the dogs for a walk before it gets hot."

Ronnie sucked at her cup. "I thought you were all about doing nothing."

"I am at home. But you townies infect me with productivity."

"A townie, eh? Listen to you. What does Carly call you? City?"

"Yeah but she can't call me that anymore."

They teased and bantered until their cups were empty then Frank stripped and got back under the covers. Seeing where their ardor would go, they cuddled and necked, interrupted often by laughter, chatter, and the dogs. Their passion stayed its placid, sensual course. Stretching luxuriously, Ronnie sighed. "I think I'm the happiest woman in the world right now."

"At least a close second," Frank murmured.

Unlike any other woman Frank had been with Ronnie was all flesh and mounds and curves, her only hard planes cheekbones like diamond points. Frank smoothed one with the ball of her thumb.

"I had a lover who used to say women with cheekbones never get old."

Ronnie laughed. "*Cariña*, women with *spirit* never get old."

She rolled over onto her elbows, her great, fleshy breasts making a chasm that swallowed Frank's wandering hand. "It's all in the eyes, *querida*. Now tell me about this old lover. I love old lover stories."

And Frank loved Ronnie's largesse of spirit, the generous heart beneath the mountains of breast. So they swapped stories and histories until Ronnie declared it was time to get lunch ready. Frank apologized to the dogs for not giving them their walk. In answer they rassled and chased each other around the kitchen island while Ronnie assembled the quiche and Frank prepped fruit.

Lunch was subdued. Char cancelled at the last minute and their other friend didn't show up. It was too hot to eat outside so the three women carried their plates into the cool living room. Dolores and Ronnie fretted about Char and decided they would take her lunch. They invited Frank but she declined.

"I don't know her well enough to intrude."

"Maybe so," Ronnie said, picking at her quiche. "When you don't feel good it's hard enough to be around anyone." Then she brightened. "Dolo, I have fun news."

"*Digame*," Dolores said. "I could use fun news."

Ronnie grabbed Frank's hand and swung it between them. "Frank and I are lovers."

"*Mijita!*" Dolores choked. "You should give an old woman warning before you spring news like that on her!"

She sipped at the fancy iced tea Ronnie had made then *tsk*ed. "At our age, that you should be about such nonsense."

"*Especially* at our age. Why should kids have all the fun?"

Spearing a grape, Dolores said, "You always were the wild one."

Ronnie threw back her great mane and roared. "That's *exactly* what Mami said!"

"*Pues, tiene razón ella.*"

"*Ay*, she *is* right!"

Ronnie kissed Frank's cheek and attacked her quiche, pleased with herself. Frank grinned. She was so playful, charismatic, delighted with life and utterly self-confident. Frank wondered why Ronnie had picked her of all the women in the world. As Dolores and Ronnie chatted Frank tried to picture herself with Ronnie prior to retirement. She couldn't. Ronnie and her great hungry love of pleasure would have been too much for Frank. Before retirement she'd been too serious, too driven. Work was always first. Pleasure was earned, reward for a job well done and never something to be indulged for its own sake. And it would have been just about the sex for Frank, the quickest, easiest way to get the only kind of intimacy she'd have allowed herself. She doubted that would have flown with Ronnie. But now that it wasn't a luxury stolen from more important pursuits, Frank was diving into the deep end of the pleasure pool.

She cleared their plates though Ronnie told her to sit and relax. When she came back into the living room she kissed

167

Ronnie's forehead and said she was leaving.

"*Ay, querida*, not already!"

"Yep. I still have to go see if Carly has that number for me. She said she'd send it to you but she still hasn't?"

"*No pero*, I could call her." Pouting, she reached for her phone. "You could get your own phone you know. What if something happens to you up there?"

"Guess the *zopilote* will find me."

Dolores raised her brows. "You really don't have a phone?"

"Left it in LA. It would be an intrusion in the mountains. Out of place. It's wild up there and I like it that way. I think I've had enough civilization to last a lifetime. Dolores," she said reaching to take the woman's hand, "it was good to see you again."

"You too. I was going to say I hope you know what you're in for with this one, but now I'm wondering if Ronnie knows what she's in for."

Frank grinned at her girlfriend who complained, "You haven't even had dessert."

Patting the little koala pouch she was getting, Frank protested, "I'm stuffed."

She bent and kissed Ronnie's mouth. "See you Thursday?"

Ronnie put her hands on Frank's face and pulled her in for another kiss. "*Si, mi amor*. Be careful up there. I'm not ready to turn you over to the *zopilotes*."

Ronnie rose to give Kook and Bone kisses too. Then at the door a longer, full body press for Frank.

"Tell my sister hi," she grinned wickedly.

"Will do. Thank you."

"For what?"

"Just being you."

She pecked Ronnie's cheek and slipped out the door. Driving to the police station she thought the odds were good that Gomez wouldn't even be there. She found a slice of shade and left the dogs with the windows down.

"Be good," she told them. "Don't attack any nuns."

She asked at the desk if Gomez was in. Luckily, she was. But she made Frank wait, spending ten minutes studying the portraits on the walls.

"Frank," she heard behind her. Not the familiar *City*, she noted.

"Hey. Sorry to bother you. I was just wondering if I could get that phone number from you."

"Right." Gomez nodded. "Come back to my office."

Gomez sat at her computer and uninvited, Frank pulled up a chair. The cop scrolled through her monitor. As she jotted the number on a Sticky Frank said, "I think you have a cold case, male Hispanic named Hernandez. A stabbing. Would have been around five years ago."

Gomez looked up at her. "How do you know that?"

"A patient."

"What's it to you?"

Frank danced around the truth. "Given my situation I don't know that I can claim patient confidentiality but this person said some things I don't feel it's my place to share. But from one cop to another, I thought I might at least be able to point you in the right direction."

Gomez studied Frank flatly then turned to her keyboard. After a couple clicks and scrolls she said, "Augustin Hernandez, fifty-seven. Assaulted by persons unknown." She nodded. "Almost five years ago."

"I don't suppose you'd let me see the murder book."

Gomez glared at her. "You know I can't do that."

"Not even for another cop?"

"Oh you didn't retire? You're still active law enforcement?"

Frank tried her most winsome smile. "You could leave it on your desk. Walk out of the room to print something."

"Don't push me."

"Okay, okay." It was good to know where Gomez' boundaries were. "Do you have any suspects?"

Gomez glanced at the file then glowered at Frank. "How about you tell *me* something. Forget all your *brujeria* patient confidentiality. You're not a doctor and you're not protected by any laws. So tell me what you have."

"It's not much. I won't give you any names because everything that was said to me was said in confidence and I won't betray that trust, but it's related to the little girl with the neck pain. Hernandez was her grandfather. And she was there when he got killed."

"How old was she then?"

Gomez started clicking the keyboard again.

"Little. Only two."

"You think she saw it happen?"

"I don't know. Even if she did I don't think she remembers it."

"What it is it you want to know?"

"I'm curious about prime suspects. Were there any?"

The cop glanced at her monitor, then shook her head. "You're something, City."

"Could you at least tell me Hernandez' wife's name? It's a matter of public record but it'd save me a trip to City Hall."

She clicked the mouse a couple times. "Justina Hortensia Hernandez."

"Was she a suspect?"

"Every spouse is a suspect. You know that."

"She was there when it happened. She was watching her granddaughter."

Gomez stayed tight-lipped. "Are you saying we should look into her?"

"I'm just wondering if you did."

"We did. We're not Big City cops like you but we know how to do our jobs."

"Okay." Frank gave a hands up. "I figured you had. Guess she checked out clean."

"If you're hiding something, Frank…"

"I'm not. It's just cop curiosity. But if I hear anything interesting I'll let you know."

She picked up the Sticky and stood. "Thanks for this. I'll

pass it along." Almost out the door she stopped and said, "Oh. Ronnie said to say hi."

CHAPTER 22

The next morning Frank woke deep in her blankets just at the first dawn. She stayed in her bedroll cuddling the dogs. As colors bled back into the land it occurred to her the heat had broken.

With the promise of a warm rather than sweltering day, and after a quick cup of coffee, she saddled Buttons and headed for the mountains. The dogs were happy to run without leashes and even the placid old mare had an extra skip in her step. Once she was under the cover of buckeye and maple Frank took her shirt off. She'd come to love the dappled sun and tender kiss of breeze on bare skin. There was always the chance she'd come upon Pork Chop or one of the other hands but she didn't give a shit. If that happened she'd just pull her shirt back on.

Approaching the downed oak where a gray fox had had her kits that spring, Frank ordered, "With me."

The dogs reluctantly came back and walked alongside. When the fallen tree came into view, Frank reined in and repeated the command. Two fox pups stood at attention on the log, alert to the intruders. Bone saw them and tensed.

"No," she growled. He relaxed slightly but kept staring. Kook still hadn't seen them and was blithely wagging his tail and gazing at her, wondering what the "no" was all about.

"With me," she repeated, slowly circumventing the log.

Buttons' ears pricked at the pups. They remained motionless, staring. Bone paused, craning his neck at them. Frank called his name and he reluctantly fell into step. Kook, so aptly named, was still oblivious. Just then one of the parents shot from behind the cover of a bush. Bone broke for it and Buttons jumped. Frank wasn't prepared for the quick sidestep and slipped in the saddle. Her right foot lost the stirrup while her left slid through. Buttons shifted the opposite way, trying to lose her awkward load.

"Whoa, *shhh*," Frank soothed, her mind simultaneously taking in two imperatives: stopping Buttons, and getting her left boot back into its stirrup.

"Easy, easy, easy," she crooned with a calm she didn't feel. Buttons snorted nervously but stilled. Frank's adrenaline kicked in and she started trembling. Pulling on the saddle, and with her right leg still over Buttons' back, she whispered, "Easy, girl," and managed to seat herself enough to slide her boot back into the stirrup. She put her weight on it and was stroking Buttons' neck, trying to find her right stirrup, when Bone burst back from his chase. Buttons pranced, just a couple steps, but it was enough to loose Frank. As she fell she thought how glad she was her foot was free.

She landed gracelessly, her breath thumping out in a whomp. Like a cartoon, she thought. Her left shoulder took most of the impact. She heard a noise she didn't like, then felt the pain. Frank didn't dare move. She just breathed for a minute, taking stock of the pain. It was about a six on a scale of ten, but climbing. From where she lay she considered Buttons, nonchalantly browsing a few feet away. Kook leant in to kiss her face and she let him, wondering if the silly beast had ever even seen the animals that caused all the commotion. She craned her head to find Bone and the pain leapt to an eight. She felt along her collarbone. It was swelling up but no bone was poking through.

She glanced around for Bone. He was snuffling and scrabbling at the hole in the log. She lost her temper and screamed his name.

"Leave it!"

He stopped and jerked his head toward her, startled at her outburst.

"Come!"

He slunk to her, cowering, and Kook jumped all over her. She swore and pushed him away with her good arm.

"Sit!"

Both dogs dropped like they'd been shot. Gingerly Frank rolled to her knees. That went well enough so she stood.

"Okay," she whispered. "Okay."

She stepped slowly to her fallen shirt. Using her teeth and her good hand she crafted a crude sling with it. Then she took a moment to just breathe into the pain. It was just pain. It would pass someday. Not right now, though. Right now she just had to endure it. Nothing else to do. Just live with the pain and get home.

Gathering Buttons' reins, she scratched under her bridle, telling her what a good girl she was. It could have been so much worse. She had done well to do no more than shy when the fox, and then Bone, had startled her, and to hold steady while Frank had freed her foot. She thought about getting back into the saddle. That's what they said you were supposed to do after a fall. But Frank had enough trouble mounting with two good arms. No way she could do it with just one.

"Christ."

It was going to be a long walk home.

Tugging on the reins she started the trudge. The pain became a mantra, a cadence to step to. She'd never felt so happy to see the little cabin rise from across the field. She managed to unsaddle Buttons then penned the dogs. They seemed to understand her mood and didn't balk or whine as usual. After slowly maneuvering a shirt on she grabbed her keys. With the seatbelt alarm screaming she eased over the bridge. Each jounce felt like someone hammering the edge of a brick into her collarbone. She took a deep breath, bracing for the trip to town.

She left the truck running at Pete's and knocked on the door. He wasn't around. No one was.

"Great."

She walked wearily to the truck and scratched out a note saying she had to run to the ER and the dogs were penned, could he feed them if she was gone long? She jammed it on the front door knocker and headed down the mountain, inching over each rut and washboard. Once she hit the blacktop at Celadores, she relaxed. Every muscle hurt but she thought that was more from tensing the whole ride down than from the fall.

Apparently lunchtime on Tuesdays was a good time to go to the Urgent Care Center—there were only three people in the waiting room and when she checked herself in they immediately ushered her to a doctor. X-rays confirmed it was a clean break. The doc rigged her up in a sling, gave her a scrip for painkillers, and sent her on her way.

Frank stood in the parking lot, looking west to the dark wall of the Santa Lucias. Her stomach fell at the thought of bouncing back up there. She considered dropping in on Ronnie, maybe spending the night. Pete would take care of the dogs. There was no reason she couldn't stay in town.

She got in the truck and rolled the windows down. Ronnie would probably make a fuss and flutter all over her. If she wasn't put out by the unexpected drop-in. If she was even home. Frank knew Tuesday was her immigrant advocacy day but she didn't know what hours Ronnie volunteered.

She tapped her fingers on the steering wheel, staring at the rangy mountains. Part of the allure of her relationship with Ronnie was that both of them were happy to have lives separate and independent of each other. Frank didn't want to start blurring the lines. She wanted Ronnie to be her friend and lover, not her nurse or a convenience. Plus, they didn't see each other that often so when they did Frank wanted to be at her best for Ronnie. Not some helpless thing with a broken wing. Frank had a sudden idea and smiled despite her throbbing bone.

She twisted the fob and used her chin to tug the seatbelt into place. She dropped her prescription at a pharmacy and while it was being filled she went to another store, emerging an hour later.

By then the day had caught up to her. She leaned into the headrest and closed her eyes. Her stomach rumbled. She wasn't hungry but hadn't eaten all day and wasn't about to go home and cook something. She roused herself, found a McDonalds, and ate in the truck, praying her prescription was ready. By the time she'd downed two cheeseburgers it mercifully was. Frank popped two of the painkillers, thinking it wasn't too late to stop at Ronnie's. But then she glanced at the cheerfully wrapped package on the passenger seat and smiled. Thursday would be soon enough. Besides, Frank thought, glancing at the mountains, she wanted to be home.

She eased back up to the ranch and as she approached Pete's house all the dogs ran out to greet her, including Kook and Bone. Pete came out of the house as she got out of the truck.

"Thanks," she called.

He nodded, taking in the sling. Figuring the dogs had had plenty of exercise for one day she let them climb into the cab. Raising a hand to Pete, she finished the drive home, glad Pete hadn't asked for an explanation. The pills had kicked in, easing the pain and making her sleepy. She'd have been content to just sit in the truck all night but after feeding everyone an early dinner she propped a bunch of pillows in Sal's old bed and nestled in with the dogs and a book.

She dozed through the night, shifting often. At one point she admired the moon climbing over the trees, awash with gratitude for its simple beauty, the night's deep silence, the company of her dogs, and relief that the day hadn't turned out so much worse. She started to think of what might have happened if Buttons had bolted while she was still trapped in the stirrup then put the thought out of her head. The horse hadn't, and other than a mending bone, Frank was fine. She wanted to get back on Buttons as soon as possible and she drifted back into sleep trying to think how she could get into the saddle one-handed.

Frank already took life at the speed of rocks but having one hand slowed her even more. From getting out of bed, to dressing, from picking up the dog bowls, to adding water to the kettle—she had to plan out the simplest moves. Being one-handed required attention and presence. And patience.

"Like living a Mary Oliver poem," she lamented to the dogs, making two trips to put their bowls down outside.

Just as she was finally settled with her coffee Pork Chop rode up. The dogs rushed to greet him and his horse whinnied to Buttons and the gelding.

He dismounted and she greeted him, "I just made coffee. Can I get you a cup?"

"That'd be great. If it's not too much trouble."

"How you like it?"

"Black's good."

She poured carefully and brought it back out to him. He was perched on the fire pit, scratching the dogs.

"This is for you," he said extracting a foil-wrapped burrito from a shirt pocket. One eye pointed at her and the other to the mountains. "Pete told me about your arm. I didn't know how you'd be feeling this morning but I made an extra this morning in case you were hungry."

"Damn. That was nice of you. I am hungry, now you mention it."

"Hurt much?"

"Not bad. Hurt my pride more."

"D'you fall?"

"Yeah. Buttons shied at a fox and then at Numb Nuts here," she said rubbing Bone's head. "A better rider wouldn't have even noticed."

"Happens to all of us," he assured. "Where'd you go down?"

"Almost to Vaquero Springs."

He grinned. "That musta been a long walk back."

She shared the grin. "It was."

She took a sip then asked, "How do I become a better rider before I kill myself out there?"

With an eye on the sky he said, "Practice, I guess. Time. Experience. Sal gave you some pointers, didn't she?"

"The basics, yeah."

"D'you ever ride bareback?"

Frank laughed. "Man, I can barely ride with a saddle."

"No, no, no," he insisted. "That's what you gotta do. To be a good rider you gotta feel your horse and the best way to feel your horse is bareback. Riding's all about balance between you and the horse and there's no better way to get that than bareback."

"Balance." Frank nodded. "Makes sense."

"Tell you what." He took an excited gulp from his cup. "When you get your arm out of that sling I'll show you."

"Yeah?"

"Yeah. You'll love it. You'll see. I'd ride bareback all day but it's too hard on a horse. Saddle distributes your weight better. Not digging into one spot all day."

"Okay. I'm gonna hold you to it."

He beamed and drained his cup. "I better get going. At least it's gonna be a nice day. Not hot like it's been."

Tipping his chin toward her sling, he asked, "You need anything?"

"Nah, I'm good. I appreciate it. And thanks for breakfast."

"Sure. Okay. See ya then."

She watched him trot off, as easy on his horse as if he were an extension of the beast. Frank unwrapped the burrito. Much as she trusted Buttons and loved the freedom that riding gave her, she was still too stiff in the saddle, too uneasy. She was already eager to get back on and try bareback.

The burrito was delicious and still warm—eggs, potatoes, onions, peppers and salsa. Frank wolfed it awkwardly, bits falling to the dirt for Bone and Kook. After she ate, she refilled her cup and tried rolling a cigarette. It came out loose and barely smokeable but she relished it nonetheless. By now the sun was up well and good and while the day might not be a scorcher it was still too warm where she sat. Especially wrapped in a sling. She wandered to the west side of the cabin where the shade was still cool. Dogs and chickens followed. She lowered herself against the trunk of an oak and took in the morning.

A woodpecker knocked high above her head and a flock of bluebirds made *pshew-pshew* sounds, like kids imitating gunfire. Hummingbirds zoomed around a patch of sage while goldfinches squeaked and wheezed from the scrub. It was the best music Frank had ever heard. She regretted it had taken her this long to hear it but she was grateful she at last had.

Her gaze found the mountains, the sun fresh upon them. Every day, every hour, each minute, it painted a new masterpiece upon the canvas of the land, a work grander than any found in a museum. Frank wondered if she'd ever tire of this, of just admiring the land and loving it so. While she looked forward to seeing Ronnie tomorrow, she was glad to have the day alone. Peace and wildness felt like the best antidote for a broken bone. There was a tiny hot spring tucked in a crack of a canyon south of the cabin but much too far to get to without a horse. She'd have liked to soak there but instead rose and walked up the hill behind the cabin. She was stiff and sore but the walking would do her good.

The dogs trotted ahead, noses to the ground. Frank absently named the bushes they passed—manzanita, buckbrush, chamise, black sage and white. They followed the faint trail to where a ledge curved east. The dogs plunged beneath the brush but Frank hesitated. It was a skinny ledge with barely enough room to edge herself past the chamise. A fall from it wouldn't kill her but this probably wasn't the best time to risk rolling down the hill. Still, she stepped out onto the thin edge. She could always turn around and come back. Walking slowly, minding each step, she made it to the spot where the ledge widened out a bit. She turned to study the wall of rock behind her, finding the crack above her head. It marked the opening of a cave. The entrance was covered by brush but Frank knew it was there. Sal had brought her, had taken her inside the narrow vault. Had shown her the animals painted on the walls, the handprints covering the ceiling.

Frank perched on the edge of the ledge. Clumsily she rolled a smoke. It had been cool in the cave. Enough light had filtered through to just make out the offerings left by the land's true people. She, an intruder, their conqueror, had touched the wall and felt them there. Had seen them huddled from fire, scared but alive. She remembered the story Sal had told her later, of the woman who had sheltered her people there, who might yet still be alive in the high and lonely peaks.

A ghost crossed her grave. Frank shivered and gave up on the cigarette. Gnats tried to settle on her face but she waved them off. It felt good to have the cave at her back, a friendly place of refuge. Her collarbone ached but she let the pain soak into the ground. Let the cave take it. She was so grateful to be able to just sit there, to not have pressing affairs and nowhere to be. Nothing to do but admire the crags of the Lucias and the golden sprawl of land before them.

Taking the pouch from her shirt pocket, Frank pinched the tobacco. She sprinkled it beside her, behind her, and on her other side. The last bits she blew off her fingertips over the ledge. It was a small enough offering, but it was thanks nonetheless.

CHAPTER 23

"*Ay, amor!* What happened?"

"Took a little spill off my horse. It's nothing serious."

Ronnie's hand flew to her mouth. "*Ay, Dios!* Were you alone?"

"I had the dogs."

"That's not funny. You see? What if something worse had happened to you? I mean, for God's sake, Frank, you don't even have a phone."

"*Amor.*" Frank ran the back of her fingers against Ronnie's soft jaw. "No lectures. Shit happens. I'm fine. I'm not going to stop living 'cause I'm scared of dying."

"I'm not asking you to." Ronnie pressed Frank's hand to her cheek. "I wouldn't do that, but you have to know I worry about you up there all alone, off *Dios* knows where. I mean, there's rattlesnakes, bears, lions, crazy men with guns. Who knows what could happen?"

"Yeah, no crazy men with guns down here. Or burglars or car wrecks." She put her mouth to Ronnie's, hushing her. They kissed tenderly, until Ronnie led her out to the patio and insisted Frank tell her everything. She did, adding, "I thought about coming by after I saw the doctor."

"Why didn't you?"

"I didn't want to bother you. Didn't want to intrude."

"Do you really think I would have been bothered?"

"I didn't know. Didn't want to risk it."

"*Pues*, let me ask you: if I broke my leg or got into a car accident, would you not want to know about it? Would you care less if that happened to me?"

"Okay, okay."

Ronnie cupped Frank's chin. "You've been too long in the wild, *querida*. You're the lone coyote straying into town and if you don't want to get shot at you'd better take the bone being offered you."

Frank grinned. "Maybe not the best analogy. A coyote is a wily creature afraid of enclosed spaces. And honestly, I was more a coyote in the city than I am here. I think I'm more the coyote happy to take the bone, but still wary enough to carry it away to its den instead of gnawing it by the fireplace."

Ronnie twisted toward her. "You think I'm trying to trap you?"

"No, my beauty. You're giving me bones, free of strings, and I even like it when you pet me, but I'm still not ready to give up my home in the woods. I'm the coyote that's been in a cage all its life and has suddenly discovered freedom."

Frank tipped her head back towards the Santa Lucias. "I was sitting up there under a tree yesterday, just watching the world around me, and I felt like I was mending more than just a broken bone. It's like I'm very slowly, very quietly mending something deeper. Like I'm taking scraps of myself that have been torn apart and I'm patching them back together." She smiled. "I'm never gonna be a shiny, seamless garment, but at least I feel like I'm becoming a whole cloth. It's a good feeling. The land is the needle, and the sun, the moon, the trees, all the animals, that incredible silence—those are the threads stitching me back together. It's why there's no room for people up there, not even anyone as special as you, or a phone, or internet. They'd interfere with the mending. Down here, it's different. I think down here is embroidery that's prettying up this old cloth."

Ronnie threw back her head and laughed, her generous

182

mouth soft and wide. "I'm your pretty stitches?"

"Yes." Frank wanted to kiss her, to hold her close and naked. Ronnie must have felt the same way because she growled, "Come here *mi coyote loco*," and planted her mouth on Frank's. She broke off long enough to say, "I don't want to tame you. I just want to love you and feed you and invite you across my threshold occasionally. Will you let me do that, my coyote?"

"Yes," Frank breathed against her neck. "Yes, yes, and yes."

Frank stood and held her hand out. Ronnie arched a brow but rose. She let Frank lead her into the cool, dim bedroom where they undressed, tenderly caressing, kissing, nuzzling. Frank was surprised to find that despite the drugs and steady pain and all the long abstinence, she suddenly wanted Ronnie. She told her, guiding Ronnie's hand between her legs. Deftly, feeling the dryness there, Ronnie sucked on her fingers and slid them into Frank.

Frank gasped. Then laughed. "I gotta sit. I can't do this standing."

Ronnie chuckled with her and together they eased onto the bed, propping Frank against piles of pillows.

"Where were we?" Ronnie said, inching down over Frank's breasts, her belly, her thighs, finally coming to rest between them. Her mouth wetting, licking, teasing, until her fingers slid in again.

"That's where we were," she whispered.

Frank nodded, breathless, letting Ronnie work magic inside her, letting Ronnie carry her, crying out, across the threshold. As she slipped out of Frank Ronnie straddled her, asking if she was okay.

"Yeah."

She rode Frank gently. "Are you sure, *querida*? It's not too much?"

"God, no." She pressed Ronnie's dimpled ass down onto her, urging her on.

"*Ay*, I'm afraid I'm going to *crush* you! Hold on."

She plumped more pillows around Frank. While they were

giggling at the calisthenics involved in accommodating a broken bone Paco jumped on the bed. Followed by Corto and Coqueta. Kook danced, looking for an invite, and two of the other little dogs started yapping.

"*Ay!*" Ronnie flopped onto her back, still laughing. "Mood killers!"

Frank laughed with her, running her fingers through Ronnie's mane. "Broken collarbone doesn't help."

"I could have managed that, but *this? This* menagerie? *Ay,* some things just shouldn't have an audience."

Ronnie rolled onto her side and swung a leg over Frank's. She nestled up under her good arm and Frank asked, "You good, my beauty?"

Ronnie tipped her head, her dark, fathomless eyes shining with delight.

"I am *so* good." She squeezed Frank and snuggled even harder into her. "It was an itch that passed. *Me vale, amor.*"

"Well, I'm not going anywhere," Frank murmured into her hair, inhaling Ronnie's scent, imprinting it.

Ronnie asked how her collarbone was and when Frank admitted it hurt, Ronnie said, "Let's call Winnie! She can make something to help."

She started to get up for her phone but Frank pulled her back down. "I don't think that's a good idea."

"Why not?"

"Think about it. How would you feel if the woman you had a crush on asked you to make something for her girlfriend?"

"I'd spit in it!"

"Exactly. I'll pass."

"*Ay,* I don't think Winnie would do that, but you're right that it may be rubbing salt in a still raw wound. *Pero* speaking of being jealous—not that Carly's jealous, she's just annoyed with me."

"How come?" Frank asked. "Is it me or would it be any woman?"

"Oh, Carly's very conservative. She likes things just so and her sister dating another woman, *pues*, that is definitely not in the natural order of things. It's not you, *amor*, it would be any woman, or for that matter anyone she thought beneath me. At any rate, she called and told me to tell you she contacted the wife of her unsolved."

"Really? She say anything else?"

"She said to call her if you want, but of course you can't do that because you don't have a phone."

"I have a girlfriend that has a phone."

"Ah, ah, ah. It's like cigarettes. You either smoke your own or you don't smoke. You don't beg them off your friends."

Frank laughed. "You're a harsh mistress. You used to smoke?"

"Like a burning house. Didn't everyone our age?"

"Probably."

Playing idly with each other's naked bodies, Ronnie circled back to Frank's interest in her sister's case. "Have you ever considered doing private investigation?"

"Why would I want to do that?"

Ronnie heaved a shoulder. "*Pues*, you seem interested enough in helping my sister and in solving mysteries. It wouldn't take anything for you to get a license. With your background hours I think all you'd have to do is pass a test. I'm always trying to get Carly to think about it. She's almost got enough time to retire with a full pension and I worry for her out there on the streets. It's a tough time for law enforcement. You two could go into business together!"

Frank wound her finger around a lock of Ronnie's silver-shot hair. "Hang out a shingle? 'Local PD Not Good Enough? Hire Your Own Homicide Investigators'?"

"There's more to being a PI than solving murders."

"Yeah, but those are probably the only cases I'd be interested in. Once you've worked homicide it's hard to go anywhere else. At least for me it would be."

"*Pues*, cold cases then. *Dios* knows there's plenty out there."

"Maybe. Something to consider."

"Of course I like having you all to myself. It's enough I have to share you with those mountains."

Frank's stomach rumbled over Ronnie's words and she asked, "When was the last time you ate, *amor*?"

"Actually, one of the ranch hands brought me a burrito this morning. But my stomach says that was a long time ago."

"I'm going to fix us something to eat, *pero* you stay right here, *mi coyote*. Let me feed you in bed."

"Let me help with the dogs." Frank started to rise but Ronnie gently pushed her back against the pillows.

"*Amor*, please. Let me."

Frank relented. But when Ronnie left the room Frank crept naked into the living room for her overnight bag. She dug the package out and placed it prominently on Ronnie's side of the bed. She thought to pop one of her pills before the last one wore off. They made her head woolly but she was hoping by tomorrow she could get away with just an OTC. She took it and by the time Ronnie came back to bed Frank had dozed off. Ronnie sliding the tray onto the night stand woke her with a start.

"*Calma, querida.* It's just me." She sat on the edge of the bed and kissed Frank's brow. "Would you like to go back to sleep?"

"No, I'm good." She patted the empty space beside her. "Let's eat."

Ronnie propped the tray on Frank's lap and came around the bed.

"What's this?" she asked, picking up the package.

"Open it and see."

Frank bit into a slice of homemade olive bread and groaned. "So good."

Waving a hand at the meat and cheese Ronnie offered, "I can make a sandwich if you want."

"No, this is beautiful. Tomatoes from your garden?"

"Yes! The first crop!"

"And these?" Frank pointed at a pale pink pile of vegetables.

"Pickled onions. And those are cornichons."

"God, Ronnie. I'm gonna get fat."

Ronnie pinched Frank's waist. "You could use it. The bone is for the dog but the meat is for the man, or in this case, the woman."

She took the bow off the package and slit the wrapping with a fingernail. Frowning at the box, taking the lid off, she said, "I already have one."

"I know," Frank mumbled around a mouthful of cold chicken. "It's mine."

Her lover's face lit up. "*De vera?* You bought yourself a phone?"

"I did. Just for you." She kissed Ronnie's temple. "The reception's shitty up there and I can't guarantee I'll have it on me all the time, but at least I'll have it in an emergency. And I'll try to find someplace with consistent reception."

"*Amor.*" Ronnie smoothed a palm over Frank's cheek. "I feel bad now, like I've nagged you into doing something you didn't want."

"You didn't. It's time. Once Coyote accepts the proffered bone she has certain obligations to the woman feeding her."

"You don't," Ronnie protested.

"I do. It's not fair for you to have no way to get in touch with me. And besides." She snagged a ring of pink onion. "That's what couples do. Safe to say we're a couple?"

Ronnie's smile lit the room. "Very safe."

"Then put your number in," Frank said reaching for another bite of onion. "Damn. These are amazing."

Ronnie intercepted the onion, kissing Frank's mouth. "*You're* amazing."

CHAPTER 24

After their picnic in bed and more canoodling, Frank used her new phone to call Gomez.

"So you've rejoined civilization?" she asked by way of greeting.

"Yeah. Your sister wore me down." Not giving Gomez a chance to respond, she continued, "Said you talked to Hernandez' wife. What did you come up with?"

"Not much. She wasn't happy to see me after all this time. She seemed scared of me, though, like I was a ghost from her past, which I guess I was. But it was still kind of an interesting reaction. Not the one I expected."

"What did you expect?"

"Curiosity? Like maybe I was coming by with news about who killed her husband. Or sadness for dragging up the past. Even being mad about it. But I wasn't expecting fear. She seemed downright afraid."

"Like maybe you'd found her out?"

"Kind of."

"Interesting."

"Yeah. Anyway, she didn't say anything more than she already had about that day. Stuck to her story all the way."

"Think she was involved?"

"It's sure possible. She was there when it happened, alone, except for the granddaughter who was just a toddler."

"Did she call it in?"

"No, that was a neighbor."

Frank heard pages flipping, then Gomez murmured, "Neighbor heard her screaming, came to see what was going on and found the wife crying over the husband on the kitchen floor."

"Did you respond?"

"No, another sergeant did."

"I sure would love to see those photographs."

There was a long silence on the line. Then a sigh. "Are you in town?"

"Sure am."

"All right. I should be back in the office around five."

Frank made a truncated fist bump with her phone hand. "See ya then."

She left the garden swing to find Ronnie in the kitchen. Leaning on the counter she said, "I've got a date with your sister."

"I can guarantee you she's not as much fun as me."

Frank laughed. "I doubt there's anyone as much fun as you, my beauty."

"*De vera*. When's this date?"

"In a little bit. Five."

Wiping her hands on her apron, Ronnie draped herself carefully against Frank. "Want to come back here after? Spend the night?"

"Tempting. It really is. But I have to sleep kinda sitting up. 'Fraid I'll be doing more fidgeting than sleeping."

"Stay anyway."

Frank shook her head. "I'd rather be restless at the cabin. The stars'll keep me company."

"They're not as beautiful as I am," Ronnie singsonged, playing a finger under Frank's waistband.

"Nor as warm, or soft, or cuddly. And they certainly don't smell as good." She inhaled deeply from Ronnie's mass of hair. "You smell like sun on clean dirt, and roses, and a wind that brings rain."

"*Ay!* A veritable Earth Goddess!"

"Yes." Frank hugged her as hard as she could with one arm. "How do you say goddess in Spanish?"

"*Diosa.*"

"*Si. Mi Diosa Salvaje.*"

Just before she kissed her, Ronnie said, "Look who's talking."

They necked until Frank glanced at the clock on the stove.

"I should get going. She said around five and I'd hate to keep her waiting. She's doing me a favor."

"How?"

"I think she's gonna let me peek at the Hernandez file."

Ronnie made a face like she was impressed. "She must not be too mad at you. I don't think she'd do that for just anybody."

"*Querida*, I'm not just anybody. I'm the woman romancing her sister."

Frank gathered the dogs and after a few last kisses at the door Ronnie asked, "Can you do me a favor?"

"Sure. Anything for my *coyote.*"

"Will you call me when you get home? Let me know you got there okay and didn't fall asleep at the wheel?"

"I can do that." She gave her a peck and started out then stopped. "Hey. See you Sunday?"

"Yes, but it'll just be us this Sunday. No family dinner."

"*Porque?*"

"My folks are going to the City for the birthday of one of my father's cousins, and lucky them, they're going to stop at my daughter's and see her."

"The City? LA?"

"*Amor, por favor*," Ronnie scoffed. "No disrespect but LA is not the City. *San Francisco* is the City."

"Hm. Tell four million people that."

"LA is not a city. It's a *sprawl.*"

"Point," Frank conceded. "Why don't you go with them?"

"*Ay, querida*, I love my family but to spend the whole weekend in a car with them? *No gracias.* Tell me how you feel about art."

The non sequitur stumped Frank. "Tell me what you mean and I'll tell you how I feel."

"There's an exhibition at the Monterey Museum of Art I'd like to see. Would you be interested in making a day of it?"

"I'd love that."

"If you're up for it," Ronnie cautioned, laying a gentle palm over Frank's broken bone. Frank closed her eyes, absorbing the touch.

"That feels good. Sure you're not a *curandera?*"

"Only for my beloveds."

"Okay, Beauty." Frank gave her a last kiss. "See you Sunday."

"Come early. We'll make a day of it. Oh, and Monday is lunch with the ladies. I'm hoping it's going to be a full house. Char, Winnie, Dolo, and two others."

"Can't wait," Frank answered in all sincerity, wondering as she left who the other two women would be.

Even though Gomez was in by the time Frank got to the station she had to wait until she was done with a meeting.

"Sorry about that," she said, coming around the corner, motioning Frank to follow.

"No worries."

"What did you do to your arm?"

"Fell off a horse."

Shaking her head, Gomez led them into a quiet room and indicated the Hernandez file she'd left on the table. They pulled chairs up to it and sat side by side. Gomez flipped straight to the pictures.

"Damn," Frank breathed, studying a close-up of Hernandez' wound. "That's exactly where my little girl has her pain." She put her hand on her own neck. "Right there."

"Do you think she saw it happen?"

"More and more convinced. And the only other person there was the wife?"

"Yep."

"Any evidence of an intruder? Prints? Murder weapon?"

"Nothing."

191

Frank skimmed the detective's interview with Justina Hernandez. It was through an interpreter and Frank knew a lot could be lost in translation.

"Is there anything in particular you're looking for?" Gomez wondered.

"Can't say there is. Mostly curious about how closely they looked at the wife."

Gomez defended her colleague. "Contreras was a good cop. I'm sure he didn't overlook her."

"Not saying he did."

"Coroner thought the angle of entry indicated a person at least as tall as the vic or taller. And the force of the wound suggested a strong assailant, likely male. And who kills their husband with their granddaughter watching? She's got no priors, nothing to suggest she'd planned this."

Frank tapped a finger on the coroner's report. "No defense wounds. No sign of a struggle. So he might have known whoever attacked him."

"Possible. He was heavy into gambling, a regular at card rooms up and down the Valley and apparently didn't always cover his debts. It's all in there."

Scouring pictures of the scene Frank asked Gomez what made her go talk to the wife.

"You got me thinking about the case. It's been a while since anyone talked to her so I thought I'd just drop in for an unannounced chat."

"You surprised her."

The cop nodded with a sly smile. "Like I was the ghost of her dead husband."

A man leaned in the doorway and interrupted. "Call for you."

"Okay." To Frank she said, "I'll be right back."

Frank nodded. She glanced at the door to make sure no one was watching and 360'd the room for cameras. Then she pulled her phone out and started snapping pictures. By the time Gomez returned Frank was innocently studying the photographs.

"So back to the wife. What did you ask her?"

"The usual. I said we were still working on her husband's case, that we hadn't forgotten him, was there anything else she could tell us?"

Frank turned in her chair.

"And?" Frank prompted. "How'd she react other than scared?"

"Well, to be fair, she's pretty sick. It sounds like her heart's giving out. She's on meds for the pain but she seemed lucid enough. She got pretty agitated even though I was just pitching softballs and the daughter asked me to leave."

"Daughter's name Maya?"

Gomez frowned, shook her head. "Pretty sure it was Rose."

"Okay. I'm wondering how she was during her initial interviews. If she was as agitated then. If that's just her personality."

"I couldn't tell you and Contreras is gone. Bought himself a cabin up to Shaver Lake and fishes all day. It was what he always wanted to do and now he's doing it."

Keenly aware of how it felt to be recently retired Frank had no interest in bothering the man. At least not yet.

"Let me ask you this. Did you run across any other cases like this in the area? Maybe there's someone out there frequenting card rooms and following winners home? Randomly robbing them?"

"That I don't know. I could do a search."

"Might not hurt. I should see her other daughter Saturday. She's become a regular and she'll probably come just to get the phone number you gave me. I'll see if I can't wiggle anything else out of her."

Gomez scrutinized Frank. "Why are you doing this?"

Frank smiled. "That's what your sister asked me. Thinks we should become PIs together."

The cop rolled her eyes. "She's always after me to retire. I just got promoted! There's no way I want to quit. I love what I do. And you didn't answer my question."

Frank wagged a finger at her. "You're good."

Leafing through the pictures, Frank considered her answer. It was certainly curiosity at this point. There was also the debt she felt she owed Sal. And she had to admit that whether in or out of uniform Frank liked if not justice, at least resolution. A shrink might have called it closure. Sal had called it deliverance. Retiring should have marked "paid" to that drive but apparently hadn't.

Whatever the reasons, to Gomez she said simply, "Who doesn't like a whodunit?"

CHAPTER 25

By Saturday Frank had eased off the painkillers. Ibuprofen managed the dull pain and her head cleared. She had spent Friday returning to the land, just hanging with the wind and sun, the creek, the horses and chickens, the high scarps, the solemn shroud of oak and scrub. The birds were in full, riotous breeding season, their songs ringing madly from the first gleam of dawn until the last glimmer of dusk. Then the night birds took over. Until living on the ranch Frank had only heard owls in movies and thought there was just one type but she'd spent many an evening on the ranch discerning the cry of barn owls from that of the great horneds, and the *toot-toot* of pygmy owls from that of screech owls.

She finished a breakfast of Ronnie's delicacies and drove the dogs to the ranch. Pete was in the habit of meeting her on the steps to take them but this time he came to the truck. When she stopped he opened the door to let them out. Kook hesitated.

"Go," she waved.

With a last look at her he leapt into the crowd of dogs, wiggling and fawning. Pete shook his head and growled, "You need a real dog up there."

"Bone's a real dog."

"He's old. Gettin' deaf."

"He is?"

195

"Try calling him when his back's turned to you. You'll see."

The pronouncement made Frank ridiculously sad. She couldn't imagine life at the cabin without him.

"Might think about easing a third dog in. Someone to take his place. I'll keep an eye out for you. Don't know why I ever brought Sal Little Bo Peep."

'Cause you're an old softie, she thought but didn't say.

"How's the arm?"

"Not bad."

"Pork Chop says he's gonna teach you to ride bareback. That'll do you good."

"Yeah. I'm looking forward to gettin' back on."

He nodded approvingly and as she drove off it dawned on her that if Pete was going to get her a third dog it meant he intended her to stay at the cabin. Her pleasure at that almost overshadowed the sudden sadness of losing Bone in the now not-so-far future. But if the ranch and thirty years of being a cop had taught her anything it was that life and death were inextricable dance partners. No one and no thing got out alive. Even the mountains rearing around her were quietly eroding down into dust.

Slowing to take a rut without joggling her arm, Frank glanced at the sawtoothed peaks in the mirror. Just like Sal, who had probably never left her beloved mountains, only changed shape to remain among them. There were no endings to life, only changes in form. Mountains became dirt; oceans, rain; and flesh, food. All went endlessly round and round. It was easy to forget that in the city but here it was the daily bread, the sustenance that made life not just bearable but a joy. Everything had a part, each had its role. Pulling in under the old Celadores oak, Frank wondered if maybe she was figuring out hers.

She was relieved to see there was no one new waiting on the bench, only Vivi, Maya, and Izzy. It would be an easy enough day. Vivi waved shyly and Frank returned the greeting. Their eyes followed her into the store but the bench remained quiet as a church pew.

Lolly was alone with her phone games and Frank said, "Morning. Start with you?"

"Nah. It's gonna be hot today. I'll wait 'til they're done."

"Okay. See you in a while."

Lolly had unlocked the shed and turned the lights on. A single sunflower stood in the Mason jar. Frank surveyed the row of candles and lit two, the Virgin of Guadalupe and a serene Madonna.

Izzy came first. She had the same complaint about her heart although she looked happy and healthy. As they chatted and settled Frank casually asked how long Izzy had known Maya's mother.

"*Ay*, a long time. She my good friend. But she sick now."

"Oh, I'm sorry," Frank said in Spanish. "Can I help?"

"She too sick to come." Izzy banged her chest with a fist. "Heart no good. It stopping. She no leave the house no more. Is very sad."

Frank nodded, an idea forming.

"Okay. Let's take care of you," she said, stretching out her able hand.

She forced herself to concentrate on the mountains, on being in the *abuela's* cave with Izzy, letting the ancient energy run through her, into Izzy, back to the land...

When their time was up, Izzy smiled. "*Gracias. Usted es muy buena.*" She added that Frank had the touch very strongly.

Not knowing what to do with a compliment she didn't feel she'd earned, Frank simply said she was happy to help.

Izzy left and was replaced by Maya and Vivi. The girl was spunky and playful and Maya explained, "She just wanted to say hi to you. Her neck's been good."

"Hi, Vivi. That's great."

"Yeah, it feels all better. I just came with Mama and Tia Izzy."

"Good. What's Mama here for?" she asked Maya.

"I was wondering if you got that number we talked about?"

"I did." Frank pulled a folded scrap of paper from her pocket.

"Here you go."

"Thanks," Maya said. She unfolded it, read the name and number. "I'll call. The other thing is, you really helped my shoulder last time and I'd like for you to work on it again."

"Sure."

Maya told Vivi to go and wait with Izzy, then sat opposite Frank. She asked about her arm and Frank told her, already bored with having to do so.

She grinned. "We'll see if this works with one hand. Might only get half the treatment."

"You think?"

"Nah, I'm just kidding. Seemed to go okay for Doña Izzy."

She reached across the table for Maya's hand, but before she took it she said casually, "It's funny, but after I saw you last time I got to thinking about my father a lot. What was yours like?"

"My father?" She lifted a shoulder. "He was ok. Just a father, you know."

"Do you miss him?"

"No," she said immediately. "I guess that sounds bad but he wasn't the kinda father you'd miss. Honestly? It was kinda a relief. That's awful, right? But I mean, he was never like a real dad. It wasn't like that."

"No, I totally get it." Frank said a silent plea to her own father for forgiveness. "Mine was like that, too. Too many beatings. Yours?"

"No, he never beat us. He beat my mom sometimes but not us." Maya looked cagey. "He did other things."

Frank grimaced. "Yeah, I know about other things, too."

Maya nodded.

"I'm sorry," Frank offered. "It's rough. And it's hard to watch your mom suffer. And your siblings."

"Yeah, well, what can you do?" Then she added fiercely, "And no one ain't ever gonna lay a hand on Vivi. No one."

Frank grinned. "Except for me I guess, but in a good way."

"Yeah." Maya laughed. "No one but you, Miss Frank. Anyone else, they better watch out!"

Frank chuckled and took Maya's hand. Again she had to force herself to concentrate but quickly eased into the slow, steady pulse of the healing time, as she had come to think of it. As the women came back to real time, Maya thanked her. Frank said she was welcome and accepted the offered twenty dollars.

"Hey, Izzy mentioned your mom was sick, but that it was too far for her to come here. I just wanted to let you know I'd be happy to make a house call if you think it'd help."

"Oh my God, really? That would be amazing."

"If you think she'd like that then sure. But I know she didn't like Sal."

Maya nodded thoughtfully. "I think that was different. I told her I was bringing Vivi to see you and she didn't get upset."

"That's good. Did you tell her what I said about Vivi? About her maybe seeing your father get stabbed?"

"No, no. She's too sick. I wouldn't upset her with that. And now that you brung it up it makes complete sense, of course she would have seen, she was there alone with her until the neighbor came over and took her. But I don't want to make her feel bad about that."

"Does it still bother her? Losing your father that way?"

"I don't know. She don't talk about it. None of us do. You know, like I said, he wasn't a great father and he couldn't have been a great husband either. You know, honestly, she was probably more worried about how to support four kids than about losing him."

"If you're any indication she seems to have managed it pretty well."

Maya brightened. "Yeah, all four of us came out okay. She was a great mom. Still is. I'll let you know what she says."

"Okay. I'll give you my number so if she's interested you can just call me instead of making a special trip."

"Oh, thank you, but it's worth it." She rubbed her shoulder. "It feels so much better."

Between Maya and Lolly Frank fell into a dreamless doze.

She woke when Lolly gently shook her.

"Hey."

"Hey, yourself. Why don't you get yourself on up to the cabin?"

"Nah, I'm good, Lolly. Just needed a little power nap. Come on." She waved at the chair. "Sit."

Lolly did. "Wasn't sure if we'd see you today or not."

"How come?"

"With that broke collarbone didn't know if you'd be up for it."

Frank grinned at the mountain gossip chain. "Wouldn't miss it for the world, Lolly."

Lolly's chuckle turned into a cough, then she said, "A month ago you was sure this was all a joke. Now look at ya. Sal done good."

"How do you mean?"

"She picked a good person to take her place."

"You think she did it deliberately?"

"Well, I don't know about deliberate, but when you're paying attention to life you see opportunities others miss. And I tell you what, Sal paid attention. She musta seen you and knew you was the one."

"Do you think she was ready to go?"

"Oh, I couldn't say. But there was always a certain sadness to Sal. Guess we know why now. Couldna been easy living with that all these years, so maybe it was finally a relief to lay it all down."

"You know, Lolly, I'm laying odds she's still up there, looking down on all of us."

Lolly gave her wet chuckle. "There's a reason the place is called Celadaores."

"Why? What's it mean?"

Bending over the table Lolly asked, "You don't know what Celadores means? You ain't never heard the stories?"

"No ma'am."

As satisfied as if she'd delivered a punchline, Lolly sat back and crossed her arms.

"*Celadores* means watchmen or door-keepers. As long as there's been people in these mountains there's been stories about men up in the peaks. Tall men in black cloaks that appear outta nowhere and just stand watching a lonely traveler, then disappear, poof, just like they came. Even Steinbeck wrote about 'em. Called 'em the dark watchers, just standing guard up there on the peaks. They say they're watching over lost souls, helping 'em find their way."

The little hairs all over Frank's body rose. Lolly made it sound like the stuff and nonsense of legend but it made perfect sense to Frank. She thought of the *zopilote*, hunched in their dark feathers, watching over lost wanderers.

"You okay? Sure this ain't too much for you, with the arm and all? Don't have to treat me if it is."

"No, no. Not at all." Frank made herself smile. "If anything it helps."

"If you're sure," Lolly said doubtfully.

"You know," Frank said, reaching for Lolly's hand, "it's one of the few things I am sure of."

CHAPTER 26

Frank was bushed by the time she got back to the cabin. She took everyone down to the creek for a drink and after soaking her feet in the cool water she sank into the cradle of the sycamore tree. She'd brought the journal with her but sleep claimed her before it could.

She dreamt of Sal riding across the bridge. She was on the horse she'd ridden the night she killed herself, the one that had slipped off the trail in the dark. Frank was so happy they were both alive and asked where they'd been. Sal smiled and said, "A long trip."

Frank answered, "I'm so glad you're back."

Sal nodded. "There's larks in the sky."

"Yes," Frank confirmed. "Larks everywhere."

"But don't tell Pete."

"No? Why?"

"He'll want to put them all in a pie. He loves lark pie."

"Oh, okay. I won't."

Frank was delighted to have a secret with Sal. It seemed like a harmless enough one. No need for Pete to stuff larks into a pie.

Sal patted the horse's rump. "Come on."

And then Frank was riding behind Sal, arms around her, her cheek resting between Sal's bony shoulder blades. She felt guilty and made Sal stop.

"I have a girlfriend now."

"I know," Sal said, somehow able to look at her even though she was sitting in front of Frank. Then they were on the couch in the cabin, watching the fire and holding hands, and it was okay they were holding hands because Sal just wanted company, nothing else. Frank fell asleep in the dream and that was what woke her.

She smiled at the watchful dogs. "Don't tell Pete," she said. "He'll eat all the larks."

Her back was kinked up and she stretched as carefully as she could. The dogs had come over to kiss her and she grasped Bone's collar. Telling him to stay, she used him to pull herself to her knees. The nap had left her groggy. She stepped gingerly. It wouldn't do to stumble amid the roots and rocks. The day's heat was fading in the face of a thick fog resting just on the other side of the Lucias. Trudging back to the cabin she tried to figure how she could sleep outside under her beloved night sky.

Frank stopped. When Bone realized she wasn't coming he stopped too and looked at her. She'd heard the growl of Pete's truck before he did. He finally cocked his head and she acknowledged Pete was right. She waited where she was until he rumbled across the bridge and cut the engine beside her.

Twisting in his seat he said, "Here you go, Chief."

He passed her, unbelievably, a pie. "Careful. It's still warm."

She tucked the journal under her bad arm and balanced the pie against her stomach. "Don't tell me there's larks in there."

He scowled. "Larks? It's pigeons. I shoot 'em down at the barn in the vineyard, first gate as you come up. They ain't real pigeons. Just those rock doves we get. They're a pest."

She stared down at the golden crust.

"Aw, don't tell me you're squeamish. I know you ain't a vegetarian. I just thought with your arm an' all. I made two."

Frank couldn't take her eyes from the pie.

"If you don't want it I'll take it back. Pork Chop'd be happy to have it."

Finally she met his gaze. "I was taking a nap by the creek.

Dreamt Sal rode up on that horse that died. She said there were larks in the sky but not to tell you 'cause you liked to put 'em in a pie."

Pete paled. They both stared at the pie.

"She loved pigeon pie."

A little shiver coursed through Frank but she smiled. "I'll be happy to eat it for her."

Pete wiped his mouth with the back of his hand.

"You wanna come in? Have a slice?"

"Naw." He started the engine. "Got my own at home."

She hefted it toward him. "Appreciate it."

He nodded. Then killed the engine. He gave her a hard stare. "You think with all your..." he waggled his hand at her, "that business you do, you think she's still around here?"

Frank returned the stare, took a deep breath. "I'm sure of it."

"Yeah." He nodded. His gaze drifted behind her to the mountains. "All right," he said, reaching again for the ignition. "Bring the pan back when you're done."

She watched the truck until it disappeared. Even then she kept looking. She smiled at the late afternoon sky.

"Come on, Sal. Let's eat."

She turned for the cabin realizing she was ravenous. The dogs got dinner and slavered at her feet when she cut into the pie. It smelled so good she almost started drooling too.

"Damn," she whispered, inhaling the rich smell of meat and onions and thyme. She slid a big wedge onto a plate and carried it outside. It was a pain getting out of the Adirondack chair with one arm so she perched on the edge of the fire pit and forked a mouthful of the pie.

"Jesus wept," she moaned to the dogs. "Who knew the tetchy old bastard could cook?"

She could have sworn she heard Sal laugh.

"Yeah," she said around another mouthful. "Guess you did."

The first slice was so good Frank went back and cut a second, slipping each dog a piece of the succulent meat.

"Who knew?" she marveled. That Pete could cook. That he'd

give her a pie. That Sal would share it with her and talk to her in dreams. That pigeon tasted kinda like duck. She covered the remaining half and texted Ronnie.

Have you made a feast yet for tomorrow?

She had to wander around until she found a signal. Halfway between the corral and the cabin seemed like a good spot.

A few minutes later she read, *Nada. I thought we'd have lunch in Monterey if yr up 4 trip.*

She typed, *Sounds good. I have dinner.*

Ronnie answered, *Do you now?* followed by lip and kiss emojis.

Frank winced. She hated emojis and typed *xxoo—mañana my beauty.*

Packing a bunch of pillows into the Adirondack chair she settled into it and opened the photo gallery on her phone. She'd had time to snap each page of Hernandez' thin file and she swiped to the coroner's report.

The timing of Sal's journal entry coincided perfectly with that of the murder, making Justina Hernandez an especially attractive suspect, but the worst thing a detective could do was to fixate on a suspect and try to fit the evidence to his guilt. She had to keep an open mind that while Hernandez' wife certainly could have killed him, it was also quite possible that anyone could have killed him—a disgruntled gambler, someone he owed, a random burglary gone sour, some other unknown vendetta. The evidence had to lead to the suspect, not the other way around.

The coroner's opinion was that Hernandez exsanguinated from transection of the right carotid due to a single stab wound, likely from a single-edged knife. He'd have bled out immediately. There were no drugs in his system, only a trace of alcohol. The report described the wound edges as even and regular, a clean slit.

Frank looked at the far crags, the calm blue sky. If Hernandez had been struggling and moving around trying to defend himself or attack the suspect, the wound margins should have been irregular, uneven. That they weren't suggested to Frank that he had either been holding still or immobilized.

She scanned through the report until she read that Hernandez' wallet had been found on him, apparently undisturbed, with $27 in it. A gold wedding ring and gold chain were also on his body. If it was a robbery, the suspect hadn't taken anything. He may not have intended to hurt Hernandez but the job went bad and he had to defend himself, then panicked and fled without taking anything.

Hernandez had been stabbed on the right side of his neck so either the attacker was right-handed and stabbed him from behind or left-handed and stabbed him from the front. If Hernandez had been rushing his attacker Frank would have expected the attacker to defend himself with an anterior rather than lateral motion. It would have wasted time to swing the knife out to the side rather than just stab upward and easily into the belly, or if the attacker was taller than Hernandez as suspected from the single blow, then beneath the collarbone into the thoracic area.

The stab wound had been exceptionally well placed for almost immediate disablement and rapid death. Had that been a lucky hit or did the suspect know his way around a body? There weren't multiple stab wounds as often found in crimes of passion so the single wound lent credence to a stranger inflicting it, a stranger who hadn't intended to hurt Hernandez.

Frank pulled the journal into her lap. She flipped through each page, scrolling for the initials JH. There were only three instances. All were straightforward patient entries, except the one Sal had expounded on:

JH - just a cleanse. Always the guilt with her. I can soothe it, maybe even make it go away for a while but it always comes back. Don't I know that. I so wish I could do more for her . . . She's never told me in so many words. She doesn't have to and I've never pushed her about what I think it is. We women endure what we have to and our reasons are our own.

Frank reread the Dash entries, that anyone who knew her couldn't help but blame her for what she did, and that Sal had done the same thing. Sal had killed someone. Not intentionally but it was murder, nonetheless. Had Justina done the same thing? Just got fed up one day and whacked her man? Assuming for the moment that Justina had killed her husband, it would have been easy for her to get close to him without arousing suspicion, close enough to jam a knife in his neck. Frank double-checked the point of entry. It was the sweet spot just behind and under his jawbone. If the attacker was behind Hernandez and acted swiftly he wouldn't have seen it coming.

She peered at a close-up of Hernandez' head and neck. The single, clean stabbing in an awkward area, if the attack was frontal, suggested that Hernandez had been approached from behind. That the wound was so simple and clean suggested he hadn't been afraid of whoever was behind him, as if someone had been in a position close enough to peer over his shoulder and simply stab him while he was fixing a sandwich or looking at his phone. He appeared to have been completely unaware of or unconcerned by his attacker. Nothing suggested speed or surprise. There were no signs of a struggle.

Frank swiped to the suspect list. To his credit, Detective Contreras had an impressive number of names. Hernandez hadn't had regular employment and relied on gambling for his income so it wasn't surprising that most of the suspects were gambling associates. Most of the names had a neat line driven through them, with detailed explanation as to why they were no longer suspected. It was interesting that each of Hernandez' four children were on the list. Each had been eliminated. Justina Hernandez was at the top of the list. There was no line through her name.

From Maya Frank knew Hernandez had somehow abused his daughter and beaten his wife. So there may have been motive for Justina to kill him. But why wait so long? The single wound indicated precision, planning, even patience. A sudden crime of passion usually had more chaos, more wounds and more random placements, not one meticulous, fatal wound.

Frank double-checked the pictures. There was no sign of drag marks. It looked like he'd been attacked and bled out in the kitchen. Photos and diagrams showed a back door right off the kitchen which anyone from the street could have used. Frank shook her head. It didn't make sense it was a stranger. He'd have had to follow Hernandez in, undiscovered and undetected, then quietly stab him from behind before Hernandez could defend himself. If someone was that pissed at Hernandez and had gone to all that trouble to kill him, the attacker most likely would have stabbed him in the back multiple times to ensure the job was done. What were the odds of success with a single wound to the neck? Unless someone had the time, skill, and trust to place it there.

Frank skimmed the suspect list. None of Hernandez' family or close friends had jobs that would have given them surgical or anatomical knowledge. Other than being a seasonal worker in the fields Justina Hernandez didn't have a job. A wife and mother, a woman who'd been cooking all her life, she surely knew about boning meat and maybe even butchering animals. It was reasonable to think she would know her way around the sharp end of a knife, where to insert it for a clean cut.

Frank sat back, absently studying the mountains. For her money, Justina was the best suspect. She read Contreras' notes again, wondering why he'd never eliminated her. According to her testimony she and the granddaughter were watching TV in the living room and she heard her husband call out when he came home through the kitchen door. She thought she should get up to make his lunch but was going to wait for a commercial. Then she heard an odd sound, like a grunt and a cry, and then scrambling noises. She was irritated and got up to see what he was doing. She found him holding his neck, bleeding all over, on his knees. For a minute she was just frozen. He fell over and that jerked her out of her spell. She ran to him to see what had happened and couldn't understand all the blood pumping from his neck. She grabbed a kitchen towel and pressed it to where all the blood was flowing but it just soaked through. Then it started to slow and she started screaming.

Contreras asked if she thought to call 911. She said no, that she didn't think of anything other than what was happening couldn't be happening. She couldn't believe it. It didn't make sense. She didn't understand it. She didn't really think of anything until the police came and pulled her away, made her stand back from her husband's body. The whole time was a blur, she said. And that she regretted that she hadn't thought of her granddaughter all alone in the living room. Had forgotten all about her. The neighbor had taken her until the girl's mother had rushed there from work.

Frank felt in her pocket for the small pouch. She took it and rolled a cigarette without moving her slinged arm. Contreras was probably a fine cop but even the finest had biases. She assumed he was Latino and if so he may have had a bias like the Marianisma influence, the notion that women should be gentle and nurturing like the Virgin Mary, the submissive and weaker sex. That, and maybe a cultural respect for his elders, especially a caregiving *abuela*. It was a stereotype of the Latino male, but also a credible possibility. He hadn't crossed Justina Hernandez off his list but neither did he seem to have done much other than two separate interviews with her. It was a leap but nonetheless Frank stashed it into her brain file.

"Sal," she said fondly to the coming dusk. "Miss Pigeon Pie Eater. Am I on the right track? Could you throw me a bone? Gimme a sign?"

Frank lit her cigarette and blew out a gray stream, the silence of the new stars her only answer.

CHAPTER 27

The next morning after she'd fed the dogs and was getting ready to head down the mountain, Frank turned her phone on. There was a call in voice mail.

"Hi, Miss Frank. It's Maya, Vivi's mom. I talked to my mother and she said she would like to see you, so whenever it's convenient for you please let me know. Thank you so much."

"Hm." Frank looked up. "Seems like a good enough sign, Sal. Thanks."

It was too early on a Sunday morning to answer Maya but it would be ideal if she could see Justina tomorrow after she left Ronnie. She drove carefully down the ranch road, cursing each of the five gates she had to unlock. Different pastures for different things. She had to admit she was impressed with Pete's operation. Far more than a cattle ranch, she knew he leased some of the bottom land for crops, grew some of his own, and had his own dry-farmed vineyard. She suspected he was a shrewd businessman who ran his outfit with an eye to the future rather than the past. Maybe someday they'd be on easier terms and she could have a real conversation with him. As it was, she followed his lead in all their dealings. So far they had been gruff and to the point. But that had been awfully thoughtful of him, to make her a pie. She suspected he was a lot more bark than bite and hoped she'd be able to stick around long enough to find out.

At Ronnie's she left the dogs in the truck while she managed the pigeon pie and her bag one-handed.

"*Ay*, let me help," Ronnie cried at the door. "Where are the dogs? You didn't bring them?"

"They're in the truck. If you can take these," Frank gave her the dish and bag, "I'll go get 'em."

There were the usual loud and excited canine greetings but Frank could only hug her lover with one arm.

"I miss holding you tight."

"Mmm, me too. How long are you going to be in that thing?"

Frank made a face. "Weeks. Lotta weeks."

"*Ay, pobrecita.* But I'm sure we can think of something." Ronnie ran her hands under Frank's shirt, nuzzling her. "I see you brought your bag. Does that mean you're staying tonight?"

"Am I invited?"

"*Pues, claro!*" Ronnie hugged her carefully. "And I even bought you something. Come see."

She pulled Frank into the bedroom and pointed at a backrest pillow propped on the bed. "The lady at the store called it a husband pillow, but I said, no *querida*, more like a *wife* pillow. See? You can sleep sitting up and the arms will keep you from rolling around. I had one for my son when he fell off his bike and it was a *huge* help."

"That's sweet," Frank said. "You didn't have to do that."

"I wanted to. I want you to be as comfortable here as you are up there."

Frank kissed her thanks, and then some. Finally she asked, "We still on for Monterey?"

"Are you up for it?"

"Absolutely. Looking forward to it."

"*Que bueno!*" Ronnie clapped her hands. "I figured we can stop in Carmel and I'll treat you to lunch at my favorite place, a little Oaxacan restaurant with food *to die for!* Then on to the museum. How's that sound?"

"Like loads of fun."

"Oh, I'm so glad. Then we'll come home and have a nice

quiet night, yes?"

"*Perfecto.*"

"*Bueno*, let me get the dogs settled and then off we'll go."

While Ronnie did that Frank called Maya back.

"Oh, thank you for calling me. I think she's excited to see you. Her pain is bad but she doesn't like to take her medication. She says it's stealing what little life she has left."

"I can't make any promises but I'll do my best to help. Would tomorrow, late afternoon, early evening work for you?"

"I think so. Let me call my sister. She lives with her so she'd know best. She watches Vivi for me while she's outta school so I go there every day after work about five if you'd like me there too."

"Sure. It'd be good for you to introduce us. Does she speak English?"

"Not much, but I'd be happy to translate."

"Okay, that'd be good. Text me directions, and we'll plan on five-thirty. If that changes just give me a call."

"Okay, I will, Miss Frank. Thank you so much."

"Happy to help."

Ronnie breezed into the room. "Who was that?"

Frank bristled a little but decided it was a fair enough question. "I'm going to see a patient tomorrow on my way home."

"*Ay*, making house calls! *Doctora*," she pursed her lips. "I have a pain right here."

Frank kissed her. "Better?"

"It still hurts a little."

Frank laughed. "You're wicked."

"You don't even know the half of it."

The lunch was as amazing as Ronnie had promised. They shared a *mole* of smoked pork cheeks and a plantain burrito. Ronnie drank a margarita with lunch but Frank noticed she didn't even finish it.

Frank hadn't been to an AA meeting since she left LA. Every time she went to the library she passed a sign with the familiar logo on it and every time felt guilty. She knew she should be going to meetings but the thought of sitting in a stuffy room with a bunch of strangers made her almost sick to her stomach so she trusted that whatever it was that had gotten her sober would keep her sober until, if and when, it was time to go back into those rooms.

Picking at the last of the still-warm tortilla chips, she asked, "Does Char go to AA meetings?"

Catching a drip of salsa Ronnie murmured, "Religiously."

"Think she'd take me someday?"

"I'm sure she'd love to! Poor dear is always trying to drag one of her sponsees to our lunches and, *pues*, we're snobs and very selective about our company."

"How'd I get into such an exclusive club?"

"*Ay*, you're perfect for us. I like to think we're the *abuelas*, women of a certain age who know ourselves and make no apologies for who and what we are."

"You're a coven of old witches."

"Close," Ronnie corrected. "We're withes."

"Withes?"

She nodded, dabbing with her napkin. "We each work *with* something—colors, plants, water, energy. Witches manipulate energy for an outcome but we work with the natural ebb and flow of what's already there, of what's present. So we're withes, not witches."

"A fine distinction I'll be sure to make come the Inquisition."

"It's a *huge* distinction," Ronnie argued. "It's like Tam said, it's what women have always done, but way back when patriarchal rule started taking over they had to make us evil, so they invented the Devil and used him against us, *ay*, they even did it to my own *abuela's* mother, Doña Serafina. She was a *powerful* curandera. The people came from all over for her healing, even from as far away as Cuernavaca, she was so famous. But then they built a church in her little town. For a while everything was okay, but then one day a new priest came and called Serafina a witch. He claimed she was doing the work of the Devil and that only God Himself could heal. At first the people ignored his foolishness.

213

He didn't know Serafina and didn't know what he was talking about. These were poor people, good people, but they struggled, and the people who still visited Serafina didn't get any of the food or gifts the priest handed out. So one by one they stopped going to see her in the open. They'd sneak to her instead, and accept her healing in shame. And what happens to people when they are ashamed? They get mean. They get ugly and want to blame others for how they feel. So one by one those good folks who used to love Doña Serafina turned against her. And they felt good in their righteousness, and that righteousness became vitriol and venom, so much so that she was forced to flee with her family in the dead of night and settle in a town far from her home."

The waitress delivered coffee and churros with chocolate fondue. Moaning over their dessert, Frank asked, "Did Doña Serafina continue working there?"

"*Ay, no, pobrecita.* The town already had a healer. From then on she kept her work to her family and passed it down to her daughters."

"But your *abuela* didn't pass it down."

Ronnie shrugged. "The times had changed by then. The old ways were passing. Everyone wanted to see the medical doctors. That's why I get so excited when people like you and Tam and Winnie do what you do. You're honoring the memory of Doña Serafina and all the wise women like her. You're keeping the old ways alive. People forget that all these one-boy-god religions are a couple thousand years old at best and before that *everything* was a part of religion—the earth and sky, all the plants and animals. We used to have relationships with everything and we worked *with* all that energy until we were forced not to, but it's still in us, that connection to everything and I think it's especially strong in women. It still lives deep down in our bones"—she waved an arm around— "but in this modern world with fake time and light, and these buildings that cut us off from the outside and make pretend weather, and our noses stuck in screens and gadgets and electronics all day and all night, *ay*, we push ourselves farther and farther away from all that beautiful natural energy that our DNA evolved with and still is so hungry for. It's no wonder we're all so sick—mentally, physically, emotionally—*ay!*"

"That's why I spend time up at the cabin doing absolutely nothing."

"*Ay, querida,* you're feeding your *soul,* and what could be more important than that?"

Frank reached across the table for Ronnie's hand. "You better be careful."

"*Por qué?*"

"You're bewitching me."

Ronnie leaned in and whispered, "Winnie makes me love potions that I drop in your food."

"You don't have to," Frank whispered back. "I'm good and caught."

As the waitress approached they dropped hands and sat back but their eyes remained joyously locked.

CHAPTER 28

Frank hadn't been to a museum since she had to interview a witness who worked at the Getty. Before that, not since a grade school field trip.

"Goddamn," she muttered, admiring an M. Evelyn McCormick. "Another thing I've missed out on all my life."

Hanging unabashedly on her arm as they walked through the collection, Ronnie said, "Maybe you just weren't ready for any of this until now."

"Maybe," Frank sighed. "Just frustrating how much I've missed. I lived ten minutes form the Huntington and Norton Simon. Probably a half hour from the Getty and never went to any of 'em. What a waste."

"Not at all," Ronnie dismissed. "You were busy becoming the woman you are today."

Frank grinned at her. "You're the kid digging in the pile of shit under the Christmas tree looking for the pony."

Laughing loud enough for a guard to start toward her, Ronnie squeezed Frank's arm and kissed her cheek. "That's me, *querida!*"

After the small but excellent museum Ronnie begged for a quick stop at her favorite bookstore.

"I won't be long, *querida*, but every time I'm in town I like to buy something from them. *Es importante* to keep our local independent bookstores alive!"

"By all means," Frank agreed.

Like the museum, the store was small but well stocked, mostly with metaphysical books and curios. While Ronnie chatted with the store owner (who didn't she know, Frank wondered?), Frank ran her hand along a selection of tarot decks. One of them fell off the shelf onto her foot. Ronnie and the owner both looked at her.

"Well," the owner laughed. "I guess that deck picked you!"

Frank was about to protest but then realized she'd barely been touching the deck. She studied the box at her feet.

"*Amor*," Ronnie called, waving her hand. "Let's see what chose you."

Gingerly, like it might explode, Frank carried the box to the counter.

"Ahh," the owner exclaimed. "The Motherpeace deck. A powerful, pre-patriarchal deck."

"Okay, that's weird. We were just talking about that at lunch."

"*Ay, amor*, you *have* to get them!"

Frank nodded, more to placate the two than because she wanted the deck. But still, it had fallen at her feet...

"Is there a book that goes with it?"

"It's got a tiny guide inside, but this," he said gliding from behind the counter and sliding a book from its shelf, "this is the one you want."

While Frank looked at it, he placed another one next to her, adding, "And this is a marvelous accompaniment. I suggest both."

"*The Great Cosmic Mother*," Ronnie cried. "I remember this! It's old! I can't believe it's still in print."

"Oh, absolutely," the owner assured. "It's a classic. It's *never* gone out of print. In fact I can barely keep it in stock."

Frank read the subtitle. "*Rediscovering the Religion of the Earth*. I like that." On impulse she said, "I'll take 'em."

Ronnie squealed and hugged her good arm. Frank laughed,

still no end to her free fall in sight. Nor did she want there to be.

The fog chased them all the way home, and once there Ronnie suggested taking the dogs for a quick walk. "But not if you're too tired."

"No, let's do it. They'd love that."

It was just a simple stroll around the block but the dogs got to sniff and pee at every tree and fencepost. Ronnie chatted with a couple neighbors and introduced Frank as her dear, dear friend. By the time they got back to the house, Frank said, "Okay. *Now* I'm done."

She apologized, collapsing onto the couch.

"*Ay, no, mi amor!* It was a busy day! Let me feed these beasts then I'll throw together a little salad and heat up the pie. Are you hungry?"

"Famished," she admitted.

"*Bueno.*" Switching on the gas fireplace, she ordered, "You sit and watch the fog roll in. I'll take care of everything."

"You're spoiling me, *diosa.*"

"You are a woman who *needs* spoiling. How else can I tame the wily coyote in you?"

Frank laid her head back, taking in the view from the broad front window, the fog painting the town in watercolors. But above it, proud and defiant, her mountains watched down upon the valley and all its little men.

For the first time since she'd moved into them, Frank was happier to be elsewhere. With her big heart and generous love Ronnie made Frank feel special and deeply cared for. Scrolling back through her previous lovers, Frank realized she was usually the one doing most of the caring for, most of the spoiling and wooing. It felt good to be on the receiving end for a change. She thought she should get up and help, but told herself it was okay to let Ronnie wait on her. The dogs ran back into the living room after their dinner and insisted on snuggling with her. She humored as many as she could under one arm until Ronnie came in and shooed them off.

She set a tray down between them and Frank said, "Ronnie."

"*Si, amor*? Do you need something?"

"No. Sit."

"Uh-oh," Ronnie said. "I don't like the sound of that."

Frank smiled. "Nothing like that. I just want to thank you."

"*Ay*, for what? You're the one who brought dinner."

"Not about dinner. About you. About how wonderful you are."

"*Ay*, stop! Eat your pie before it gets cold."

"No, I'm serious. I realized sitting here how generous you are with your love—not just to me, but to the waitress, your neighbors, the guy at the store, your critters—everyone. And you're not afraid to show it. I love that. It's a first for me. All my other girlfriends were pretty closeted, but you, your heart's right there on your sleeve where everyone can see it."

"*Querida*," Ronnie demurred. "You bring out the best in me. Do you know how hard it is to find someone alive in this world? Someone with their heart and soul wide open? Someone willing to take chances? That's you, *amor*. I knew it the second I laid eyes on you. *Ay, si*, there was all that dark stuff, but under it? *Pura sol.* You're one of those rare people that glows. I couldn't have stayed away from you if I'd tried."

"I'm glad you didn't try too hard."

They picked up their forks and Ronnie said, "In case you hadn't noticed I didn't try at all."

"True." Frank chuckled.

"*Ay, dios*, this is *divine*. Pete made it for you?"

"He didn't make it just for me but he had two and gave me one."

"He sounds sweet."

Frank almost choked. "I wouldn't say that. He's a crusty old fart but I think there's a pretty decent guy under all his bluster."

"And he just lets you stay there at the cabin? A total stranger?"

"Sal left him a letter. Asked him to. He did it for her, not me."

"Why would she ask him to do that?"

"She felt I belonged there."

219

"*En serio?*" Ronnie lowered her fork.

Frank nodded. "Seriously."

"That's *spooky.*"

"*Por qué?*" Frank stabbed a tomato.

"*Pues*, it was true, right? And that she knew you that well. It's not spooky scary, just…uncanny. She was remarkably gifted."

"Did you see her often? For healing?"

"No, rarely. To tell you the truth, Sal kind of scared me. The few times I let myself see her, her colors, she was *so* dark. Not in a bad way, just very depressed, very sad. I liked her. She seemed very kind, but I was always a little unnerved when she came to our lunches. There was something terribly private around her, like a wall I couldn't get past. And I have to admit I didn't try too hard. She and Winnie were close, very good friends."

Frank nodded, gathering as much from Sal's journal.

"Hmm." Ronnie smacked her lips. "Tell Pete thank you for me."

Frank almost said she could tell him herself, but wasn't quite ready to. Someday she would be, just not today. They piled their plates on the tray and when Frank stood to help with the dishes Ronnie told her to sit and stay, just like one of the dogs. When she came back from the kitchen Ronnie drew the curtains and they snuggled back into the couch, dogs tucked between them. When they both got sleepy Ronnie propped Frank up in bed with her new pillow and fluffed her own up beside her. "So I can cuddle you as best as I can."

Frank slept off and on, but well enough. By the time she got up to make coffee Ronnie had burrowed down into the blankets. Frank let her sleep, taking advantage of the quiet morning to watch the sun trying to beat back the fog. By the time Ronnie shuffled into the living room, wild-haired and puffy-eyed, the sun was gaining the upper hand.

She slumped against Frank's good side.

"*Buenos dias, amor.*"

Frank kissed her head. "*Buenos dias, diosa.* Let me get you some coffee."

Ronnie grunted, her dogs crowding into Frank's seat the minute she stood. Frank returned with her cup. Ronnie took it with both hands and ordered the dogs down. They all complied except Paco, who crawled into Ronnie's lap. She slurped noisily. "Now who's spoiling who?"

"How'd you sleep?" Frank asked.

"Like the dead. I don't even remember lying down. And you? Did the pillow help?"

"It did. Thanks again."

Nursing a second cup, Frank asked how she could help with lunch.

"I knew we'd be busy between the museum and other things," she winked at Frank, "so I made most of it Saturday. The soup is in the fridge and I just have to make a salad. Oh! And take the bread dough out of the freezer."

"You sit," Frank said. "I'll get it."

"*Ay, amor, gracias.*"

"Save my seat."

After coffee Ronnie helped Frank take a shower, stepping in to soap her up. Frank reciprocated, delighting in Ronnie's mounds and creases.

"I've *never* had so much fun in the shower!" she cried, kissing Frank wetly. "Or such a water bill! Come on. Let me dry you off."

After walking the dogs they got lunch ready. The fog had mostly gone but it was still cool enough that Ronnie had Frank set the table inside. It felt good to be useful, and by the time the women arrived everything was ready.

Char came first, then Winnie. She shook her bangs as she came into the living room and handed Frank a paper bag.

"Ronnie told me you broke your collarbone so I made you a couple things."

"Winnie, that is so sweet. Thank you."

In answer she twitched her bangs and started to move off, but Frank patted the sofa. "Tell me what's in here," she said, pulling a jar from the bag.

"That's a salve made with boneset. It doesn't grow around

here but I grow my own. And arnica, too. The salve should ease the pain and help your bone mend faster."

Making a silly, nervous face, she added, "That's why it's called boneset. The Latin name is *Eupatorium perfoliatum* if you want to look it up."

"That's okay." Frank laughed. "I trust you. And this?"

"These are tea balls of comfrey," she made her goofy face again, "also known as knitbone, and nettle. Comfrey helps the bone heal from the outside in and boneset speeds healing from the inside out so they work really well together."

Winnie was almost bouncing with excitement as she explained her medicines and Frank hadn't the heart to interrupt her impressive discourse on bone growth and cell regeneration. Finally she added, "Let them steep in boiling water until they're cool then drink them down right away." She ducked her head. "It should help."

To show her appreciation, Frank stood up and said, "I'm sure it will. I'm going to put some water on right now and brew a cup of this."

Winnie beamed like a little kid that'd just been given an early Christmas present. When Frank came back into the living room, Ronnie introduced her friend Gloria.

"Gloria *es una partera*, a midwife."

"Pleasure to meet you."

She took Frank's hand and said, "The pleasure is mine." Adding in a giggly singsong, "I've heard wonderful things about you."

She and Ronnie sniggered.

"All *good* things," Ronnie assured, kissing Frank's cheek.

"Okay, girls." Char announced, "As long as we've got a quorum I'm making a pitch to bring one of my sponsees to our soirées."

Ronnie smirked at Frank.

"She's a super nice gal, just a little shy. She's part Esselen if you can believe that. Not many of 'em left. She practices the old ways, when she's sober, and I think it'd do her a world of good to be around women like us."

"How old is she?" Gloria asked.

"Well, she's young. Late thirties."

Ronnie shook her head and Dolores dismissed Char with a wave.

Gloria laughed. "She's hardly out of diapers."

"Aw, come on. She needs the support of wise old gals like us."

"She's got you," Winnie piped up.

"Boomers," Char grumbled. "You're just a bunch of ageists."

"Damn right," Ronnie said. "I've raised all the children I want to."

"*Yo también*," Gloria chimed in. "That's my job! I come here to relax with my peers, my friends."

"Aw." Char waved at them.

"*Ay*, saved by the Dolo," Ronnie cried, jumping up to greet her. "Char's trying to drag another sponsee into the group. A baby!"

Dolores shook her head, muttering, "How many times…"

"You have to give me credit for trying," Char said.

"True." Gloria applauded. "A thousand gold stars."

Ronnie waved at the festive dining room table. "Everyone sit. There's wine and tea on the table, *chicas*, help yourselves."

Gloria was almost as lively as Ronnie, but a quarter the size. She was a tiny little thing that didn't look strong enough to pull a fly from a bowl of pudding yet she had helped deliver hundreds of babies. She'd been an RN before she became a doula, and her husband had retired from practicing medicine to become a death doula.

"That's like a hospice worker?" Frank asked.

"Not quite. An end-of-life doula is more of an emotional, spiritual support for the dying person and their family members, while hospice supports their medical and physical needs. They're tremendous compliments to each other."

"That's awesome. You're there at the start of someone's journey and your husband's there at the end. It must be very gratifying work."

"Oh, it is. I'm so glad I left nursing for this. Not that nursing wasn't a great profession, but I'd just had it up to here," she patted the top of her head, "with doctors telling us how we should have our babies. As if we hadn't been doing it for millennia all by ourselves!"

The ladies bobbed their heads in unison.

Turning to Frank, Gloria said, "Is that right, you used to be a detective?"

"Yep."

"And so what do you do now?"

Frank looked around the circle of women. She'd enjoyed the company of lovers and colleagues but had never had the simple pleasure of girlfriends; yet each of these women had willingly shared themselves with her. Each had given freely of their gifts and their struggles.

Deciding to trust this circle of "withes" she'd been thrown in with, Frank admitted, "I think I've spent the last year fixing parts of me I didn't even know were broken."

"How so?" Char rumbled.

Frank thought a moment. "It's like I've been two Franks—the Frank I was before I moved here and the Frank I am now. For the Frank I am now there's nothing more satisfying than just hanging out and being a tiny part of the world. It's like for the first time in my life I'm *in* life instead of racing around the edge of it. I'm part of it instead of dancing on the periphery. Now when I see a tree, I know its name. I know if it drops its leaves in winter or keeps 'em. I know where it likes to grow and what animals eat it, what birds nest in it. I *know* that tree. I have a relationship with it. I have relationships with things I never even knew existed.

"The old me never would have even seen the tree. I was always looking somewhere else, always ahead. Always waiting for something—waiting to leave home and my crazy mom; waiting to graduate school then the police academy; waiting to trip up a bad guy or for him to trip me up; waiting in traffic; waiting to earn my detective badge; waiting for a coroner's report; waiting for end of watch; waiting for a drink—just always waiting for something else. Always anticipating a moment just outta my grasp instead of appreciating the one I was in. But being up there in the mountains changed all that. It's like they've stripped me clean and pared me down to the essentials. I wonder sometimes if that's why all the healing stuff's happening. Because there's nothing in the way of it."

The women were all watching her and she suddenly felt as shy as Winnie.

She grinned. "That's probably more than I've said in a whole year."

"It was beautiful," Winnie breathed.

"It was, *querida*." Ronnie reached across the table and squeezed her hand.

Frank had been wondering if Ronnie was going to announce their status as lovers but the look they shared pretty much said it all.

Char picked up her glass of water and toasted, "To the present, 'cause there's no guarantee of a future."

"*Ay*," Dolores said, lifting her wineglass. "*Los muertos al cajón y los vivos al fiestón.*"

"Yes!" Ronnie translated, "The dead to their coffins and the living to their parties!"

"Here, here!" Winnie cried.

The circle of women clinked their glasses and laughed.

CHAPTER 29

After Frank had helped Ronnie clean up and kissed her lingeringly goodbye, she'd packed up the dogs and headed for Maya's sister's house. It wasn't far but a nagging, unpleasant sensation crept over Frank as she drove. Only a short time ago she'd been excited about meeting Justina and maybe getting some answers about her husband's murder. Now all Frank wanted to do was turn around. Call Maya and tell her it had been a mistake, she couldn't come.

But she didn't. Instead she pulled over. The thing about recovery was that it taught an alcoholic or junkie not to ignore their feelings, but rather to dig into and identify them before they were tempted to use over them. Frank wasn't at all worried she was going to go on a bender but habit spurred her to tease out what was going on.

She rolled the windows down and tried to name the sensation. It wasn't quite dread. It wasn't nerves. She was curious about Justina and very much wanted to meet her. She kept digging until the word *conflicted* sprang to mind. She stopped drumming the steering wheel.

Conflicted, she realized, because she was visiting Justina for all the wrong reasons. She was visiting her as a cop, not a healer. She'd arranged the visit to get more information from the woman, not to help her. Frank gave a tiny nod, admitting there was a little shame mixed in there too. She was playing Maya and her mother. She was being the old Frank, Frank the relentless detective.

She thought about Ronnie's explanation of witches, how they manipulated energy for a desired outcome. That's what she was doing by visiting Justina under false pretenses. Frank the cop would manipulate the hell out of her. But if Frank truly was a healer she had to meet Justina on her terms alone, taking only what the woman gave her. The two roles were diametrically opposed—one bent the energy to her will and the other worked with it however it came. Before she set one foot in Justina's house she had to decide whether she was going in as cop or healer.

Frank took a deep breath. It was a pretty clear choice. She wasn't a cop anymore. She would go to Justina's to help, not sniff out her secrets. If she even had any.

Frank felt easier for the decision and finished the drive with a much lighter heart. When she knocked on Justina's door, Maya opened. Vivi stood beside her.

"Look at my neck," she said, wobbling it around like a bobblehead doll.

"It looks great."

Vivi skipped off and Maya ushered her in. She introduced Frank to her sister then led her down the hall. Opening a door, they stepped quietly into a small bedroom. Frank took in an altar on a dresser. It burned with votives before a plaster Virgin of Guadalupe surrounded by fresh roses. The shades were drawn and the only other light came from a dim lamp beside Justina's narrow bed.

Maya whispered, "She likes it dark because it helps her pretend she's in church."

Frank's first impression of Justina Hernandez was that she was too small to kill anybody. But for the wizened face she looked like a child under the drawn covers.

"*Hola, Mami. Esta es la curandera.*"

Frank bristled. She didn't like being called a *curandera*. It felt fraudulent. It wasn't the right name for who she was or what she did but for now there probably wasn't a better one.

"*Encantada de conocerla, Señora Hernandez.*"

Justina greeted her with wide, anxious eyes.

Maya asked Frank, "Would you like me to stay or should I wait outside?"

"I think outside would be better. I'll call if I need anything."

"Okay. I'll be right out there."

Frank took the chair by the bed. She explained in her halting Spanish that she wasn't sure if she could help the Señora's pain but would she like for Frank to try?

The old woman's skeletal hand was on top of the covers and she inched it toward Frank.

"*Por favor.*"

Frank nodded and reached for it but Justina withdrew a little. The black eyes swimming in her skull grew even larger.

"*Puede ver cosas? Cosas malas?*"

"*No, Señora.*" She assured her she couldn't see anything, good or bad, making it a point to add she wasn't like Sal. That alone seemed to alleviate the woman's anxiety. But the cop in Frank couldn't help but note that Justina's first concern on meeting her was to make sure Frank couldn't see anything bad.

Frank continued that she didn't know what she was doing or how, but that it seemed to help. She guessed it was just a gift from God that she could touch people and ease their pain. She had nothing to do with it and was just his vessel. That seemed to relieve the old gal even more and her hand fluttered across the covers toward Frank.

Questions skittered through Frank's mind, questions perfectly appropriate for a cop but not a healer. She closed her eyes and forced herself to concentrate on the mountains, the cave, her breathing. Nothing else mattered right now. She was here for Justina Hernandez alone, not for her husband, not for Sal, not for Gomez. Only Justina.

She slid her palm under the woman's dry and raspy bones, lighter than dead leaves. And she knew Justina Hernandez was leaving soon. Very soon. Frank saw a great door gaping open for her with only light beyond. Frank was a little startled but it seemed welcoming, even warm. Frank wanted to go toward it but quickly pulled herself into the safety of her cave. She got the sense that was where she needed to be and also felt it was okay to help Justina toward the door. So for an untold time she did just that, picturing herself high in her circle of boulders, Justina in front of her, facing the bright, wide door beyond.

Eventually Frank pulled her hand away. Justina opened her eyes. She smiled at Frank.

"*Gracias.*"

"*El gusto es mio, Doña Justina.*"

The old woman seemed to sleep. Bracing herself for the light and noise beyond the bedroom, Frank quietly slipped out. Maya was perched on the edge of the couch at the end of the hall.

"How is she?"

"Sleeping, I think. She seems peaceful."

Maya's hand flew to her heart and tears sprang into her eyes. "Oh, thank you. Thank you so much."

"I'm glad I could help. I hope you'll feel free to call me if she'd like to see me again. I'd be happy to come back."

"Would you? Oh my God, that would be wonderful. I know she's in a lot of pain. She says everything hurts."

"Well, I think I helped a little, so whatever I can do. Just call."

"I don't know how to thank you."

"None necessary. It really is my pleasure."

"Here." Maya grabbed for her purse. "Let me at least—"

"No," Frank said, stilling Maya's hand. "I couldn't. It's an honor to be with someone who is passing."

Maya looked up with her mother's eyes. "She is, isn't she?"

Frank nodded. Maya's tears fell.

"Call me," Frank told her. "I'll be happy to come."

She let herself out. An orange sun skimmed the Lucias, flirting with the peaks, teasing them with her touch. Frank felt that soon Justina would be up there with them, another *celadora* looking down upon her children and grandchildren. Watching

229

over them. She took a moment to remember the vision of the door. She wanted to chalk it up to imagination, because who hadn't heard of near death experiences and the white light? But the image had been so sharp and sudden it felt like it had been received rather than conjured. She wondered if that was how Sal had seen the things she saw, if they just popped into her head like that.

Kook was in her seat when she opened the door. She petted him before climbing in. Bone stretched in the backseat and licked her hand. She waited before starting the truck, then turned around and drove back through town. A minute later she was knocking on Ronnie's door.

"*Amor*! You're back!"

"Yeah," Frank said, sheepish. "You got a minute?"

"*Pero claro, amor*! What's going on? You want to get the dogs?"

"No, they're okay. I just wanted to see you for a sec."

Frank cupped Ronnie's warm, soft face, her thumb caressing the keen cheekbone. "Christ, but you're a beauty," she whispered.

Hugging her as carefully as she could Ronnie asked, "Did you come back just to tell me that?"

Frank shook her head. "I just sat with a dying woman. I've been with a lot of dying people but I've never just *been* with one. It was so beautiful. It was…an honor. It was profound."

"*Amor*," Ronnie whispered. "What a gift you gave her."

"I hope so. What a gift we gave each other. I just had to tell someone."

Ronnie kissed her deeply, tenderly. "I'm glad you told me."

"Yeah. Thanks for hearing it."

"Do you want to stay?"

"Nah, I should get home. I want to tell the stars too. But I wanted to tell you first."

"What an honor," Ronnie said sincerely, "to be placed before the stars."

"See you Thursday," Frank said.

"Will you text me when you get home?"

Frank nodded, stepping toward the door. Part of her wanted to stay, but she knew she needed to be home, home where her other lover could cradle her, empty and fill her like no mortal could.

She kissed her finger and planted it on Ronnie's lips.

"*Hasta jueves,* my beauty."

Ronnie blew a kiss back. "Thursday, *mi coyote.*"

CHAPTER 30

Frank was so glad to be home. She fed the dogs who trotted off to smell what had visited while they were gone, and though it was almost bedtime for the chickens she let them out and raked their cage. With just one arm she had to work slowly but it was peaceful, tranquil work. The hens pecked right outside the coop and when she was finished, one by one they trooped inside, took an approving look around, and disappeared into the henhouse.

Next she went to the barn. The corral was open so the horses could graze in the pasture but they waited for her by the barn gate. They whinnied as she approached with two fat flakes of alfalfa wrangled under her arm. She dropped them on the ground and tossed one in. Buttons claimed it immediately, pinning her ears and warning the gelding away. He trotted off a safe distance and Frank chucked him the second flake with a pained grunt. He dug in with a contented snort.

Bone and Kook found her leaning against the corral and wiggled merrily as if they had all been playing a great game of hide-and-seek. Scratched and rubbed in turn, their territory cased and secured, they plopped beside her as happy as the horses and hens.

A light wind sang through the oak and around the barn. Dusk had settled, smudging the colors of the day, priming the land for night. From a nest by the creek a pair of juvenile great horned owls started begging for their parents to bring food. And soon they would. Frank had often seen the adults glide in to the tall sycamore with a rabbit or skunk clutched beneath them.

Be it chickens, dogs, horses, or people, Frank had never understood how gratifying it was to care for another's life. She'd always cleaned up after a life was over, not cared for one while it was still going on. It was still a marvel and a mystery how she'd morphed from the old city Frank into this new mountain Frank. But it made sense—the same coin, just two different sides.

An unfamiliar pressure filled her chest. It swelled like a balloon then popped. Frank let surprising tears fall. Glancing around to make sure Pork Chop or Pete hadn't ridden up on her, she caught one with a fingertip. She couldn't remember the last time she had cried. Not for Sal, not Dez, or any of her lovers. Certainly not her mother. Maybe her father? All her life she had been stoic, sucking everything up and stuffing it down. But these inexplicable tears weren't from grief or loss but rather pure joy.

She'd heard of such tears but never experienced them. They seemed to have come from a gratitude so immense she couldn't contain it, gratitude she had only broken a collarbone and that her corpse wasn't rotting out at Vaquero Springs; gratitude for Ronnie's big body and bigger spirit; gratitude for all the animals around her, tame and wild. For the oak with its wind songs, the dusky meadow and darkening escarpment. Gratitude for the cabin's humble shelter, for Sal and Pete and all the women at the store. Gratitude for being able to just sit with Justina Hernandez and help her toward her next journey. Gratitude for this bend in the road she'd been shown and by whatever miracle she'd had the sense to take.

She palmed the wetness from her cheeks and took a steadying breath. She settled with her back against the solid oak and Kook wormed his way onto her lap. She kissed his curly head, inhaling his dusty doggy smell. Even Bone finally gave up his dignity and came to her for kisses. He licked her salty cheek and she laughed, hugging him hard.

Ronnie was right—Frank's heart and soul had been cracked

wide open. Here in the heart of the watchful mountains she had tipped the scales away from death and toward life, and while there was certainly death here it was purposeful. Here when the fox snatched the quail or the owl sunk its talons into a rabbit death was sustaining life, it was *good* death and Frank had forgotten such a balance existed. Justina dying of old age was a good death. It was the natural order of life that the old made room for the new. There was nothing good about the senseless, wasted death of a schoolkid stabbing a classmate or a pedophile strangling a six-year-old. Random drive-bys and revenge killings had no purpose. They gave back nothing to life.

Frank sat with the dogs until she got cold but she didn't want to go inside. Unwilling to miss a second of the night she carried blankets and pillows out to the chair and made herself as comfortable as possible. Even the stars contributed, she thought as she fell asleep, wondering how dark the world would be without their light.

Hours later she woke beneath them, chilled and cramped. Wishing she'd slept inside, she dragged everything into the cabin and cursed herself for being so damn stubborn. Winnie had warned that resting was the best thing she could do to heal and it seemed she'd have plenty more chances to sleep under the stars. Debating between the couch and the bed, she passed the phone on the table. It was blinking. Frank stopped. Deciding on the bedroom she dumped the bedding and went back to check the phone, assuming Ronnie had left her a message.

But it was a voicemail from Maya. Semi-hysterical. Her mother had asked for Frank. The priest had given her last rites and could Frank please come quick. Maya knew it was late and that she might not get the message until morning but if she did get it before then, could she possibly come as fast as she could.

It felt like the old days, being jolted awake in the middle of the night by a call-out. But in the old days Frank wouldn't have hesitated. She pulled out a chair and dropped into it. What exactly was her responsibility to Justina Hernandez? None, she decided, but she had told Maya to call her. And Maya had.

"Goddamn it."

Frank was tired, sore, and fuddled. The very last thing she wanted to do was make the trek to Soledad. But she had foolishly said, "Call me. I'd be happy to come."

She swore again and pulled on her jeans.

"Come on," she told the dogs. "If I gotta go you're going with me."

They had commandeered the couch when she came in and both stared at her.

"Come on," she said louder, jiggling the keys. "Let's go."

They stepped down reluctantly and she commiserated. Her and her big mouth. "I'll be happy to come," she mimicked.

Bone didn't want to jump into the truck and she had to heft him onto the floorboard with her one arm. Kook at least was willing. Bone crawled in back and curled up but Kook was a stalwart companion, standing on the armrest, nosing the air out the window. Frank drove slowly, mindful of nocturnal animals. She wished she'd thought to make a cup of coffee. She rolled her window down and let the night air wake her as best as it could. A shooting star with a long tail cheered her and once she hit blacktop two more shot to earth making the drive almost worth it.

She concentrated on being present, on the strength of the mountains behind her and the living night sky. Losing a little sleep wouldn't kill her and now that she was more awake she was glad Maya had called. Frank had been sincere when she'd told Maya she wanted to help.

The lights were all on when she pulled up to Justina's house. She sat a moment, steeling herself for the familiar chaos around death. But alone in her dark and quiet cab, she could have sworn Sal whispered, *Don't do that.*

Frank nodded. This was a time to soften, not harden, to be open instead of closed. She thought of Ronnie and smiled. She needed to be a withe, not a witch. Frank encircled herself in her trusty defilade of rock and stone. Imagining Justina standing before her, eager to face the wide and well-lit door, Frank stepped from the truck.

A woman met her and ushered Frank down the hall. Justina's room was crowded with her family and Maya had to press through to greet Frank. She thanked her profusely for coming and led her to the bed.

If possible Justina had shrunk even more. Her mouth hung open and she gasped in long, steady intervals. Her eyes were closed. Maya leant over her mother and whispered into her ear. Her eyes opened slowly, working to focus. Then she turned her skull to Frank. The dark eyes widened and Justina grew agitated. Her bony hand flapped on the covers. Frank bent to take it. Justina calmed but her eyes roamed fearfully around the milling people.

"*Vayanse . . . todos,*" she gasped.

Maya looked dubiously at Frank.

She nodded. "Let's give her some space. I'll call you if anything changes. We won't be long," she assured with an authority she didn't feel.

"Okay."

Maya made sweeping motions and herded everyone from the room amid some grumbles about the *gabacho.*

When the door closed, Frank pulled a chair closer to the bed. She bent to the old woman and asked gently how she could serve her. Justina's hand fluttered. Frank took it as if it were a baby bird.

"*Hizo...algo,*" she rasped. Gripping Frank's hand, she continued in Spanish. "I did... something...terrible. I need... to tell you."

The hair on Frank's neck stood up. The cop in her wanted to grab her phone to record whatever Justina was about to say. If she'd had two hands she might have been able to turn it on but Justina held her in a literal death grip. And that was just as well because again Frank had to remind herself she was there as a healer, not a detective.

After a deep breath, she said, "*Digame, Doña.*"

The old woman shuddered and closed her eyes. She licked

her lips and swallowed.

"*Quiere agua?*"

The old woman shook her head once. Frank gave the bones in her hand a tender squeeze.

"*Algo horrible,*" she moaned. She spoke so slowly Frank had no trouble comprehending her words. "The father . . . of my children . . . bad man. Did . . . terrible . . . things . . . to my daughters . . . and I . . ."

Justina closed her eyes. Frank waited. A lone tear slid down Justina's temple.

"I let him. I let him . . . do . . . those things. I had . . . such fear . . . that I let him . . . . do . . . despicable . . . things . . . to my babies."

Another tear followed the first.

"The day . . . I caught him . . . with . . ."

She faltered. Frank waited her out.

"*Con mi nieta.*"

Frank couldn't help it; the old thrill surged through her. She knew Justina had a couple granddaughters.

"*Cual?*" she whispered. Which one?

"*Mi . . . amorcita. Vivi.*"

Frank nodded though Justina's eyes were closed. The old woman labored for breath. Freeing her hand she made a weak stabbing motion. She said something Frank didn't understand but quickly committed to memory.

"It was . . . easy . . . like killing . . . a chicken. But . . . the worst thing?"

She shifted her frail head to look squarely at Frank.

"I don't . . . regret it."

Frank nodded. Justina's whole body softened under the blankets. She tried to find Frank's hand. Frank found hers. Justina's breathing slowed. Frank thought she slept. When she tried to remove her hand Justina held it tight.

"*Esta alla? El?*"

"No," she answered. "He's not there. He's somewhere else."

Justina gave the hint of a nod. "I'll see him...there. In Hell."

"*No, Señora.*"

237

Frank told her she was going to the open door, the door with all the light. "Shall we look for it?"

Justina's lips curved in the trace of a smile.

"*Por favor.*"

Frank went into her cave. She called on her mountains and calmed her breathing. Justina's wavered, grew more faint, more irregular. Her hand was limp in Frank's. After some time Frank placed it on the bed. She rose and quietly left the room.

The family all stood as she came out. Maya asked, "Is she . . . ?"

"She's alive. She's calm."

Frank saw herself out. She didn't know how long she'd sat with Justina but the sun was pinking the sky over the Gabilan Range. It was all she could do to get herself into the truck. Stroking the dogs, grateful for their simple, undemanding company, she watched the sun grow brighter and brighter.

There was no joy in Justina's confession, no triumph. The old Frank would have been thrilled but this Frank was just weary. Bone weary at the mess, the waste, the sorrow that a woman had felt the need to kill her husband to keep him from molesting little girls. Augustin Hernandez had contributed nothing to life. Then Frank corrected herself. He had helped create Maya who in turn had created Vivi, so no, although he had been deeply flawed, he had indeed contributed to life.

The thought heartened Frank enough to start the truck. She drove to McDonalds and let the dogs out to pee, then bought a sandwich for each of them. Driving back into the mountains, the dogs hung out the windows and she sipped a warming cup of coffee. She drove slowly, steering with her knee. Glancing ahead at the sharp bones of the Lucias she wondered if Justina had joined Sal yet.

CHAPTER 31

Where Frank should have turned left onto the Celadores road she kept straight. The coffee had given her a second wind and she took the curving canyon road north, through to Carmel then south into Big Sur. Fog hung over the coast but when she let the dogs out to romp in a grove of redwoods she could see flashes of bright blue above the tall trees. It was going to be a beautiful day. Maybe the first for Maya without her mother and Vivi, her grandmother. She hoped they would find comfort in Justina's peaceful transition.

"Okay," she called the dogs. "Back in."

They leapt into the truck and she continued south. When the fog lifted it revealed the ocean rushing in to kiss the feet of the Lucias. Frank drove slowly, absorbing the untamed ocean on her right, and on her left the mountains rising sharply to the sky. She didn't think about Justina or her admission. She concentrated solely on the endless ocean, the grandeur of sheer cliff, and how infinitesimal she was amid the enduring drama of sea, stone, and sky.

About an hour later she came to a little sign that welcomed her to the hermitage. A steep road twisted up and around to finally end at a cluster of buildings. She parked at the main office and looked around. The hermitage was nestled against the back of the mountain on a wide, lush shelf with stunning views of the

Pacific. As she was admiring the view a robed monk came out of the office and turned the "closed" sign to "open."

"Good morning," he called.

She gave a little wave and followed him into a bookstore. She told the monk she wasn't sure what the protocol was but asked if it would be possible to speak to Kevin.

"Well, let's see." The monk slipped on a pair of glasses and seemed to consult a schedule. "He may be available this morning. Who should I say is here to see him?"

"Tell him Detective Frank."

"Ah-hah." He frowned. "Give me a minute to find him."

He disappeared into a back office and while he was gone she browsed the book titles. Most were over her head, concerned with religion and faith, but she found a couple shelves that featured poetry and novels. She recognized one of the poets and was leafing through her book when she heard Kevin behind her.

"Well, hello!"

"Hey." She reached for his hand and he took it with gusto, guiding her outside. "Hope I'm not bothering you."

"Not at all, not at all. You're a marvelous interruption and I'm terrible but," he lowered his voice and said with a gleam, "Brother Elias thinks I'm in trouble with the law! We'll see how fast the rumor gets around that a detective wants to see me!"

Frank grinned and he offered her the five-cent tour.

"I'd love it." She said.

He showed her around the public grounds, giving a brief history of the place. At a bench overlooking the lengthy sprawl of coast and sea he said, "Now tell me. What brings you all the way here at eight in the morning?"

"Cops and priests," she offered. "Always trying to suss out the truth."

He nodded, and just like a cop, he waited out her silence.

"You hear confessions, Kevin?"

"I have," he answered solemnly.

She studied the flat sea below, the fog retreating to the horizon. "I heard a deathbed confession this morning."

If Kevin was surprised he didn't show it. "Go on."

Frank explained how she'd fallen into healing, then about Sal's journal, Vivi and her grandfather's murder and finally about Justina.

"She asked for me in the middle of the night. She was dying and called for me. I think she just wanted to tell one other person. I guess I was the right person."

"That's quite an honor."

Frank kept her eyes on the sea.

"A priest had been there. Gave her last rites. But she didn't tell him. I think because she did a very bad thing. She knew it was bad, but said she didn't regret it."

Kevin nodded.

They stood in comfortable silence until Kevin remarked, "Being entrusted with confession is a great honor but it can also be a terrible burden."

"Yeah. So see, here's the thing. I got one of the local cops involved, got her looking into what this woman did. If I was active duty I'd be legally sworn to tell her but as a civilian I have no such obligation."

"Nor," Kevin pointed out, "are you bound by canonical law to keep her confession secret."

"No, of course not. But what's my moral obligation?"

Kevin stroked his beard. "A sticky wicket indeed. Is there an active crime involved? Can anyone else be hurt by what this woman did?"

"No."

"All right. Now did you go to this woman as a law enforcement professional or a healer?"

She shot him a rueful grin. "Funny you should ask. At first I was all excited to see what I could find out from her, but when I got there I realized she had called for me as a healer. So I went as that. I doubt she even knew I was a cop."

"In that case it seems to me your obligation is to your patient."

Frank turned to face him. "What about the victim's family

and friends? Don't they deserve answers? Closure?"

"There are many mysteries in life. Not all can be solved. Some just have to be borne. That's what I love about the life I've chosen; it offers such a broad perspective. It makes the small mysteries of men seem so trivial and fleeting. There's a wonderful book by a young woman who died in the Holocaust. Her name was Etty Hillesum and she wrote that soul and spirit are so eternal and infinite compared to the tiny bit of suffering she was enduring that her pain and fear really didn't add up to much. Can you imagine? I try to remember that when one of the brothers shirks his duties or takes the last piece of pizza."

Frank gave a wan smile.

"How long ago did this bad thing happen?"

"About five years ago."

"I see. Have the victim's friends and family moved on? Do they still suffer from what happened to the victim?"

"I don't think they do. I'm pretty sure his wife and kids don't. The victim was molesting his own children, then his granddaughter. Not exactly a stand-up guy. But he's probably got siblings. Who knows? Maybe a parent still alive?"

They studied the horizon together.

"You know, Frank, I'm blessed that whatever happens to me I have the comfort of my God. That's where I turn in all my trials and tribulations. Hopefully this man's people have a faith to turn to."

"I think some of them do. He's been dead a while. People seemed to have moved on, but as a cop, even a retired one, I still feel obligated to help a fellow officer."

Kevin pulled his gaze from the horizon. "Let's suppose you reveal this woman's secret. How will that be for her children and grandchildren? Will it bring peace or turmoil?"

"Turmoil." Unless they had already suspected Justina but Frank didn't think they had.

Frank's shoulder ached and she was suddenly exhausted. She wanted to sink into the bench but she knew she was intruding on Kevin's time.

"There's a wonderful line in the book of Luke, two actually, that concern Mary, who as you can imagine was subject to the most unbelievable tests and trials. I mean can you imagine an angel coming down from on high and telling you, 'Hey, Frank, you've been chosen to bear the son of God'?"

"That'd be a rough one," she agreed.

"Exactly. But what does Mary in her faith do? She takes that incredible mystery into her heart and ponders it there. Quietly, and alone with her faith, she trusts in the mystery of it. The unknowableness of it. She does the same when Jesus is older and they're traveling home from Jerusalem but she can't find him. She and Joseph look for three days and they finally find their twelve-year-old son back in Jerusalem discoursing in the temple with teachers and wise men. Everyone's astonished at the depth of his understanding and though Mary herself cannot fathom his comprehension, she again takes this mystery to her heart and quietly holds it there. I find that so deeply courageous."

Kevin placed his palms over his heart. "'She treasured all these things and pondered them in her heart.' She embraced the unfathomable and lived with it."

"So I shouldn't tell anyone."

Kevin opened his arms. "You must do what you feel is right. Only you know what that is. But hearing a confession is a sacred responsibility, clergy or not. She entrusted you with her greatest secret. What do you think she would want you to do with it?"

Frank studied a glistening macadamia tree. She felt Kevin looking at her but had no answer.

After a while, he asked gently, "Do you have a god?"

She took a long time before replying, "None I can name."

He nodded.

"Could those be my gods?" she asked, tipping her head back toward the mountains.

"Ah." Kevin turned to smile at the peaks rising beyond the enclave. "St. Augustine said that we could read the 'Book of Nature' to understand God, and Christianity is rife with stories of people finding God in the wilderness—the desert Fathers,

243

John the Baptist, St. Kevin—my namesake," he added. "Moses on Mt. Sinai, Elijah in his cave." He chuckled. "Benedictines in Big Sur. It's a wonder I'm a Benedictine and not a Franciscan."

"Lost me again."

"Sorry. That was a rude in-joke. Franciscans see Nature as a manifestation of God whereas some other orders see Nature as more mundane and base, more of the Devil's territory than God's."

"Is that how you Benedictines see it?"

"Oh, no, not at all. The order's founder, St. Benedict, abandoned life in the city, at the tender age of fourteen, to go live in a cave. He was basically the founder of monasticism, and the point of monastic life is to be separate from the world in order to better know God. What better place to be separate from the mundane affairs of men than in wilderness?"

"Is that your purpose? To become closer to God?"

"It is."

"Would you say you've had a successful career?"

Kevin laughed and his whole body heaved. "Oh, goodness. I feel such a failure at times, but I would say that if living in awareness of the Divine is any measure of success, then yes, I have been fairly successful. I struggled in my early years with wanting to know God, to understand Him in my head, but He has come to me slowly and gently. He's filled me here," Kevin touched his heart, "instead of here." He moved his hand to his head.

"As far as *knowing* God, I must confess I'm an abject failure. The older I get I feel the less I know. But," he wagged a finger at her, "the older I get the more I absolutely *feel* His mystery and presence all around me."

"How so? What's that like for you?"

He spread his chubby arms. "It's luminous. It's a sense of expansion and infinity. I'll be doing something completely mundane, pulling weeds or scrubbing a pot, and I will be completely overcome with a sense of oneness with every living thing. There's just a sudden, sharp *knowing,* a crystal-clear realization that there is no us or them, no separations, no boundaries. I'm just in this great stew with everyone and everything else. It's such a marvelous sense of unity and just *being* that it often leaves me in tears, what I call sacred tears, tears of an immense joy and gratitude."

"Hey." She gawped at him. "That happened to me yesterday. I was hanging out at the corral watching the horses and all of a sudden I was just overcome with . . . with like what you just said. Like everything was perfect and exactly in its place. It was just like this absolute joy welled up in me from outta nowhere. Honestly? It left me in tears. It was the weirdest thing."

"Yes!" He was nodding excitedly. "That's it. That was your soul popping in to say hello. For as long as that moment lasted you were experiencing life through your soul—not your ego, your mind or body, just your total soul. There's a marvelous Zen koan that asks, show me your original face, the face you had before you were born. That face, *that* is your soul. That is your pure, eternal essence and that is where God resides in all of us."

"Damn." Frank chuckled. "I had a religious experience."

"You did, indeed." Kevin beamed. "Maybe you have more of a god than you think."

"I guess if I were going to find one anywhere it'd be there." Frank jutted her chin toward the peaks. "I had a friend who said that's where the last of the rough old gods hang out."

"Indeed," Kevin murmured. "The last redoubt of the *numina*."

"Why does that sound vaguely heretical to my untrained ear?"

He laughed and looked around guiltily. "Can I confess?"

"Why not?" She grinned. "I'm on a roll."

"You asked if the mountains could be God. Well, I think—and yes, this is definitely heretical—I think God appears to us in the form we find most palatable. For me it's Christ. For another it's Allah, or Shiva, or one of the world's old goddesses, and for you and many others, you might find God in nature. I think there are infinite expressions of the Divine and as long as it embraces reverence and awareness I don't think it matters how the form comes to a person."

"Reverence and awareness," she repeated.

Kevin nodded. "Reverence for whatever moment you are in and awareness of that moment. Participation in and full engagement with the present."

"You believe in coincidence?"

He gave her a cheery smile. "Einstein said coincidences were God's way of staying anonymous."

"God knows when a sparrow falls and all that?"

"All that and more."

They gazed out over the long slope of cliff. Behind them a bell clanged.

"I shouldn't keep you. You must have a lot of *ora et labora.*"

"It's unending," he agreed. "But I am very glad you came by. I don't know if I've helped at all."

"You have. I appreciate your listening. You're a good listener."

He winked. "Cops and priests."

"Yeah. Hey, when am I going to get that letter from you?"

"Oh, soon! I've been composing one, adding questions as I think of them. Did you see my books in the bookstore?"

"I didn't."

"Well, come on." He turned back to the office. "Let me get you the first in the series. You don't have to read it but I'd love to know what I got right and what I didn't."

He pressed a book on her and when she offered to pay he demurred that the least the abbot could do was give a copy away for the sake of improving the product. He walked her to the Tacoma and greeted the dogs.

As she got in Kevin said, "Please let me know what you decide. It's a difficult decision but I trust you will make the right one for your circumstances."

"Thanks. I appreciate your faith."

He lifted his hands with a wide smile. "That's all I've got."

CHAPTER 32

The loss of sleep, her aching collarbone, the long drive to the hermitage—all of it caught up to Frank. By the time she reached the cabin she could do no more than throw dog food into the bowls and collapse on the bed. She slept until the sun was hard on the west side of the cabin. Back in the day she'd been used to sleeping at odd hours, napping when she could, but here it was disorienting to wake in full daylight. When the dogs heard her stir they left the cool floor and jumped up to snuggle.

They got her up and outside. She opened the coop and the chickens followed her to the corral. She called the horses over for oats and they came trotting. She tossed them their flakes then ambled to the creek. She rolled a cigarette sitting on the edge of the bridge. The dogs splashed below and the hens foraged on the bank. The *picogrueso* sang merrily. Frank smoked.

Surely Justina had passed by now. Frank wondered if she had walked through that wide and beckoning door.

With no malice, she asked the sky, "Happy now?"

Not that the matter with Justina was a happy one but as Sal would have said, she was freed. And there was peace in that. Peace was good, Frank thought. Happiness and pleasure were well and fine, but Frank thought peace might be the better deal. As if to underscore that she thought of Gomez.

Frank blew a stream of smoke and watched it dissipate like

a miniature contrail.

"*Apuñalé*," she said. "What the hell does that mean?"

Reluctantly she got to her feet. Back in the cabin she browsed through Sal's books until she found a well-worn Spanish-English dictionary. Squinting, she swiped through the *A*s looking for the unknown word Justina had said. Wondering where the cheaters were, she squinted harder. The word came into focus: *Apuñala*, to stab.

Peace, Frank thought, shelving the book; peace was vastly underrated.

She wandered back to the bridge and dangled her legs above the gurgling water. She watched it flow, clear and clean and cool. It would flow all the way to the Salinas River and then out to the ocean somewhere north of Monterey. Each molecule would be absorbed by the sea, carried south past LA and down to Mexico. Frank didn't know where it went after that. Swirled around the world maybe and came back to start all over again in Alaska.

She sighed.

Gomez was a fellow cop. Frank owed her the truth so she could close out the Hernandez case, mark paid to it. But where would Gomez go with that truth? Even if Gomez quietly closed the case she'd at least have to tell her boss, and Soledad was a small town. How long before word leaked out?

Or maybe she'd insist on digging deeper than a secondhand deathbed confession. And where would be the proof of that? Who could corroborate Justina's confession?

Frank considered what Kevin had asked: how would it help the family to know that their mother, sister, grandmother had killed her husband? Was it worth the cost of Justina's memory to discover who had killed him?

She thought about her own father's murder. It had always haunted her that some unknown junkie had ripped him off and killed him. In the end, it had helped her to know who had done it but then again, it wasn't her mother who had killed him. If it had been she didn't think it would have been worth the price of knowing. Especially without her alive to ask about it.

248

Augustin Hernandez didn't seem like a particularly upstanding citizen. Not the kind of guy a lot of people would mourn. Maya certainly didn't miss him. Frank wondered if anyone did. Surely they deserved justice. But what can of worms would such justice open? Turning families against families? His people against Justina's?

Picking leaves and stickers from Kook's coat, she dropped them into the water and watched them either swirl away or sink.

Swirl away, she thought. Drop the truth in Gomez' lap and let her figure out what to do with it. Let her deal with the consequences.

Or sink. Take the truth into her heart. Hold it there and let the water close over it.

She suddenly wanted to see Ronnie. To smell her rich, warm scent, feel her wiry hair against her cheek, Ronnie's skin on hers, to see the hunger for life in her eyes, the shine and sparkle there, to hear her whisper, *"Ay, mi amor."*

She went back to the cabin and texted, *How's my lover?*

A few minutes later Ronnie wrote, *Lonely :(Is it Thursday yet?*

Frank hesitated before typing, *It could be*

She was startled when the phone rang in her hand.

"Hello, my beauty."

"Mi, amor. What does that mean, *It could be?"*

"It means I'd like it to be Thursday too. Maybe we could make today Thursday?"

"En serio? You'll come today?"

"Would you like that?"

"I'd *love* that!"

Frank smiled. "Then so it shall be, *mi diosa."*

Frank had to hold the phone away as Ronnie squealed.

"Ay, I just made a veggie lasagna for dinner. Are you hungry?"

"Aren't I always? I'm leaving now."

Ronnie squealed again and Frank laughed.

"Drive carefully, *mi amor."*

"I will. I'd hate to miss that lasagna."

She lured the chickens back into their coop and left them with plenty of food.

"Wanna go for a ride?" she asked the dogs. They looked excited but unsure. "I know, I know. Lots of trips lately. Wanna go see Ronnie? Paco?"

Bone cocked his head.

"Paco?" Frank repeated. Bone craned his head to the other side and wagged his stump. She opened the truck and Kook jumped in. Bone waited for help and she obliged as best she could. The ride down was the opposite of the morning's bright light on the way home. Now the sun lay subdued and shadowed, the trees and grasses dull and dusty. She drove faster than she should have.

Just like a local, she thought. She checked the clock. There was a place by the police station that sold flowers and she could probably get there before they closed. Suddenly Frank braked hard. She whipped the truck around and drove back a couple miles to the rosebush. It was still covered with yellow blooms. She parked and climbed carefully up the hill. The dogs watched as she awkwardly sliced a generous bouquet.

"There we go," she told them, setting the stems into a littered plastic cup, filling it from their stash of water. The fragrance of the roses filled the truck, even with the windows down. Frank couldn't help but think of Sal.

She was almost to the freeway entrance when her phone rang. Frank glanced at the number and pulled over.

"Hey, Maya."

"Hi, Miss Frank." Maya's voice was calm, resigned. "I just wanted to let you know my mother passed this morning not long after you left. We're very grateful for you. She passed peaceful and easy."

"I'm glad for that," Frank said. "Thank you for letting me know."

"You're welcome."

"How are you doing?"

"Oh, you know, okay. I'm sad but she's at peace now and that

250

gives me comfort."

"Good. How's Vivi?"

"She's fine. Her neck's good. I got an appointment with that therapist."

"That's great. I hope it helps."

There was a long pause and Frank knew what was coming. "Did my mother....did she say anything to you? About... anything?"

A successful cop was like a successful bad guy—she could lie, cheat, prevaricate, evade, and finagle with the best of the worst. It came with the territory and was a skill Frank hadn't lost.

"She was pretty agitated but when I held her hand that seemed to calm her a lot. She said a couple things I didn't understand. I'm sorry my Spanish isn't better."

"No, no, that's fine. I was just wondering."

"She was at peace," Frank reminded her.

"Yeah. That's a blessing. Okay. Well, I just wanted you to know and to thank you again."

"I'm glad I could be there, Maya. I hope you take care of yourself."

"I will. You too."

Frank got back on the road and was soon at Ronnie's. She knocked, flowers in hand, and Ronnie yanked the door open.

"*Amor!*" she cried. "I can't believe you're here! *Ay*, these roses! For me? *Perritos!*" She bent to kiss the dogs. "I've missed you! Come, come, come," she said shepherding Frank inside. "*Ay, dios*, those smell *amazing*. How are you? How's your collarbone? I don't see your bag. Are you staying?"

Frank laughed at the dizzying flurry of pronouncements and questions. "The arm is good; the roses are for you; yes, I'm staying. If you'll have me."

"*Amor*," Ronnie said squeezing up against Frank's good side. "I'll have you a thousand times over."

They stood kissing until Frank pulled back. She melted into Ronnie's eyes, as dark and deep as an ancient well, and like a well, shining and reflecting the sun.

"I think you've ensorcelled me."

Ronnie gave a low chuckle and pressed tighter into Frank. "I think you've been reading too much Harry Potter. Come. Let's get these beautiful roses in a vase. Where'd you get them? They smell so good I want to *eat* them! Are you hungry, *amor*? I was just going to sit down and savage that lasagna all by itself but I made a salad for us. *Tienes hambre?*"

"I'm starving. The roses are wild. They grow by the side of the road."

"*Ay*, such beauties! The best things are wild." She winked.

Frank watched Ronnie arrange them in a wide bowl. She didn't want to tell her where they came from, didn't want to share her old, albeit brief lover with her new. It was enough that the roses brought them together, incorporating the two wildly different women. Hugely different in their outward expression, but oddly alike in that both were deeply reverent and present. Even when Ronnie walked all over her own questions she always came back to them. They weren't tossed out and forgotten, merely stepped on in her exuberance.

Frank was sitting at the dining room table and Ronnie started to put the overflowing bowl in front of her then said, "No, not here. We won't be able to taste our dinner! The living room. We'll be able to smell them later *quando abrazamos*."

"Don't know what that means but I think I like it."

Ronnie called over her shoulder, "When we cuddle, baby."

They sat down to eat and after exclaiming over the lasagna, Frank said, "I went and saw Justina Hernandez again. Her daughter called in the middle of the night and asked me to come."

Ronnie exclaimed indignantly, "You answered your phone in the middle of the night for *her*?"

"*Calma, celosa*. She left a message. I happened to see it."

"Okay, that's better, *porque* you told me you turned it off at night, and here I think you're taking some strange woman's calls at midnight."

Frank grinned and shook her head. "Such a green-eyed monster."

"*Ay*, go on. You went to this strange woman's house in the middle of the night..."

"I did. I sat with her mother."

"And?" Ronnie paused and leaned toward Frank. "How was it? Did she say anything? Did she confess?"

"Well, even if she had I couldn't very well tell you, now, could I?"

"*Pues, claro*, of course you could. You're not a priest!"

"What if she had?" Frank asked slyly. "Do you think I should tell your sister?"

"Of course! How could you even think not to?"

"What would come of that but shame for Justina's family?"

"For one thing they'd have resolution, but more to the point, Frank, she broke the law. You'd have to tell Carly. Or someone. How could you even think not to?" she said chewing with her hand over her mouth. "And she should pay the price. And the husband, too, he should pay for what he did, wherever he is."

"I suspect he's beyond paying now. Justina too. So who would pay except her family? The sins of the father and all that?"

"I can't even believe we're having this discussion. Can you look me in the eye and tell me you wouldn't turn her in?"

"No." Frank kept her eyes on her plate. "But can you look me in the eye and tell me there weren't any cases you didn't want to prosecute?"

"Of course not, but I had to. It was my job."

Frank nodded. "Your job was dispensing justice to someone. Mine was just finding that someone."

"And then you turned them over to someone like me. Need I remind you that is how the justice system works?"

"No. But I think a lot of times justice is pretty unjust."

"*No es perfecto*," Ronnie allowed. "And if she had whacked her husband, I could sympathize, I could. We old ladies, we get *crazy*. We get to a point where we just don't care anymore what people think of us. The jiggly arms, the muffin tops and chin hairs."

253

Frank laughed and Ronnie beamed.

"Am I right, I mean, who cares? Who are we trying to impress? At a certain age we've earned the right to be exactly who we are and you have to take us as we are or not at all. And I understand how that applies to rules, believe me, I do. All our lives we've followed them, but one day, we just," Ronnie snapped her fingers, "we break like an old tree in the forest falling over to give light to the baby trees and make food for them. That's what we old women do. We nourish the babies even at the cost of our lives."

Nodding, glad to have moved away from Justina, Frank said, "I had a grandma killed her daughter's boyfriend. Popped him with a cast iron skillet a couple times. Made sure he never got up. She'd asked the daughter to leave him. Thought he was molesting her grand-baby but the daughter wouldn't give him up. Even defended him. But when Grandma caught him in the act, *bam*, game over."

"*Ya ves*? And at that point we're so close to the end anyway, it doesn't matter what happens to us. It's an easy sacrifice. I've seen it too. Grandmothers protecting their babies. It's no wonder men are so scared of old ladies. We just stop giving a shit what they think."

"What a contradiction you are. Upholding the law with one hand yet disregarding it with the other."

"I know, I know." Ronnie sighed. "*La vida es* messy. I didn't always like my job but I did it to my fullest capacity. And I *believe* in the law. We would have chaos without it. But I'll grant you that sometimes there is a chasm between justice and the law."

"Doña Veronica?"

"S*i, mi amor*."

Frank reached across the table to take Ronnie's hand. "I think you'd be a fun woman to get old with."

"Why, *Doña* Frank, is that a proposal?"

Frank grinned. "As close as you'll get to one."

Ronnie came around the table. She squeezed herself onto

Frank's lap and kissed her. "I'll take it."

Later that night, after *muchos abrazos y besos,* Frank woke to the sound of a car door being beeped open, then slammed shut. She listened to an engine start then fade. Street light filtered in through the curtains and half a dozen electronic gadgets glowed red and blue and green. It was like trying to sleep in a Christmas tree. She glanced down at Ronnie, snoring lightly. Frank smiled. She wanted to kiss her unruly mane but instead she quietly slipped out of bed. A couple of the dogs padded behind her to the patio. Frank clicked off the party lights swagged all over and eased onto the porch swing. Bone laid with a grunt at her feet and Paco went back inside. Kook and Corto jumped up and curled beside her.

Frank lifted her head to the night, to the light of the cool and implacable stars. In all her pondering about whether or not to tell Gomez Frank hadn't considered the one thing Kevin had asked her.

"Justina," she said, barely audibly. "*¿Qué quiere usted?*"

Frank closed her eyes. She laid her hand on the closest dog, felt Corto's short hair, his warm, rising and falling body. The stars continued across the sky. A cricket rubbed its wings together in song. Another answered. Down the street a rooster crowed.

She had gone to Justina as a cop, but she'd had to lay the cop aside so she could be with Justina simply as one human to another. Justina's confession hadn't been about the law, or justice. It had been about being *known.* If only for the briefest of moments Justina and Frank had shared what Kevin called their original faces. They had met soul to soul. Justina had been seen. It was all she had wanted. Sal had written as much in her journal, that sometimes her patients just wanted to be heard. They wanted a place to lay their burdens. Sal had diligently shouldered their burdens, baring them only to the mountains. She had kept them quietly in her heart.

The sky began to lighten, from pearly gray to soft pink. Frank thought of her father and the man who'd killed him. She thought of her half-mad mother, of the grandma who'd killed

255

her daughter's boyfriend, of Justina and Maya and Vivi, of Ronnie and Sal. Of Kevin.

He must have been asked a lot: if God was so great why did he allow suffering? As Ronnie had pointed out, Frank was no priest, but she was pretty sure that if there was a God the poor bastard didn't have anything to do with suffering. If there was one thing Frank knew for sure, it was that people made other people suffer. God had nothing to do with it and was probably looking down all day long in tears at what people did to each other.

But—and surely this must have given whatever gods there were hope—there was also goodness. Frank had lost sight of that. Steeped for so long in the banal meanness of people she had forgotten there was so much beauty in the world. Love and kindness. Compassion and joy. Laughter and generosity.

She was discovering it in the people who came to see her at the store, in Ronnie's arms and at her family's dinner table, and amid her circle of friends. She found it in Kevin and Pork Chop. Even Pete. Most surprisingly of all, she was finding it in herself.

Frank pressed her hand to her heart. Where she would keep Justina's confession. To share it only with mountain and star. She smiled at the pink new day. A familiar sensation rose in her chest, the swelling joy and keen awareness of being held in grace, the thrall of devotion to this singular moment. Frank let the sacred tears fall. She let them course down her original face, the face she had before she was born.

ABOUT THE AUTHOR

Baxter Clare Trautman is the Lambda Literary Award-nominated author of the six LA Franco mysteries. Her other works include *The River Within* and *Spirit of the Valley*. She lives with her wife at the tail end of the still wild Santa Lucia Mountains in Central California.

At Bywater Books, we love good books just like you do, and we're committed to bringing the best of contemporary writing to our growing community of avid readers. Our editorial team is dedicated to finding and developing outstanding writers who create books you won't want to put down.

For more information about Bywater Books, our authors and our titles, please visit our website.

www.bywaterbooks.com

CPSIA information can be obtained
at www.ICGtesting.com
Printed in the USA
JSHW022352150623
43333JS00001B/2